ALSO BY APRIL GENEVIEVE TUCHOLKE

The Boneless Mercies

SEVEN ENDLESS FORESTS

SEVEN ENDLESS
FORESTS

APRIL GENEVIEVE TUCHOLKE

FARRAR STRAUS GIROUX · NEW YORK

SQUARE
FISH

An imprint of Macmillan Publishing Group, LLC
120 Broadway, New York, NY 10271
fiercereads.com

Square Fish and the Square Fish logo are trademarks of Macmillan and
are used by Farrar Straus Giroux under license from Macmillan.

Our books may be purchased in bulk for promotional, educational,
or business use. Please contact your local bookseller or the Macmillan
Corporate and Premium Sales Department at (800) 221-7945 ext. 5442
or by email at MacmillanSpecialMarkets@macmillan.com.

Library of Congress Control Number: 2019940838

ISBN 9781250762917 (paperback)

Originally published in the United States by Farrar Straus Giroux
First Square Fish edition, 2021
Book designed by Elizabeth H. Clark
Square Fish logo designed by Filomena Tuosto

1   3   5   7   9   10   8   6   4   2

To all those who seek a quest

SEVEN ENDLESS FORESTS

THE WOLVES

ONE

The Gothi nuns will not travel to remote places, so when the snow sickness sweeps through the forgotten mountain hamlet, or the secluded steading, or the lonely, isolated Hall, we burn our own.

We bury our own.

We thought we were safe, another dark winter behind us. The festival of Ostara had come and gone. Spring had arrived, jade-green buds, emerald-green grass, bright blue skies.

Our steading was in the Middlelands, remote and quiet, far from any sea, far from any major town, far from any jarls with their Great Halls and shifting laws. Here, in the region of Cloven Tell, the soft green Ranger Hills rippled across our horizon, and cold, clear lakes marked our landscape like sparkling jewels.

My sister, Morgunn, and I had spent our childhood running

wild and free, without a thought to the world beyond the hills—it was no more real to us than the stories of the Green Women of Elshland or the tales of Frey and the giant Logafell. We were isolated. We were happy.

Aslaug, our cook, used to tell me I had too much happiness in me. She said only witches and Fremish wolf-priests were truly happy, because they cast spells and drank poison, because they made pacts with the gods in pursuit of their own joy.

I'd heard of these magic pacts from the sagas and the songs. I've never stolen an infant, or tricked a jarl into marriage, or slain a sleeping Elver, or burned a village. I've never taken to the air, floating across the night sky, fingers cupping the stars. I've never made all the children of Vorseland scream, as one, in the middle of the night. Yet I've been happy. Happy as a witch. Happy as a wolf.

I'd shrugged off Aslaug's warnings as I'd shrugged off the warnings of Elna, our pretty, apple-cheeked servant, who used to say that the moon was the eye of a great dragon and that one day he would look down and see us and burn our world to ash.

Now Elna was burning to ash, her body on the pile in the east field.

The snow sickness struck a few Middleland villages each winter. It would blow in with a storm and stay as long as the white flakes fell from the sky. It would start with sweating and a fever and end in death. Some people lived, and most people died, and only the gods knew why.

Snow had come in the night and turned the world white again.

At supper, my mother began to shake and sweat until she fell from the bench and lay writhing in pain on the floor beside the hearth fire. The servants began to scream. They knew that only the snow sickness could do this, only the snow sickness could take down such a strong Vorse woman.

I dragged my mother to her bed and awoke at dawn to find her dead in my arms.

The servants died in the night as well. I carried their bodies to the field and set them on fire, gray smoke floating up past the trees.

Gray.

Gray was the color of the winter sky. It was the color of a pair of cooing mourning doves, my father's beard, and the thick wool tunic my mother used to wear on feast days.

Gray was the color of Viggo's eyes.

And now gray was the color of death.

I took a half-empty jug of *Vite* from a table near the main doors of the Hall and drank. I wiped my hand across my mouth and took another sip.

I had two more bodies to see to, and these I would not burn.

I dug two graves by the rowan trees until blisters wept across my palms, stinging, bleeding. I straightened, pressed my hands to my aching lower back and then to my heart.

My heart pushed back. I was alive.

Blood from my palms seeped into the front of my tunic. I wiped my hands on my leather leggings and picked up my shovel. I needed to finish this task before the morning's sorrow could sear itself so deeply into my mind that it would be the only thing I would ever think about. The only thing I would ever remember.

I returned to the Hall, propped open the main doors with two large stones, and then walked slowly to her chamber. My mother had been six feet tall, sinewy, broad-shouldered, made of muscle and steel. I pulled her body out of the bed, strong limbs woven between furs, fingers in tangled hair. Panting, muscles straining, I carried her past the central hearth, past the long feast table, out of the building, into the fresh air.

The Hall smelled of thick smoke—sour, acrid sickness and sweet, rotting death. The air outside smelled of sun and wet earth. It smelled of life.

I glanced toward the five rowan trees in the northeast corner of our estate.

Mother was Elsh. She would go in the ground, not the fire.

The bright sun had melted most of the snow, and my boots were soaked through. Sweat blurred my vision, and my bones ached with my mother's weight.

I set her in the first grave and picked up the shovel. The hole filled slowly.

Now . . .

Viggo.

I'd found the shepherd collapsed outside the Hall at dawn, his tunic covered in blood.

His body should have been in the east field, burning alongside Aslaug and Elna and Ivar the field hand and old Haftor the woodcutter.

The shepherd wasn't Elsh, but I would bury him by my mother all the same.

I tossed the first shovel of half-frozen dirt onto Viggo's body. It fell on his hair, a black clump that would never be washed clean.

I dropped to my knees and howled like wolves on the hunt, crying to the moon.

I yelled my voice into dust . . . and then I rose to my feet and finished burying him.

I knew it was selfish to keep Viggo here with me on the steading, to not burn him in the way of the Vorse. But then, the living are selfish.

When it was done, I threw the shovel into the snow between two of the rowan trees. Let it rust. I would never use it again.

I wasn't full Vorse, and I didn't believe that life was simply a long journey toward a good death. All the same, Viggo had been more than a shepherd, more than my lover, more than a wise, quiet Vorselander who ran across the Ranger Hills with the strength and grace of a young god.

He'd had the heart of a hero, noble, wise, and brave. He deserved a hero's life and a hero's death. Instead, he died alone, in the night, a victim of a passing plague.

I would not let the same fate claim me. If I had a speck of heroism in my heart, then I would find it. I would honor it. I would sacrifice for it.

A memory surfaced. I was a child, ten or eleven, out in the hills with my mother, collecting green winterberries by moonlight for Elsh frost-brew. We stumbled upon a white arctic bear—it came roaring out of a nearby cave, jaws wide, teeth the size of my fist, white fur stained with old blood.

I hid behind my mother and shook with fear. She leaned over slowly, eyes on the bear, and pulled a knife from its sheath on her right calf.

"*Fortune favors brave women,*" she said. "*We rise up, while the meek women cower.*" She ran forward and sank her dagger into the bear's throat.

She slept under that bear's snow-white hide for years. It still lay on her empty bed. Each time she caught me looking at it, she reminded me that I had cowered while she killed the bear, that I had flinched when she took its life. It didn't matter to her that I'd only been a child.

"You have a soft heart," she'd say whenever I hesitated to wring a hen's neck or slit a lamb's throat. It wasn't a compliment. "You take too much after your father, Torvi. Your sister is the true Vorse."

I wiped my bleeding palms on the front of my tunic, and then I walked to the cold, fast-moving stream that wove through our farm, down from the Ranger Hills. I tore off my tunic and boots and underclothes—there was no one to see, no one to care. I slid my naked body into the water, feet slipping over stones, limbs pressing into the silky current. I let it wash away all the blood, all the dirt, all the death. I let it cleanse me of my old life.

When I climbed out of the water, I was numb with cold. I ran to the line of laundry strung behind the Hall, near the vegetable garden. Elna never had a chance to gather the clothing before the storm hit. I beat the blood back into my thighs with my palms, and then I grabbed a large wool cloth, wrapped it around myself, and went inside.

I crossed the Hall, leaving a trail of wet footprints. I walked down the east corridor, stopped at the second door, and knocked.

The door opened slowly. "Is it over?"

I nodded, and my sister grabbed me. Her face pressed into my shoulder, and her fingers clenched my tunic at the waist, squeezing the cloth into her fists.

TWO

———————— ✦ ————————

Aslaug used to say that all great tales begin with a journey and a quest.

She would lower her voice and whisper stories of Vorseland and the world beyond our steading. She told me of the Jade Fells, a wild, secretive people who lived in the Skal Mountains. They slept during the day and roamed the night like wolves, drinking blood and eating the hearts of their dead.

She told me of the wolf-priests of Frem and the Relic Hunters of Finnmark and the hedge-fighters and Butcher Bards of Elshland.

She told me of the evil Pig Witches, of the mysterious Drakes, of the Bone Women and the Whistlers and the Gothi nuns.

Each winter, her rich voice blended with the sound of the crackling wood in the hearth fire as she recounted the tragedy of the Child Wizards and the Moss Witch Massacre of the Western Hills.

She told me the stories of the Thirteen Crones—a fellowship of cunning female jarls who ruled Vorseland when Aslaug's grandmother was a child.

She told me all the tales, both ancient and modern. She told me of the first Witch War, and the second, which was called the Salt and Marsh War. She told me how, on a warm summer night during a rainstorm, the Cut-Queen and her army of Pig Witches attacked the Sea Witches of the Merrows in a great battle of magic and blood. The Salt and Marsh Witch War raged across Vorseland for years. The Cut-Queen would die in battle, and peace would return for a handful of seasons, but there was always another resurrection, always another battle.

Finally, after the Battle of the Hawk and Hummingbird, the green-cloaked Sea Witches defeated the brown-cloaked Cut-Queen and her followers. They captured the queen, and this time the Sea Witches beheaded her, boiled her body down to the bone, and crushed her bones into dust. She did not rise again.

Juniper, the Sea Witch queen, took her women back to the famous Scorch Trees in the Merrows, and the second Vorse Witch War came to an end.

I would press my cheek to Aslaug's neck as she spoke and breathe in the smell of leather and wool and straw. I would tell her that I wanted to be a Sea Witch like Juniper when I grew older. I would tell her that I wanted to fight wolf-priests and go on quests and find adventure and cross an Endless Forest. I would tell her I wanted to win a jarldom, like one of the Thirteen Crones.

"You can do anything you set your mind to, little Torvi," she'd say. Unlike my mother, Aslaug believed I was capable of great things.

Her stories had thrilled me as a child, made my blood sing. I would shiver, despite being near the fire, and Aslaug would wrap me in her strong arms and tell me of the Boneless Mercies—women who had roamed Vorseland for centuries, killing the old and the sick and then finally dying themselves, forgotten, poor, and alone. On and on and on, until a young Boneless Mercy named Frey pursued glory and found a monster.

Bards in Great Halls everywhere sang of Frey and her companions—Aslaug said she knew a dozen or so Frey songs, and there were at least a dozen more.

My favorite stories were always about Frey. Her fight with the last Vorseland giant Logafell in a cave under the Skal Mountains. Her cunning and bravery during the second Witch War. Her travels with the Aradia Witches through the Sand Sea. Her time roaming the Green Wild Forest with Indigo and the Quicks.

"Will there ever be another Vorse hero like Frey?" I'd ask Aslaug, not for the first time.

"Yes," she'd whisper. "When we need her, she will come."

———————————

Morgunn and I sat on a thick wool rug in the main room of the Hall, near the central hearth. We were eating a simple supper of bread and aged cheese.

Outside, a spring thunderstorm howled unhindered across our stretch of green Ranger Hills.

I used my thumb to pick up crumbs from my wooden plate, my elbow touching my sister's. The two of us were alone on a thousand-acre farm. We hadn't seen another living soul in four weeks.

I hadn't been to Trow since the snow sickness, though it was only ten miles to the north. I'd watched smoke rising from that direction a dozen times over the last several days.

Before he died, Viggo told me that a pack of marauding Fremish wolf-priests was moving through Vorseland. The wolf-priests did this every few years, but never had they stayed so long or burned so many hamlets.

"I was at the Evil Stepmother Tavern in Trow last night, Torvi, and I spoke to some neighboring shepherds."

I was wrapped in Viggo's arms, my chest pressed into his, and his low voice vibrated through my body when he spoke.

"Those flame-hungry wolf-priests set a village on fire thirty miles from here. They've left the Borders and are moving through Cloven Tell."

"Should we be worried? I thought they burned only a few villages, never isolated farms. One came to the Hall a few months ago, but Mother quickly took care of her."

Viggo sighed and moved his hands over my hips. "I don't think so. The other shepherds at the tavern informed me that Jarl Meath had hired bands of Quicks to roam the Middlelands, slaying wolves." He paused. "Usually the wolf-priests are too high on yew berry poison to do much more than set a few fires before the Quicks drive them back south. But I gather that one of their leaders is more tenacious than in previous years, less poison-addled, more ambitious. I'll keep an eye out for them from the hills—your farm is hidden from the main road, and all should be well. Just be ready to flee the Hall if needed."

I nodded, my lips sliding against his skin. "Stop worrying, shepherd. You've got a naked girl in your bed. Do something about it."

He turned me over and kissed me from my chin to my ankles. Cold skin and warm lips and beating hearts. I forgot about wolves and fires and the rest of the world.

Two days later, Viggo was dead.

I sat up and threw another log onto the hearth fire. Morgunn inched closer to the flames. She was fourteen, four years younger than me and shorter by five inches. We had the same dark, curly hair, but she had a small, short nose and round cheeks, whereas my nose was long and straight, and my chin as pointed as my ears, like an Elver. Morgunn was short and soft, and I was tall and strong.

My sister's eyes were an odd shade of indigo like my own. Our irises shone violet in moonlight, a trait we'd inherited from our father.

Morgunn's eyes looked innocent still, in a way I knew mine no longer did.

We shared the work now. We cooked and cleaned and fed the animals and scrubbed our clothes clean in the stream. We were surviving. More than surviving.

We slept when we wanted, ate when we wanted, and no one from the outside world bothered us. So far.

"Torvi?"

"Yes?"

"You're worried. I can see it in your eyes. It's the smoke, isn't it."

I knew Morgunn had seen the smoke rising from the north. We hadn't spoken of it, but it was there, a dark thread of fear stretching between us. "Yes," I replied. "Jarl Meath hired Quicks to hunt the wolf-priests this year, but I've never seen them burn so close to our farm. I've heard them howl at night. It carries far across the hills, on the high winds."

Morgunn wrapped her arms around her knees, moved her bare feet closer to the fire. "The Quicks will drive them out. And when the smoke stops, we can go into Trow again and get news."

The Quicks were skilled archers who roamed the Seven Endless Forests of Vorseland. It was said that they were indifferent to all politics, religion, and law. They were known to be fierce hunters during the day, but genial, carefree rogues at night beside the fire. They despised the wolf-priests for bringing fire and death to their peaceful woods, and they killed the Fremish beasts as swiftly and quietly as they killed deer, quick arrows shot into dark wolf hearts.

I moved closer to my sister. "Aslaug once told me that the Quicks were blessed by the gods and brought luck to any place they roamed. Our farm will be safe, Morgunn. No one will find us."

My sister nodded and then ate her last piece of cheese slowly, savoring it. We savored all our food now. Our storeroom had been low after the long winter, and now it was near empty.

I wished our mother were still alive.

And Aslaug.

And Viggo.

"You need a quest, Torvi," he whispered to me once after we lay together in his bed, still shaking with love. "You need to travel, to roam, to see new things, new people. It's in your blood, in your breath, in your bones. You can't stay here with me forever." He looked at me for a long moment, his hands moving across the small of my back. "I'm happy here in these hills. I'm content. But you need to pursue something larger than yourself. I can smell it on you—you smell of risk and adventure. You smell of dark forests, of gloomy caves, of exotic spices, of danger, of battle, of sacrifice, of hard-won victory."

I wove my fingers into his. "You can't possibly smell all of this on me, Viggo."

He kissed my forehead and smiled. "I do. Your skin smells of the open road." He paused. "You have buried a part of yourself, perhaps from fear, and perhaps from love, but it's there. You hunger for something more. You're starving for want of it. And if you refuse to seek it out, it will come to you instead. There's no hiding from life, just as there is no hiding from death."

I pushed back the furs and moved into a sitting position. "As a child, I used to say I wanted to be a witch when I grew up, or a warrior like Frey, or a jarl like the Thirteen Crones. Aslaug

16

would laugh and stroke my hair, but my mother would shake her head and tell me I was destined to marry one of the Tather boys."

I raised my gaze to Viggo's. "She believes that my sister, Morgunn, has the capacity for greatness, that she has the courage and determination that I lack. Morgunn is a natural leader and true Vorse, and the only thing I'm good for is marrying."

Viggo put his palm to my cheek and stroked my face with his thumb. "She is wrong, Torvi."

"She is not a woman who is often wrong," I said softly. "I am lazy and pleasure-loving. I enjoy peace and quiet and safety. I dislike killing animals. Morgunn has always been more daring, more reckless, more bold. She was killing chickens nearly as soon as she could walk. My mother had a little ax made just for her to cut their necks."

"You respond to peace and simplicity, Torvi, like all wise, thoughtful people. But this is not all of who you are. You have steel in your blood. Your mother can't sense it. She can't smell the glory on you as I can. She is wrong."

I've thought about that night and what Viggo said time and time again since I buried the shepherd back by the rowan trees.

I let my mind drift then to simpler memories, to the way Viggo's hut felt after a summer thunderstorm—clean, fresh, and cool—to the smell of his sun-warmed skin, to the taste of *Vite* on his tongue—

"Are you thinking about the shepherd?"

Morgunn was watching me. I realized suddenly that I was smiling. I stopped.

My sister had caught me sneaking out one night last autumn and demanded to know where I was going. I told her, and she kept my secret. I think she enjoyed the recklessness of it.

Thunder roared outside, ripping open the night sky. I felt it pulse inside my chest, echoing my heartbeat.

Morgunn tilted her head back and laughed—thunder always put her in a good mood. She had a cheery laugh, and I often felt the sound of it alone could see me through a lot of darkness.

"Thunder needs mead," she said a moment later. "Let's open the last cask in the storeroom, Torvi, and drink until the rain stops."

Morgunn had inherited our father's taste for honey-wine and other spirits. One summer's night a few years past, I'd gone to fetch my sister for supper and spent the next hour searching the Hall and the hills and the barn. I finally found her in the winter storeroom, stumbling drunk in the dark—she'd unearthed a dusty jug of long-forgotten *Vite*. I took the half-empty jug and put Morgunn to bed, hoping a pounding head the next morning would serve as her punishment. But my sister was lively and hale the next morning, and since then, her thirst seemed to have grown by the day.

"No, Morgunn." She'd been on me about that cask for some time. "It's all the mead we have left until I visit Trow."

Morgunn rubbed the end of her button nose with her palm

and sighed. "Something inside me wants the mead, Torvi. All the time. It's a beast, always hungry, never satisfied."

My eyes met hers. "I worry about you."

She shrugged. "And I worry about you as well, and your broken heart. But you can't stop me from drinking, Torvi, just as I can't bring a shepherd back to life."

My sister was blunt, a trait she'd learned from our mother. I admired her for it, even when I disagreed with her.

Morgunn rose to her feet and walked to the front of the Hall. She gave the two main doors a shove, and they opened wide into the dark, wet night. She stood, staring out into the storm, the wind whipping her hair, the rain licking her face.

Lightning flashed—

Morgunn let out a small gasp and stumbled backward. "Look, Torvi." She pointed into the dark beyond the doors.

"What is it? What did you see?"

"There's someone outside."

I grabbed the sharp cheese knife from the nearby table. I went to the doorway and peered out. I could see nothing but darkness, hear nothing but rain.

I drew a cross over my heart with one finger—the Elsh gesture of warning, of all things sinister and ominous.

We waited for the lightning to strike again.

"I keep dreaming that Mother will come back." Morgunn's voice was soft, but her fingers were clenched into fists. "She crawls out of her grave and enters my room, covered in mud.

She wants to take me back with her, wants me to get down under the dirt with her." She paused. "Why didn't you burn her, Torvi?"

"You know why." I handed Morgunn the cheese knife, then grabbed a hunting dagger from a shelf on the nearby wall. "I buried her as she would have wanted."

Morgunn clutched the knife to her chest and met my gaze. "There is someone outside, I swear it."

I nodded. I grabbed my cloak from the nail by the left door and pulled the hood over my head. No flame would withstand the rain, so I left the lamps and kept my dagger. I walked down the Hall steps slowly, then moved forward into the shadows, one foot after the other, toward the barn and the low, sod-covered summer storehouse.

Ten steps, twenty, fifty . . .

My eyes began to adjust to the dark.

I saw her.

A girl my own age, perhaps younger. She was slumped on the ground, her back pressed to the outer wall of the barn. She wore a dark cloak over an undyed tunic, no boots. Her bare feet were slick with mud.

"Are you a priest?" I shouted.

She didn't move. Lightning blazed, and I saw the girl's face, bloodied and bruised.

"Are you a priest?" I asked again. "One of the Fremish wolves?"

Her arm snapped forward. She grabbed the edge of my tunic

and yanked me to the ground. I dropped the dagger, and mud smacked against my open palms. My knees sank into the muck, and rain hit the back of my neck.

The girl turned her head, and her hood fell back. Her scalp was naked, scraped bare to the skin.

She was no wolf-priest.

She was a shaven-skulled Pig Witch.

"Witch," I said, shouting it into her face, into the rain, into the wind. "*Witch.*"

"*No*," she screamed back. "*It's not what you think.*"

We stared at each other in the dark. Raindrops splashed the top of her skull and slid down her brow. She wiped them away with a flick of her hand.

"They were going to burn us," she said. "They were going to burn us alive."

THREE

The Pig Witches were Stregas—sorcerers—who lived on the Boar Islands in the Quell Sea. They scraped their heads clean and powdered their faces and scalps with coral dust.

My mother had often warned me never to speak to a Pig Witch, never to let one near me, never to witness their prophecies, or buy their pig magic. She'd said that their spells were unnatural and evil and that even a Strega's shadow had power.

But my mother was dead, and I would make my own decisions now.

I brought the girl into the Hall, silent and dripping, and sat her at the long table near the fire. I put a plate of bread and cheese in front of her and then poured her a small horn of *Vite*.

She loosened the clasp of her cloak, and it dropped to the floor. She downed the liquor in one long drink and then began to eat quietly and quickly. She'd been hungry. Very hungry.

The girl had a strong chin and clever eyes that seemed very large under her bare skull. She was my height and had the elegant, graceful bearing of a jarl's wife, with the strong arms and hard waist of a farm laborer. Four purple bruises lined her neck, each the size of a finger.

She finished the last of the food, pushed back the plate, and then looked at me with a direct gaze that displayed both gratitude and pride. Her eyes were the same smoky shade as Viggo's and rimmed with red from exhaustion.

She's been through Hel, I thought, *but she's not beaten yet.*

"My name is Gyda," she said.

"I'm Torvi, and this is my sister, Morgunn."

Morgunn leaned against the far edge of the table, chin down, black curls hiding her face. She still held the cheese knife in her right hand, blade at her side, where the girl could see it.

My sister looked up when I said her name. She narrowed her eyes and turned to Gyda. "You've eaten our food and drunk our liquor. It's time to talk, Strega. Who tried to burn you, and why?"

"A pack of wolf-priests tried to burn me, the same ones who've been ransacking the Middlelands this last month." Gyda glanced toward me, then back to Morgunn. "The yew berry poison makes them love the smell of fire and the sound of screams. Burning me would have brought those filthy curs great joy. I'm glad the gods denied them the pleasure."

The girl ran her palms over her bare scalp and suddenly began to laugh. It was deep and hearty, a full, body-shaking laugh that echoed down the hall and bounced off the rafters.

Morgunn and I began to laugh with her. We couldn't help it—her laughter was such a cheerful sound. Free and wild.

Who was this strange girl we'd plucked from the storm and taken into our home?

Gyda rose to her feet and looked at Morgunn. "Put down your knife, girl. I won't harm you." She paused. "I'm out of the rain. I'm fed and warm and away from those wolves. I may look exhausted, but my heart beats with jubilation. I didn't expect to live through the night."

Morgunn set her knife down slowly but kept it within reach.

"And I'm no Pig Witch," Gyda added. "I'm a druid—I was born on the Boar Islands, but we druids are no friends to the Stregas. We shave our heads to protect ourselves from their magic, but that is all you will find in common between us."

"Tell us how a Boar Island druid ended up outside our Hall in the middle of a rainstorm," I said, "and we'll stop pestering you with questions, at least for the night. I swear it."

Gyda paused so long I thought she wasn't going to answer. She took a sip of *Vite* and then looked at me. "This pack of wolf-priests is led by a woman named Uther. She's as tall as the goddess Howl and as brawny as the goddess Tor. She leads a band of ragged, starving girls. They are all fearlessly devoted to the wolf-priest goddess Skroll. I've been tracking this pack since Owl Lake, seventy miles to the south."

"Have you sworn an oath to hunt wolves, like the Quicks?" I scanned the girl's body, but I saw no dagger sheathed at her waist and none at either calf.

"No. I'm looking for a sword, not vengeance—but I will tell

you more about this later." She paused again. "I finally caught up with the wolf-priests in the nearby town of Jord, where they stopped long enough to set a fire."

I felt Morgunn tense next to me. "What did they burn?" she asked.

"Everyone. Everything. Uther believed the town to be sheltering a Quick who had killed seven of her wolves."

"Were they?" I asked.

"Yes." Gyda drew closer to the hearth and stretched out her palms to warm them. The mud on her feet had dried and was starting to flake off onto the floor. "The Quick was just a boy of seventeen, with deep blue eyes and a smile like sunshine. I know because I tried to rescue him. I stole a dagger and stabbed two of the howling, poison-drunk guards before they caught me."

"How did you escape?" I asked.

Gyda ran her palm across her skull. She did not want to answer my questions—the strain of it was making her right hand twitch. "Uther stripped us of our blades and our boots and tied us to two stakes so that the wolves could watch us burn. But before the fire began to lick our feet and turn our skin to ash . . ." She paused. "A thunderstorm blew in and put out the flames."

Morgunn shifted slightly. "Did you raise the thunderstorm, Pig Witch?"

"I'm no Pig Witch, damn it all." Gyda laughed, but it was quieter this time, with a touch of sadness. "The clouds covered the moon. A strong wind and a hard rain hid everything else.

The night went as dark as death. Lightning sparked across the sky and struck one of the wolves. She burst into flames. In the chaos, I wriggled free of my bonds and then cut the Quick's. We ran together full out for miles. A group of the wolves followed us, despite the storm."

"What happened?" I prodded when she didn't continue.

"We finally decided to split up at the Bergen crossroads. The Quick's name was Melient. He continued north, and I turned east—we hoped it would give one of us a chance. The wolves took the bait and followed me. And I lost them in the hills." She bowed her head and brought her thumbs to her lips and then her forehead. "Tonight I will say a prayer to the Rover King that Melient has reached his Quick companions by now and is safely on his way to the Brocee Leon Forest."

"You pray to the Rover King?" I asked. He was mostly a Fremish god, though it was said he was friendly to all roamers.

"No, but some of the Quicks do. Melient shouted his name when Uther touched her torch to the pile of straw beneath our feet."

Morgunn picked up the knife again. "Are you sure you lost the wolves, Gyda?" She watched the druid closely, all laughter gone. "Did you lead a pack of dogs right to our doorstep?"

Gyda shook her head and put her fist to her heart. "Your steading is far from the Stretch and hidden by the surrounding hills. I wouldn't have discovered it myself except by chance. They won't find us here."

"I'm not sure I believe you, druid. If you found our farm, so will they." Morgunn's eyes moved from Gyda's to mine.

I read my own thoughts echoed in her gaze. *So we survived the snow sickness just to end up dying at the hands of some dirty, stinking wolf-priests?*

Ten years before, I watched my father march off to sea, though he'd sworn to my mother when he married her that he was done with ship-life for good. He never came home.

Four weeks before, I burned the servants in the east field and then buried my mother and a shepherd named Viggo.

Now I was alone on a farm with my sister and a bare-skulled druid, with a pack of Fremish wolf-priests burning nearby villages.

I let Morgunn open the cask that night. I didn't want my sister to drink, but neither did I want her to be terrified and melancholy.

When I brought the mead from the storeroom, my sister grinned. When I poured her a tall mug, amber liquid dripping down the sides, she laughed.

Gyda drank the mead as well. We all did. We ate the last of the cheese, and we drained the cask. We forgot about the wolf-priests. We forgot about the snow sickness. We forgot about everything.

The druid proved a good drinking companion. We sang bawdy songs at the top of our lungs and danced, arm in arm, down the length of the hall. Morgunn built up the fire, and we stripped to our shifts. We sweated and drank and laughed.

It's easy to become friends with a stranger when everyone else you know is dead.

Sometime near dawn we staggered down the east corridor. Morgunn stumbled into her room and fell onto a pile of sheepskins, asleep as soon as her body hit the bed. I took Gyda to Aslaug's old room at the far end. She fell onto the furs there, closed her eyes, and slept.

I returned to the long, dark corridor alone. It smelled of dust and cold air. I didn't stop at the door to my mother's room as I passed. I didn't even look at it.

I thought back to that frigid day last winter, crisp air and an indigo sky. A messenger had come that morning with an offer of marriage from Eric Tather.

Mother and I had been fishing in the stream, casting our lines between chunks of ice.

The Tather steading was five times the size of our own, and their Great Hall was nearly the size of a jarl's. All the Tathers were large men, tall with broad shoulders, thick arms, and slim hips. They were a wealthy family, dating back to the days of the Elshland raids. They had a handful of Iber horses and enough gold to pay a band of Quicks to protect their land. They had ties to Jarl Sindri at Black Dyre, and the oldest of the Tather brothers had married one of the jarl's seven daughters.

"I will not wed him, Mother," I said. "I will not marry Eric."

She threw her net onto the bank and put her hands on her hips.

"Torvi, your only chance at greatness will be to marry this

Tather. You are too lazy, too cautious, to do anything else. Your heart is too soft. You are not Vorse."

She paused, just long enough to make sure that I wasn't going to weep at her cruel words, that I was at least Vorse enough not to cry.

"You have big dreams," she said, "like all young girls. But mark my words, you will live out your days on these hills, drifting through life, sunset after sunset, season after season. This is all you will ever do." She paused. "Aslaug has filled your head with tales from the sagas, of simple farm girls who grow up to win themselves a jarldom, but the few Vorse jarldoms that were ruled by women were obtained through magic or war, and you are neither a wizard nor a witch nor a warrior."

It was true. I was none of those things.

Not yet.

I did not fall asleep as easily as my sister and the druid. I sat on the end of my bed and watched the moonlight flow in through the square window. I tried to keep my mind light and simple, as it had been before, when we were drinking, but I sobered up quickly in the quiet and the dark.

I thought of Gyda, knifing two wolf-priests to rescue a Quick she didn't know. I thought of my father on the deck of a ship, sailing some foreign sea. I thought of my mother, her tall, strong body trapped forever under the earth by the rowan trees.

I heard a howl outside the window. It was faint but real. Then I heard another. And another.

Morgunn was right. They would find us eventually.

I took a deep breath and sighed. I stretched out and pressed my cheek into the soft sheepskins that covered my bed. I imagined myself sinking down . . .

. . . into the ground, under the dirt.

I curled up with Viggo, relaxed, and fell asleep.

FOUR

I squinted in the sunshine. *My head hurt—from too much mead, from lack of sleep.* Gyda looked as bad as I felt: red eyes, swollen face, the bruises still a vivid purple across her neck. Morgunn, by contrast, was bright-eyed and cheerful.

We were eating boiled eggs outside on the front steps of the Hall. The morning light was clear, slanting across our knees, striking the brown eggshells at our bare feet.

I gave Gyda another egg and then handed her the pitcher of cold water I'd collected from the spring. "How did you sleep?"

She let out a low laugh and shrugged. "Deep and dreamless for a while. Then I tossed and turned . . . I can still smell the wolf-smoke on my skin. Even after all the rain. The scent echoed through my dreams."

I leaned toward her and put my nose to her wrist. "You're right. I smell it, too. I'll take you to the stream for a bath, and you can use Aslaug's yarrow soap and juniper skin oil. I'll fetch you a new tunic to wear as well."

"Burn this one," she said.

We all bathed in the beck, the water frigid but the sun warm. Afterward, we stretched out naked on the grassy banks, waiting for our skin to dry, soaking in the sunshine after all the months of cold and dark.

Gyda eyed my hair, the dripping-wet curls cascading down my spine. She ran her hands over her own bare head, palms moving from her temples to the base of her skull. "My hair has never been long enough for me to know its true color. Perhaps I will let it grow now that I've left the Boar Islands."

"Why did you leave?" I asked.

"It's a long story, better told on a dark night in front of a roaring fire."

I turned and rested my cheek on my arm, blinking in the sharp sun. "Tell me what you know of Uther, then. I want to learn more about this wolf leader who is burning Cloven Tell."

Gyda rose and began to dress, sighing with pleasure as the clean, well-made clothes slid over her skin. "Uther is one of the Fremish bishops—meaning she leads her own wolf-priest pack. The bishops answer to no higher moral power, no pontiff, no jarl. They drink yew berry juice, they practice their wolf magic, and they burn. They are unorganized bands of marauding beasts and thus have never posed much of a threat to Vorseland. But Uther is different. She isn't as addled with poison as the rest of the Skroll followers and hence is much more dangerous."

I began to dress as well, unconsciously running my eyes across the circle of green hills that surrounded our farm, searching for dark shadows. "What does she want?"

"What all the bishops want—more power, more priests, more flames for their god. Only, Uther wants it more than the rest." Gyda paused. "Uther has a way about her, something that draws the girls in—a look in her eye, a way of holding her head, a tone to her voice . . ."

Gyda pulled wool leggings up over her knees and then flicked her chin northward. "Uther and her wolves plan to set up camp along the shores of Lake Le Fay, some fifty miles north. She will head into the Skal Mountains by winter—she wants to recruit among the Jade Fells."

Morgunn and I looked at each other, eyebrows raised. So the wolf-priests were going to leave the Middlelands. This was good news.

A cloud moved, and a ray of sunlight hit my cheeks. I turned my face back and forth, letting the light pass over my eyelids, across my nose, to the tips of my ears. "Aslaug once told me that the people on the Iber Islands live in perpetual summer," I said. "Azure skies encircled by an azure sea. And no one dies from the snow sickness, because there is no snow."

"Could such a place exist?" Morgunn knelt by the stream,

dipped in her palm, and drank the cold, clear water. "Could anything be so beautiful?"

Gyda nodded. "The Boar Islands do not lie as far south as the Iber Islands, but even we have better weather than Vorseland— sunny summers and gentle winters of rain instead of snow."

"Maybe we should all travel to Iber." Morgunn's voice was soft, almost lazy, but I felt the determination behind it. "We can make our way to the edge of Vorseland. Hop a ship to the islands and never leave."

"The thought has also occurred to me," I said.

Morgunn's eyes met mine. "You want to wander? I thought you wanted to live and die in these Ranger Hills."

"I've considered taking to the road, just as you have, Morgunn. What is left here for us? Just know that if you and I became roamers, if we leave this steading, we will have nothing. No land, no home, only each other. The gold from last year's wool harvest might get us as far as Elshland or Frem, but once there, we'd have to find a way to earn food and shelter."

Morgunn stared at me for a moment, then laughed in a carefree, open way. "It's still a risk I would take, Torvi. We could always come back to these hills. We aren't losing our home forever. You're making too big a thing of it."

I smiled at this. "You would say that about practically anything. If a pack of Drakes arrived on our doorstep, and I hesitated to drop everything and join them in their mystic rambles, you'd call me timid, just as Mother used to do."

Morgunn laughed again. "I wish a pack of Drakes would wander by. I would welcome them."

I turned to Gyda. "And what about you? Will you go rambling with us?"

Gyda shook her head. "I would go with you south, but my path lies north, past the Skal Mountains, into the seventh Endless Forest." The druid tilted her head and looked at me. "You are Elsh, yes?"

"Our mother was. How did you know?"

"I saw the fresh graves by the rowan trees. I tripped and fell over the second mound last night in the rain." She paused. "You could join the Butcher Bards."

The Butcher Bards were bands of nomadic artists from Elshland, so called because of the knives they wore around their necks. They were something like our Vorse Quicks—though they roamed from town to town instead of forest to forest, seeking artistic commissions rather than the next hunt. Some were painters, some weavers, some musicians, some mystics, some storytellers. The groups changed as members found long-term employment, while others finished projects and took to the road again. Most were young, and many were women.

One of the tapestries in our Hall depicted a scene of five wolves howling into the night sky, white moonlight on a black field, gray stones stained with blood. Mother had bought it from a handsome Butcher Bard some years ago, and I'd often caught

Morgunn staring at it, an odd expression on her face, and her eyes full of yearning.

It gave her the same feeling it did me—a longing to stand at a lonely crossroads and pick a path based on nothing more than gut feeling and a shift in the wind. A desire to climb a tree town's steps and drink with strangers. An ache to travel through dark forests and witness great magic. An urge to see the Sea Witches in the Merrows, to visit a Night Wild, to take up a blade and fight monsters.

Viggo had been right. He'd known me better than my own mother had. A love of peace did not quench a hunger for adventure.

"The Bards often travel this way in the spring," I said. "I've heard they take in anyone who can claim Elsh blood, as long as the person is brave and honest and has an art to share." I turned to my sister. "I could tell stories. I know all of Aslaug's tales by heart."

Morgunn clapped her hands and spun in a quick, tight circle. "And Mother taught us all the old Elsh steps, the Lone Traveler spins, the nomadic dances. I could teach them to the other Bards."

I shrugged. "It might work."

"It might, Torvi."

A band of Butcher Bards came to the Ostara festival in Trow the year before, traveling east. A mystic was with them, one with bright red hair. Some people shunned him—it's said the redheaded mystics often go down dark paths and bring forth dangerous magic. This Bard didn't seem to notice the stares or the whispers. He wandered the festival with his companions, drinking mead from large, polished horns. I took an instant liking to his quick smile and the sharp look in his green eyes.

On the second day of the festival, he set up a blue tent at the edge of the stalls, near three twisted, ancient oak trees.

"Sit down," he said when I entered. "Hold out your hand."

His voice hummed with the low, purring accent of the Elsh. He sat on a plain wooden bench next to a small table covered with a simple linen cloth. I sat down on the opposite bench, hooked my feet behind its legs, and held out my hand.

He wore no hood, letting his red hair flow straight to his shoulders. It flashed a dozen shades of scarlet in the light from the three candles on the table—wine, brick, cherry, ruby, blood. He took a stack of Elsh Fortune Cards from the pocket of his wool cloak, leaned forward, and placed them in my palm.

I looked down at the pile. The backs of the cards were painted black, with a yellow-eyed owl in the center of each, staring out at the viewer. They felt warm, as if they'd been left out in the sun. I itched to turn them over and see the beautiful illustrations on the other side.

"Shuffle, and then cut the deck."

I did as he asked, and then he swept the cards up with one long-fingered hand. He held the cards in his cupped palm for a moment, tapped the sheathed Butcher Bard knife that hung from his neck, then placed the top five cards on the table. "Your past, your present, your future, and two more for good measure." He flipped them over.

A man in a black cloak, staring down, five goblets at his feet.

A black wheel floating among clouds, guarded by a lion.

A black stone tower, ribbons of fire spurting from three high windows.

A hand holding an upright sword, a great white tree in the background.

A woman hanging upside down from a tree, a rope tied to one foot, arms tied behind her back, the tips of her hair touching the ground.

The illustrations were haunting, etched in black and red on a white background.

"The Five of Cups." He paused. "You lost someone close to you."

I nodded. "My father."

"The Wheel of Fortune." His eyes met mine. "You are happy and secure . . . but it will not last. It never does. The wheel is turning. Enjoy it while you can."

He pointed to the next card.

"The Tower. You need to prepare yourself for a great change. It might be tomorrow or three years from now. But it is coming."

He pushed the next card toward me. "The Ace of Swords. In the future, you will come to a crossroads, and you will need to choose a path. Which path you decide will cast a shadow over the rest of your life and influence it in ways large and small. Choose wisely. Trust in yourself."

He picked up the last card and then let it drop to the ground. "The Hanged Woman."

"What does it mean?" I asked when he stayed silent.

He merely shook his head, red hair dancing in the candles' light. "Be careful, Torvi," he said as I rose from the table, though I hadn't told him my name.

I had dark dreams that night and for many afterward. Sometimes I believed that the Butcher Bard was a trickster and a liar and that his prophecy would all come to nothing. Sometimes I believed in his cards, his reading, every word of it.

Lately I'd been wondering if the great, dark change from the Tower card was the snow sickness.

Have I weathered the worst, or are there more changes to come?

Morgunn rose from the grass and began to dress. She pulled her tunic over her head and glanced at me. "You would really be willing to join the Butcher Bards, Torvi?"

"Yes. But we'd have to find them first, which won't prove easy, isolated out here on this steading."

"We can tie a red cloth to one of the trees on those green hills." Gyda squinted her eyes against the noonday sun. "My grandmother was Elsh and taught me many things. A blue cloth tied to the uppermost branches of a tree will let passing Bards know that a steading is friendly and that they can shelter there for the night. A green cloth means that the region's jarl is suspicious of wanderers and that they should keep moving. A red cloth means there is danger nearby and help is needed." She bent to tighten the lacing of her boots—they were an old pair of mine and fit her well enough. "It might work, if they come this way."

I nodded, thinking on this.

Morgunn leaned down and grabbed the basket by her feet. "Chickens," she said. "Join me, Pig Witch? Do pigs know how to gather eggs?"

Gyda laughed, head tilted back, cheeks pink in the sun. "Call me that again and I'll cast a spell on you, girl. A pig spell, full of prophecy and blood and entrails."

"Looking forward to it, Pig Witch. I enjoy prophecies and entrails."

They moved off toward the barn, laughing.

I watched my sister as she walked away. She had braided her wet hair into two fat plaits down her back, her too-short blue tunic swinging just above her dimpled knees. She seemed younger than fourteen, especially next to Gyda's mature, muscular frame.

The chickens clucked, and a soft wind brushed the back of my neck. I looked around our steading, taking in all the open space, all the emptiness. It seemed as if Gyda, Morgunn, and I were utterly alone. The last three people in all of Vorseland.

The thought had a sort of peaceful carelessness to it, like

falling asleep outside on a warm day, body on the green grass, gentle breeze, bare toes.

But peace is just a season. Like the Wheel of Fortune card from the Butcher Bard's deck, life spins on, and nothing lasts forever.

FIVE

❧

I woke at midnight, when the crows began to caw.

I crawled out from under my furs and went to the window. Something felt wrong—the air smelled odd. Thick. I drew a sheepskin across my shoulders and walked down the corridor and through the main hall. I opened the front doors and looked out across our steading to the north.

Fire.

Trow was burning.

"We go up into the hills," I said. "Today."

The three of us stood outside, blinking in the dawn light, hands on our hips, watching the smoke rise on the far horizon.

"We are moving into Viggo's hut. Pack as if you aren't planning to return."

"Yes, Torvi," Morgunn said, eyes on the sky.

Gyda rubbed her bare skull. "Who's Viggo?"

"A shepherd I used to know."

"And where is he now that we can move into his hut?"

"You tripped over his grave on your first night here. By the rowan trees."

Gyda gave me a long look and then nodded.

We gathered together furs, sheepskins, flasks of *Vite*, bread, and the last of the smoked lamb sausages. We stuffed the food into leather packs and flung them over our shoulders. We didn't need much, only what we could carry.

I turned and traced my steps back down the east corridor. I went to my mother's room and put my right hand on the door. I pressed my left hand to my heart and said a prayer to Stray, the Elsh god of luck and fortune.

Watch over this Hall while we are gone. Watch over my mother's grave. Watch over Viggo's grave. Do this and I swear that I will not live meekly, and die meekly, in these Ranger Hills. I will not hide from the world. If adventure comes my way, I will run to greet it. I will grab the world by its leash and make it heel.

Aslaug would have told me not to bargain with the gods, and she would have been right. Yet I couldn't leave our steading without calling down a blessing. It was the only home I'd ever known.

I opened the fenced-in pasture near the barn and freed the chickens before we left. We kept no pigs, instead buying our pork from the market in Trow. We ate mutton mostly, butchered for us by Viggo. I supposed that gruesome task would fall to Morgunn now. Unlike me, she didn't mind slaughtering the poor creatures.

Our steading's large garden would have to be abandoned, but Viggo kept his own small patch of cabbages, leeks, carrots, peas, and herbs. It would be enough.

I took a deep breath. The air smelled of ash.

We followed the nearby stream as it wound north into the hills, past the rowan trees and across the endless blanket of soft spring grass. Morgunn released her hair from its braids as we walked, and the black shone almost blue in the sunlight. I supposed mine did as well. Indigo hair, indigo eyes.

We spoke little, pausing only to count sheep. The woolly beasts seemed to be flourishing, even without Viggo to watch over them. It was comforting to know that something survived and did well after all the death.

I enjoyed watching the sun move over the hills, changing the color from jade to gold to amber and back again, shadow and light moving across the land. A family of grouse ran in front of us, and I smiled.

We ascended the first hill, sweat gathering at our temples. A grove of black pines was at the crest—Viggo and I had spent time there one warm summer afternoon. My stomach fluttered pleasurably at the memory, but the feeling faded quickly, leaving only a deep heartache.

I selected the tallest tree and walked to its base.

Gyda gave me a wary look. "Are you sure you can do this?"

"Every Vorse girl worth her salt can climb trees," I said.

The druid shrugged. "The trees don't grow this tall on the Boar Islands. And I don't appreciate heights."

"Can't you just magic your way to the high branches?" Morgunn asked. "Chant a bit of druid gibberish, blink your eyes three times, throw a pebble over a shoulder, and whoosh, you're up a tree?"

Gyda and I laughed.

The druid brought out my sister's sardonic side, and I found it delightful.

"Yes, that is just how druid magic works," Gyda replied. "How clever you are, Morgunn."

They kept up the banter as I dropped my pack and furs and grabbed the red cloth from my pocket—it had once been a tunic of Aslaug's, one she wore for feast days.

I scrambled up, ten feet, twenty, thirty, fifty, seventy, gripping the bark with my knees and my feet, my hands clutching branches. I gave a yell of victory when I reached the top. Morgunn and Gyda echoed my yell from the base.

"I've conquered the tree," I shouted.

"What can you see from up there?" Morgunn asked.

I shielded my eyes and looked out, scanning the Cloven Tell Valley. It was a sea of green, pitted with a group of blackened lumps that used to be Trow. The smoke had weakened into thin gray wisps. I saw no one moving among the ash . . . not a soul.

"Nothing," I called down. "Nothing but trees and hills and birds." I didn't mention Trow.

I tied the cloth to a high branch, tight. The Butcher Bards would see it if we were lucky. If the gods were on our side.

45

We continued to follow the stream as it wound between hills, the sunlight dancing across the water's soft curves. It soon joined up with another beck and formed a proper river, loud and fast, a thousand shades of blue pouring over gray stones.

I'd first met Viggo on a day such as this in spring—warm sun, cool breeze, wild green hills, my life stretching out before me in an endless flow of lazy, quiet days.

My father had left on a beautiful day in spring, and each year my mother mourned his return to the sea during this season. She didn't suffer from a broken heart—she suffered from fury, fury that he'd left and that he'd broken his promise. She would wander the steading, searching for ways to relieve her rage.

My features resembled my father's. I have my mother's physical strength and height, but I have my father's straight nose, high cheekbones, and pointed Elver ears.

I have his soft heart as well.

Aslaug pulled me aside one day and told me to take a walk into the hills so that my mother could find some peace, for seeing my face every day fueled her anger.

Morgunn wasn't asked to leave. Unlike me, she didn't take after Father, with his serene, amiable gentleness. She was Vorse.

I spent the next weeks wandering like a stray dog until I turned half wild with it. I went farther away from home and stayed away longer than I'd ever done in the past. I walked and walked and walked.

That spring day, the sky was blue, with wispy, feathery

clouds, and the birds seemed to sing louder than usual. I followed our steading's stream to a nearby waterfall—I would often sit beside it and let the cold mist settle on my cheeks.

As I drew closer, I caught sight of something behind the cascading water, a glint of sun off something smooth.

He stepped out of the falls, naked from the waist up, tossing his wet head like a wild red stag.

Our shepherd was something of a legend among the women of Trow. They often whispered that Viggo was as shy as a deer and as handsome as a god. Aslaug had hired him a few months before to replace the old shepherd, Magda, who had decided to spend her last good years wandering Vorseland, as long as her ancient legs would allow.

I had yet to meet Viggo. He kept to his hut and his sheep, rarely coming to the Hall and appearing in the village only when he needed food and supplies. He was young for a shepherd, not much older than me, but I'd known younger—one of the Tathers' shepherds was a wiry girl of twelve, with wild red hair and a feisty temperament that matched any sharp-tongued village elder's.

I took one step toward him and then another. He shook his long hair again, and droplets hit my face.

"Viggo," I said, and then flinched when he opened his eyes.

He paused for a long moment and then whispered, "Torvi."

So he knew who I was.

His thick hair bled thin streams of water down his bare

sides. He had a wide forehead and piercing eyes under a deep brow. Classic Vorse. There was a pink scar on his left cheek, two inches long, and another of the same length down his right forearm.

"I'm not used to visitors," Viggo said finally, "but I can offer you some *Vite* or nettle tea."

I nodded. "Yes, to both."

He lifted a calloused hand and rubbed a palm up and down his cheek. "Come," he said.

Viggo took me to his stone cottage. It was hidden in a small grove of pine and juniper trees, hard to see unless you were really looking for it. I could feel his eyes on me as I walked in front, and I was suddenly aware of the way my thighs moved against my long tunic, and how my black curls swung between my shoulders.

The shepherd made me nettle tea over an open-hearth fire. His hut was small but clean, with a thick sod roof. I sat on a simple bench, my knees almost touching the flames. We sipped and didn't talk, but it was a soft and comfortable silence.

I emptied my cup but didn't leave. Viggo began to whittle a piece of brierroot into one of the fat, short-stemmed pipes Vorse shepherds smoke. He occasionally glanced at me but remained silent. He seemed at ease, despite what he'd said earlier about being little used to other people.

Viggo retrieved a small jug from a shelf in the corner, and we started sipping *Vite*. He passed the vessel to me, his fingers grazing mine, and I passed it back.

It grew dark. Morgunn would wonder where I was, but I couldn't seem to make myself care.

"A god," I said.

"What?" Viggo asked softly.

"The women in Trow say you look like a Vorse god, one of the strong, quiet ones—Obin or Ved. They say you were cast out of Holhalla for a love crime and are now in hiding, disguised as a shepherd."

Viggo smiled as he leaned over to stoke the fire, then broke into a low laugh. "Do they really, Torvi?"

"Yes," I said. "And now I see why."

———————————

I thought it would be easy to go back to Viggo's hut. I thought my memories of the place would fill me with happiness and peace. I was wrong.

He was everywhere. In the firewood stacked in neat piles against the outside wall. In the gray wool cloak that hung on a nail by the door. In the carved wooden mugs stacked on a small shelf, in the wooden bench by the stone hearth.

I climbed the narrow stairs to the loft. Viggo's spare tunic lay draped over the hand-carved wooden bed frame, right where he'd left it. He'd worn his other one to the grave.

I picked up the tunic, and it felt warm, as if he'd just taken it off. It smelled of grass and rain and wool and boy.

That last night before the snow sickness, we'd sat together outside his hut, huddled under furs, watching the stars.

"A storm's coming," he whispered. "I can smell it." He took a deep breath and let it out slowly. It turned to white fog in the cold spring air.

"This late in spring?" I sniffed the air. He was right. I smelled snow.

Viggo held me in the crook of his arm and wove his fingers deep into my curls, his palm cupping my skull. His eyes met mine. "I don't like the look of the sky. Go home, Torvi. I'll come to the Hall at dawn and make sure you're well."

I never saw him alive again.

I left the loft, went back downstairs, and started cleaning. I opened the front door wide to bring in fresh air. I built a fire in the hearth, and soon the crackling of the wood was harmonizing with the gentle wind outside. It made a sweet, natural song.

We prepared our supper just after the sun started sinking low, slanting off the grassy roof of the hut and glowing orange. We cooked soft-boiled eggs in river water and nibbled on thin slices of dried sausage.

Afterward, Morgunn curled up next to me underneath Viggo's double-pelt sheepskin. I'd caught her sipping from one of the flasks of *Vite* earlier, while we were cleaning the hut, but I'd said nothing. The wolf-priests had burned Trow. I'd let her take what comfort she could.

"We live in sod-roofed cottages like this on the Boar Islands."

Gyda held a wooden cup of warm spiced milk in the palm of her hand, sipping from it slowly. "The Pig Witches live on the beaches in huts with long stilts, to keep the ocean from flooding in. They share their homes with their pigs, and their villages are cold, dirty places." She paused and refilled her mug from the pot near the hearth fire. "But we druids live in the high, lonely hills in neat cottages tucked deep into dark forests. I feel at home here."

"And yet you will soon leave us," I replied. "You are on a quest for a sword. Are you ready yet to tell us this story?"

The druid smiled slowly. "No, not yet." She finished the milk and crawled under the sheepskin next to Morgunn. A few moments later, both she and my sister were sleeping, fluttering eyelids, soft breaths.

Viggo's short-stemmed pipe sat on a shelf on the nearby wall. I rose and took it in my hand. I ran my fingertips over the round bowl and thought about the time I'd spent watching him carve it.

The Ranger Hills get into your blood, he used to say. *Once you've seen them and spent time among them, they stay with you forever.*

Morgunn turned over and opened her eyes. She began to sleepily twist her hair between her fingers. "You can talk about him sometimes. Viggo, I mean."

I shook my head. "It's best that I don't."

Morgunn paused for a moment, then glanced over at Gyda. The druid slept deeply, chest moving rhythmically in and out. My sister lowered her voice to a whisper. "We are safe here, yes?"

"We are."

"Don't you think we should take to the road and go south, away from the wolf-priests?"

"No. Not yet. I want to see if the Butcher Bards find our signal. It would be much more prudent to join them than strike out on our own. As a druid, Gyda may know a bit of magic. But none of us are warriors. We haven't trained in the Seventh Degree. We don't even know archery. I wish Mother had taught us some weaponry."

Morgunn nodded. "She always meant to, I think, but she never found the time—"

She flinched suddenly, and I froze, listening.

Howling. It echoed through the hills, eerie and melancholy. I couldn't tell from which direction it originated or from how far away.

I sat down next to Morgunn. "The wolf-priests won't stay here long. The jarls may not care about a few villages burning in the Middlelands, but the Quicks will track the beasts down soon enough."

"But I've heard that Jarl Meath is near ninety and was on his deathbed last spring. The old bastard might be dead by now." She paused. "According to Gyda, this wolf leader Uther will not be easy to kill."

"The wolves come every year, and every year the Quicks drive them out again. Have faith, Morgunn."

She nodded and closed her eyes again. I walked around her curled-up body, opened the front door, and stepped outside.

The breeze lifted my hair and sent it flying. I scanned the dark silhouette of the hills and breathed in deeply. The air smelled fresh and soft and verdant. It smelled of Viggo.

I turned my back to the strong night wind and watched dark gray clouds move against a black sky.

SIX

※

A lone Fremish *wolf-priest had come to our steading the winter before.* She crept into our Hall one winter twilight, sneaking through the doors and hugging the shadows like a rat.

I was in the west corridor, returning from the barn, when I heard our servant Elna scream. I found the wolf holding a rusty dagger to the girl's throat, the doors of the Hall wide open, snow drifting in on a light evening breeze.

She was short and bone-thin, with bulging blue eyes peering out between thick, tangled hair, a grim mouth in a face streaked with mud. In her right hand she held the dagger, and her left gripped Elna's braid in a tight fist. She wore a shaggy wolf-pelt cloak, and her pupils were large and glossy—she was flying high on yew berry poison.

She was young, fifteen at most. Her forehead barely reached Elna's nose. Wolf-priests usually move in packs, and they rarely bother with steadings—we didn't provide enough sport. I figured this girl must be a rogue—cast out for some wolf crime.

"What do you want, wolf? We've no gold. We raise sheep, and the wool harvest isn't until spring."

"I didn't come for gold." She spat on the floor. "We care nothing for it. We seek only meat and screams and fire and blood."

We stared at each other, neither moving. With a quick jerk, the wolf-priest released Elna's braid and reached into her tunic. She pulled out a small vial filled with a thin, orange-hued liquid. "Drink this," she said, "and I'll let you both live."

"I'm not going to drink your poison, wolf."

"It won't hurt you. It will just let you *see*."

The vial contained yew berry juice. I'd heard the wolves would negotiate only with people who drank their poison. The girl didn't lie—it wouldn't harm me. It would likely only turn me senseless for a while, or perhaps give me a vision or two. Nothing worse than eating a Sly Barbaric Mushroom, which I'd done once before.

I looked from the wolf to Elna and back again. "Hand it here."

I pulled the small cork and sniffed. It smelled of sweet, ripe fruit and cold winter storms. I drained the vial and then threw it into the fire, where it shattered against the logs. I licked my lips. The poison tasted of crisp apples and fresh snow.

The wolf-priest released her dagger. It hit the floor, and I kicked it with the toe of my boot into the far corner. I grabbed Elna by the waist and pulled her to my side. She shuddered, as if to shake off the wolf's touch, and then leaned into me.

"Go," I whispered in her ear. "I don't know what will happen now—stay well clear of it."

Elna gave me a long look and then slid out of my arms. She crossed the hall and disappeared down the west corridor.

The poison began to work. I felt it creep into me, into my blood, into my heart. I felt my skin flush with the poison-heat.

The wolf turned to the side and whispered something under her breath. A cold sweep of air blew past me, colder even than the winter breeze from outside. I heard a strange whispering sound, and the fires in the braziers died, leaving only thin wisps of smoke.

The Hall went dark.

I caught movement in the far corners and flicked my gaze across the long room. Shadows, long and spindly, danced over the walls. I watched them, entranced, as they began to shift from shadows into . . . *creatures*, dark, furry animals, snaking across the floor, black eyes, black paws.

I took a step back. Then another. One of the shadows opened its black mouth and let out a squawk, like that of some poor hen after Aslaug had sliced off its head, one hard strike of her sharp ax.

So this was wolf magic.

It was vile.

It was wonderful.

The rogue wolf-priest whistled, high and shrill, and the shadow-creatures jerked left. They began to crawl up the nearest wall, oily black stains dancing to the wolf's tune.

Her bulging eyes met mine, and she hissed, two pink lips opening to reveal small, sharp teeth.

"Do you see my magic? Do you see my power?"

"*Yes*," I said.

I saw fear in her eyes, and hunger . . . not for food or safety or family, but for power. For *fire*.

She lifted her arm and drew a finger across the air in a short arc. The shadow-creatures fell back to the corners, like a gust of wind blowing dirt into a wall. They were simple, bland patches of dark once more.

I stood still, frozen, *savalikk*. My mind ached with the yew berry haze. It was hard to think . . .

The wolf spat again. The flames in the hearth rose up, two feet, three, until the entire Hall was as bright as daylight.

She craned her small, dirty neck and looked me in the eye. "Skroll craves a sacrifice. You will do."

She fetched her knife from the far corner and returned to me. She reached up and put the blade to my throat. She smelled of unwashed skin, raw meat, and ash. I tilted my neck backward to give her more room . . .

Let her slit my neck, I thought as my mind sank deeper into the poison. *Who cares? Who cares about anything but the blood and the screams and the life and the death and the fire . . .*

A shadow appeared in the open front doors. A real one. My mother moved to the left, as silent as the stars, and took the bow and quiver from the hook on the nearby wall.

"Let the girl go, wolf. I know your magic, and its limits, and your grubby wolf spells can't stop me from putting this arrow through your skull."

The wolf hissed, and the hearth flames flickered and died,

leaving only bright red embers. The Hall fell back into gloom. She hissed again and kept her knife to my neck. "I came here with a purpose, and I won't leave until it's done."

My mother loosed her arrow. It flew past the girl's head and nicked her ear.

The wolf muttered a string of curses as blood began to drip down onto her shoulder. She tossed her head, drops of blood splattering across my cheeks, and then lowered the knife.

I reached up and rubbed my neck with my palm.

The wolf slunk to the left, cloak swinging. She wiped a grimy hand down one of the Hall's tapestries, leaving black marks across yellow thread. "I need a sacrifice," she whispered. "Either I take one of these girls with me or I set this tapestry on fire and watch as this Hall burns to the ground. You choose."

My mother turned to me. "Torvi. Come here."

I went to her, and we stood shoulder to shoulder. The cold winter wind hit my back, and it made me feel strong. Vorse. I shook my head and rubbed my eyes. I felt my mind begin to ease off the poison.

The wolf watched us, her expression cunning and cold. "I've sworn an oath to Skroll. One of you in this Hall will die by morning."

"No. We won't." My mother raised the bow.

The wolf-priest dropped into a crouch. She began to howl like the wolf she thought she was, a high-pitched wail. She writhed, back arched, head thrust forward.

The hearth flames flared up, higher this time, four feet, then five. Her keening grew louder, and the air began to sizzle, to *crackle*, as if the Hall were on fire . . .

I felt my hair lift up, spread out, roots pulled tight. I felt the heat, felt the skin of my face begin to burn . . .

The arrow pierced the wolf's neck clean through and came out the other side. She swayed back and forth on her heels, then slumped over onto the floor. I heard a loud sigh, and the flames went out—not just the hearth fire, but all the braziers as well.

I walked forward and stared down at the dead wolf. Her blood began to pool near my feet, inching toward me. I watched it grow closer and closer, until it caressed the tips of my boots, a red-black shadow kissing my toes.

"Torvi?"

I looked up from the blood. "Yes?"

"Leave."

I nodded. I turned and walked down the hall, through the front doors, and cleaned my boots in the snow.

My mother burned the wolf beside the carcass of a dead sheep out in the east field. I stood nearby and watched the flames until the girl crumbled into ash.

The Fremish priests burn, the same as the rest of us Vorse, fire, ash, soot, dust.

I saw smoke again a few days later, a gray-black cloud about fifteen miles to the north. I didn't mention it to Gyda or Morgunn.

We shared Viggo's one bed in the loft or slept on sheepskin rugs in front of the hearth. We didn't talk about Uther or the wolves. We spent our days gathering food from the hills—wild celery and garlic, dill, amber cloudberries, pale-orange oak mushrooms. We spent our nights drinking and singing. Gyda was hardworking and focused when needed, but mostly she preferred drinking and jesting around the fire to anything else. She was cut from the same cloth as my sister in this way, and I adored it.

The druid was starting to fill the hole left in me after the snow sickness—she had Mother's strength, Aslaug's cheerfulness, Viggo's depth, and Morgunn's love of all things loud and boisterous.

I returned to the Hall during the day and brought the chickens to the cottage, carrying them two at a time, one under each arm, until we had all eight. They roamed freely and roosted on the roof after dark. So we had fresh eggs to go with the dried sausage, as well as early carrots from Viggo's garden.

"Show me how to do your magic," Morgunn demanded of Gyda one night after we'd all had too much *Vite* and sung too many of the old songs.

The druid swallowed a swig of liquor and flashed a mischievous grin, her eyes full of fun and fire. "No. Never."

"Is it like the Stregas?" Morgunn opened her eyes wide and

bent her hands into claws. "Do you gut pigs and weave your fingers through their innards? Do you bathe in blood and run shrieking through the night, screaming prophecies and making dirty Pig Witch love under the moon?"

Morgunn's words were starting to slur. My sister was lively and helpful during the day, when the sun was high, but when it grew dark, she started drinking. And she drank until she collapsed into sleep.

It worried me, but not as much as what she would do when the *Vite* ran out.

Gyda chuckled at Morgunn's gruesome depiction of Strega magic, which only encouraged my sister to continue her gory descriptions until the two of them were helpless with laughter.

Gyda finally held up a hand. "The truth is, I despise senseless killing, even of pigs. The Stregas are an ancient sect, and they are feared prophets and sorcerers. But I abhor the lot of them. They worship the Boar god Arcana—he is one of the old gods, from the time of the giants, when Vorseland was nothing but darkness and ice. Arcana is vengeful and secretive, and the Stregas' magic is violent, unpredictable, and unbalanced."

I nodded. "I also dislike killing animals. My mother called me soft for it. She said it was a weakness. She called it un-Vorse."

Gyda and I exchanged a look.

Morgunn shrugged. "I don't mind killing things. Chopping off chicken heads or slitting sheep throats is more interesting than pulling weeds in the garden or washing soiled tunics."

"You would make an excellent Pig Witch, then, Morgunn." Gyda rose and picked up Viggo's pipe from the shelf. "May I use this, Torvi?"

I nodded. "There's a pouch of dried kettle-leaf hanging in the corner. It was soaked in apple liquor before drying, and it smells like autumn. It was Viggo's favorite."

She filled the bowl of the pipe, lit it with a piece of coal, and breathed in deeply.

"You've done this before," I said.

"Yes." She grinned at me as she held the short stem cupped in one hand, her right side leaning against the wall. Soft rings of smoke flowed out between her lips, toward the ceiling. "Druids don't commit murder for their magic," she continued. "We look to nature for our spells, and we honor it by remembering the old ways—we sing to the wind, we dance in the moonlight, we make love in the rain, we feast under the sun." She paused, and a series of smoke rings filled the room. "Before I left, I was studying to be a Strick Rish—a high druid."

I looked into Gyda's death-gray eyes. "Show us something of your magic. I'm as curious as my sister, in truth."

Gyda glanced from me to Morgunn and then shrugged. She opened her free hand, palm down. She reached out over the hearth fire, a few feet from the peak of the flames, and then pursed her lips.

"Watch closely," she said.

The druid breathed in, and the flames rose up until they

touched her skin. She pulled her hand back to her side, and the flames dropped. Gyda pursed her lips again and whistled, long and low. The flames began to dance now, spinning and flowing until they formed into the shapes of three young women, arms entwined, faces tilted toward the sky.

Morgunn and I stared, mesmerized, as the flame-women twitched and spun.

Gyda whistled again.

I blinked, then turned to Morgunn and shook her gently. She blinked, once, twice.

"It takes years to master the studies of the Strick Rish." Gyda still leaned against the wall, eyes glinting in the firelight, hand holding the pipe. "Most druids don't reach their full potential until sometime in their forties. I've learned the basics of hypnosis, visions, apparitions, hallucinations. Not much more."

"That's enough," I said softly.

Gyda laughed. "It's a limited magic. I need darkness and shadows for it to work, and my victim needs to be fixed on me and under my gaze. I could have learned much more if I'd stayed."

Morgunn went to Gyda's side. She raised an arm and began to flutter her fingers through the curls of smoke floating from Viggo's pipe. "So why did you leave?"

Gyda finished her pipe, tapped the ashes into the hearth fire, and refilled the bowl. "There is an old druid story," she said finally, "that tells of a magical sword belonging to a Vorselander named

Esca. It is held captive in an ancient ash tree, one so old it has turned to stone."

I rose, fetched the *Vite*, and refilled our three small drinking horns. "The *Moon Serpent Saga* mentions Esca and this sword—Esca's forgotten lands lie somewhere in the Green Wild Forest, but the location has been lost for generations. Aslaug used to tell me the story. Some say Esca's jarldom is hidden by magic, and some say the jarldom disappeared into another world, and some say it never existed at all."

Morgunn took the *Vite* from me. "Whoever can find the sword and pull it from the tree will inherit Esca's lost throne."

Gyda nodded. Her head was a soft stubble of golden blond now. I often caught myself wanting to reach out and touch it. "The druids have a name for Esca's forgotten lands. We refer to them as *Avalon*. I was tracking Uther because—" She held up her hand. "Listen."

Howling.

It was far off, miles away . . . But I heard it clearly, the echo ringing off the hills.

I remembered that night in the Hall with the rogue wolf-priest, the yew berry poison flowing through my veins, my mind swirling, the girl calling up the shadows, knife in hand, her eerie, violent howls . . .

"That is no real wolf," Gyda said.

"It's them." I opened the door of Viggo's hut and looked out into the dark Ranger Hills. "No more songs tonight, sisters—the air is clear, and sound carries. And put out the fire."

Morgunn doused the flames, then turned to Gyda, voice low. "Why were you tracking Uther? What do the wolves have to do with Esca's sword?"

"There is a rumor among us druids that the Fremish wolf-priests know the hidden path to Esca's forgotten lands."

"Why would they know this?"

"Because Fremish wizards built the path and shared its se-crets with the wolves. Or so I'm told." She paused. "I intended to join their pack, learn what I could, and maybe kill a few wolves while I was at it, dark blades in soft throats on quiet nights." She paused and took a swig of *Vite*. "Then Uther threatened to burn a captured Quick, and my plans changed."

Morgunn grabbed the jug of *Vite* and refilled our horns.

"Enjoy it," I said to her. "This is the last of the fire liquor."

Gyda went to the door and motioned for us to follow her out-side. She raised her arm to the moon above and then put her fist to her heart. "Back on the Boar Islands, I had a vision of a female jarl sitting on Esca's throne. I discussed it with my elders, and they decided I should leave and discover Avalon."

"A woman on Esca's throne . . . Aslaug and Mother used to talk of such a thing, late at night, when they were relaxed and dreamy after a long day's work." I paused. "They used to day-dream about setting off and trying to find Esca's forgotten lands themselves."

"I remember," Morgunn said. "They used to complain that the current jarls were too busy expanding their lands or building trade to concern themselves with the poison-drinking wolves who burned their way across the Middlelands. They throw some coin at the Quicks and then mostly let us fend for ourselves. Mother encouraged me to seek Esca's sword when I grew older and win myself a jarldom—she used to whisper it to me late at night as I was falling asleep."

"And she used to whisper to me that I should never stand in the way of your glory."

Gyda's eyes met mine. "Your mother sounds cruel."

"She was . . . complex."

"Aren't we all."

The howling began again, unearthly wails that sounded like a child screaming in pain.

Morgunn crossed her arms and shivered in the chill night air. "I hope you are right, druid, and a woman will pull Esca's sword. Perhaps she could stop these wolf-priests from crossing the border."

I glanced over my shoulder at Viggo's hut, at the shepherd's crook that still leaned against the far side. "Perhaps she could hire an Orate Healer from Santor to create a cure for the snow sickness."

Gyda nodded. "She could do these things and much else besides, I think. If I can't pull the sword from the stone tree, then I will find the woman who can. The time has come."

I put my fist to my heart. "*Heltar*."

It was an Old Vorse word meaning "hero." It had been shouted in Halls across Vorseland for centuries, to move men and women to fight, to battle, to war.

"*Heltar*," I shouted again. I didn't care if the wolves heard me. I didn't care if the gods heard me. "*Heltar*."

"*Heltar*," Morgunn echoed.

Gyda raised her strong chin to the dark sky. "*Heltar*, to the woman who pulls Esca's sword. *Heltar, heltar*."

We finished the last of the *Vite* that night, nodding off one by one.

I woke some time later, startled by some unidentifiable sound out in the dark. Gyda was next to me, wrapped in her cloak, deep asleep.

Morgunn was gone.

SEVEN

❧

*S*he went to fetch more Vite, no doubt . . . She likely had some stashed in the Hall." Gyda's voice was calm, but she looked worried. "That girl is probably drunk right now and sleeping it off in some dark corner."

I'd woken the druid when I found Morgunn missing. The two of us stood by the hearth, embers glowing bright orange. Gyda lit Viggo's pipe and began to smoke it in long, slow puffs, waiting for me to make up my mind.

I took Viggo's gray wool cloak, threw it over my shoulders, and then handed my own to Gyda. "I'm not waiting until morning. Let's go get her."

The moon was fat and round, but its milky rays were weak and didn't cut through the dark night. The druid and I trod along in silence, listening to the calls of a pair of ravens overhead. Gyda was in front, the edge of her tunic rustling softly against the tall grass. I kept my eyes on the trail, not wanting to lose my footing in the dim light.

We'd walked a mile in silence, our attention focused on the

path in front of us, when Gyda made a low noise and halted. She turned and grabbed my arm, fingers pressing into my flesh.

She pointed at the horizon with her free hand—

I followed her gaze—

Fire.

We ran.

We ran, knowing it would do no good, knowing we were too late.

We reached the last hill and peered out over the edge—

The Hall—

My home—

Gone.

The roof caved in as I watched, flames leaping through the gap, climbing up the sky.

I howled. I howled like the day I buried my mother and Viggo. I screamed my sister's name into the smoke and flames.

Gyda grabbed me by the waist and yanked me to the ground. *"Be quiet, for Hel's sake, Torvi. Do you want them to find us, too?"*

I struggled for a few moments and then went limp, my cheek pressed into the dirt.

Gyda shook me and pointed toward the burning Hall with her chin. "Look."

I sat up and stared at the ruins of my Hall. I saw a dozen shadows weaving back and forth in front of the flames, shaggy cloaks, long, tangled hair.

As I watched, the wolves began to dance in front of my

burning Hall, their limbs wild, their movements reckless, unrestrained, primal. They spun and twitched and sang out their love for the flames.

Despite my sadness, despite my horror, I couldn't turn away.

The druid and I were enthralled by the wolf dance, and we sat, *savalikk*, as the moments passed, as clouds rubbed against the moon and blocked its light.

Everything was darkness and fire.

We didn't see the figures slinking toward us, didn't hear them, didn't smell them.

Hard arms encircled mine, and I felt a cold blade touch my throat. I heard Gyda gasp and saw a shadow pull her backward, a knife pressed to her heart.

Fear flared to life in me, hard, instinctual, a rabbit caught in a wolf's jaw—

I kicked and thrashed, elbows, fists, knees. I was tall and strong, and yet the arms around me did not budge. I heard Gyda swear next to me in the dark.

I slowed my breath and went still. "Do it quick," I said. "Open my neck and spill my blood, let it splash down my chest, let it cover us both. Just kill me already, you filthy wolf."

I tensed, waiting to feel the sting of a dagger slicing open my skin.

Stay strong, Torvi. Stay Vorse.

Instead of a blade, I felt soft lips touch my ear. *"I'm no wolf-priest. And lower your voice, damn it. Those wolves already got their hands on one girl tonight. Do you want them to get you as well?"*

"Let her go, Madoc," a voice whispered off to my right. "Let her see who we are." The arms dropped from my sides. I spun around and saw three knives strung on three cords around three necks.

Butcher Bards.

They'd seen the red cloth. They'd come.

I closed my eyes, bowed my head, and touched two fingertips to my heart. *Thank you, Stray.*

The tallest of the Bards made a quick, slicing motion with his hand. "We need to leave here. Do you have somewhere safe to go?"

"You said the wolves took a girl," I whispered, ignoring his question. "What happened to her? Did they burn her?"

"They bound her and drugged her with poison. They will take her with them, north, to Lake Le Fay."

I touched two fingertips to my heart again. *Morgunn.* Hope flickered in me—a hot, dark pulse, dangerous and steely.

The shortest of the three Bards leaned toward me. "I'm Stefan. Everyone in our camp was slaughtered by the same wolf-priests who just set that fire. We've been tracking them for three weeks—Uther's band is the last in the Middlelands. All the rest have headed into the mountains. We saw the red cloth tied to the tree, but we arrived too late to save the Hall."

My eyes met his. "Damn the Hall. Save my sister."

The taller Bard shook his head. "We've killed a dozen of the wolves, and we're nowhere near done. But we pick them off one by one—we can't attack the whole horde to rescue a single person." He paused. "We need to find a place to hide for the night. I slit the lookout's neck, but they will have another scout somewhere. We need to leave. Now."

"There's a shepherd's hut, hidden in the hills," I said. "You can stay with us."

––––––––––––––

I fed the three Bards wild mushroom soup from wooden bowls. They ate fast, standing close around the fire.

I kept the hood of my cloak raised, my face in shadow. I'd spent the last few weeks praying the Bards would come, and here they were. Yet I felt nothing.

Mother dead, Viggo dead, Father gone, Morgunn gone. I was alone, standing in a dead shepherd's hut with a druid and three Butcher Bards.

I feel nothing.

I turned to the three strangers and truly looked at them for the first time. The Bard named Stefan had smooth skin and soft, curly black hair. He was my height and strongly built. He wore simple wool trousers in the Elsh style, a short tunic of undyed linen, open at the neck, and a forest-green cloak.

He was younger than I'd first thought when I saw him in the firelight on the hill. My age, maybe, perhaps younger.

Stefan noticed my eyeing him and smiled. He set his empty bowl on the table and stepped forward. We gripped each other's forearms in greeting, and his touch reminded me of Viggo, fingers rough and steady from days spent outside.

"I'm Torvi," I said, then nodded toward the fire. "That's Gyda."

"I'm Stefan," he replied, though he'd already told me this back on the hill. "I sing. This here is Madoc and Ink. Madoc sings as well, and Ink tells stories. We roam the world, practicing our art . . . when we aren't killing wolves, that is."

Madoc gave me a nod but said nothing. His hair was a rich, dark brown, reaching almost to his shoulders. He wore the same clothes as Stefan, plus a cloak of dark gray.

The third Butcher Bard held out his hand. He was tall and thin and the youngest by far. He wore the hood of his rust-colored cloak pulled low over his face—it was half in shadow, like my own.

My fingers wrapped around Ink's, and he shook my hand firmly—he was strong, despite his bony frame.

"As Stefan said, I'm the storyteller." He gave me a shy smile. "My real name is Aeron, but you can call me Ink."

I returned the smile, glad to have a storyteller in my life again, for however long it would last.

Gyda brewed a pot of spiced walnut milk and then moved among us, handing out warm mugs. I saw the Bards watch her, eyes on the blond stubble of her hair.

"She's no Pig Witch," I said before they could ask. "She's a druid from the Boar Islands."

"And how is that any different?" Madoc stared at Gyda, eyebrows raised.

Gyda simply grinned. "When I get to know you better, Bard, I'll tell you."

Madoc laughed softly. "Fair enough."

Gyda emptied her mug of milk, then leaned against the wall and pulled out Viggo's pipe. Madoc glanced toward her again and then pulled out his own, thinner, with a longer stem.

"We Bards use myrtle-wood pipes," he said. "We like the taste the wood gives to the smoke. You are using a Vorse shepherd's pipe. Hand-carved, I think."

Gyda nodded. "Not by me. It belonged to someone Torvi knew—the shepherd who used to live in this hut."

Madoc's eyes met mine, and I saw compassion in his gaze. He was no fool.

The two of them smoked quietly, soft tendrils floating upward. Madoc's tunic was open at the top, and I saw the black hilt of a dagger nestled against soft, tanned skin.

I remembered the conversation I'd had with Morgunn, of how our mother had refused to let us learn weaponry. I reached forward and touched the knife at Madoc's sternum. "Could you teach me how to use this blade?"

The Bard took a step backward. "I would, truly, but we teach the Amber Dance only to other Bards."

The Amber Dance was the name of the Butcher Bards' fighting sequences—it was a variant of our own Seventh Degree.

This dance of blades was what allowed the Bards to be such skilled fighters.

Feared for their violence, loved for their arts. It seemed a good life.

"So take us in," I said. "Let me join you as a Butcher Bard. I have nothing left for me here."

Madoc shook his head. "This life is not for you. You are settled, and we are roamers."

Stefan raised a hand. "That is not for you to say, Madoc." He pulled out a pipe of his own and began to fill the bowl with dried leaves from a small leather pouch. "Things are changing. We take in anyone courageous and honorable, Torvi."

"And look where that got us." Madoc's voice was sharp. Cold.

Stefan glanced toward me. "Some members of our company thought at first that Ink was too young to be a Bard, too skinny, just another dirty orphan starving on the outskirts of Roark. But Ink can spin a tale that will haunt you the rest of your days. This was the right choice. I have never steered this troupe wrong."

Madoc swiped a palm across his cheek. He looked up, and I was startled to see that the Bard had tears in his eyes.

Vorselanders do not weep, not with others, and not alone.

But these Butcher Bards were Elsh. The Elsh wept if they wished.

"Yes," Madoc said. "Ink will be able to spin a lovely tale of how our companions died . . . how the wolves attacked our camp because we sheltered a band of Quicks. Of how little

Isobel—who was only fourteen and had the prettiest voice this side of the Quell Sea—died choking on her own blood. Of how young Emmelian told a story with the skill of the Old Ones, until a wolf put a knife between his ribs. Of how our friends looked when we found them the next day, stiff and blue and blood-soaked."

"*Enough, Madoc.*" Stefan's fingers went to his knife. "You know it wasn't anyone's fault. We took in those Quicks just as we took in Ink. And you. Bring this up again and there will be a skin-fight. We are in Vorseland, after all."

Madoc paused. "You're right," he said softly.

He went to Ink and put an arm around the Bard's shoulders. "Sorry, Ink."

Ink nodded. "You're upset. We all are."

Madoc turned and met my gaze. "You knew to tie the red cloth to that tree on the hill so that we would see it. You must be Elsh."

"I'm half Elsh. My mother was from Elshland. As was Gyda's grandmother."

"Do you know the Elsh Luck Lullaby?"

I tilted my head. "Why?"

"Sing it and then I'll tell you."

I shrugged. Mother used to sing this song at night by the fire. I knew it by heart.

> "*Sleep deep my child of luck,*
> *Tomorrow we run away.*

Sleep deep my child of luck,
Tomorrow we follow Stray.
Dream deep my child of luck,
Tomorrow we face the beast.
Dream deep my child of luck,
Tomorrow we head east."

Gyda joined in on the third line, her voice low, mine higher. It was a beautiful song, melancholy and tender, with a hypnotic melody that made the listener crave the next note.

Madoc watched me closely as I sang. When we finished, he turned to Stefan. "You see? We are Elsh. These songs are in our blood—it unites us, ties us together with a common thread. Those Quicks were full Vorse and had no place among us. They were the reason our friends were killed."

"You're wrong, Madoc," I said. "It's us against the wolf-priests now. It's us against Uther."

Gyda put down her pipe and came to my side. "Elsh, Vorse, what does it matter? We all wish to drive these wolves back to Frem."

Madoc stared at the fire for a long moment, then swiped his cheeks with his right palm again. "True enough."

Stefan's posture relaxed. He went to Madoc and put his palm on his companion's heart. "You must find peace, Madoc. You could slay Uther and every wolf-priest in Frem, but it will never be enough until you leave this rage behind."

He turned to Gyda and me. "Madoc sings so well you'd

think he sold his soul to the gods for the gift. But he takes death hard—he's concerned about your sister right now, despite the fact that he's never even met her. That's Madoc."

"Don't talk about me as though I'm not standing right here, Stefan."

"I'll do anything I damn well please." Stefan grinned good-naturedly, and his eyes met mine. "Madoc feels things deeply, but he is a demon with that knife of his. He's killed eight wolves to my two."

Madoc smiled and then gestured toward the Bard with his pipe. "And Stefan is the most lighthearted person I've ever met. He will laugh in the face of danger, failure, and tragedy."

"They balance each other," Ink said with another shy smile.

I picked up Viggo's pipe and began to take small puffs, letting my lungs grow accustomed to the feel. "Do you know why Uther took my sister?"

Ink stood near the fire, and I watched as he lowered his hood and removed his cloak. The shadows fell from his face. *Her* face—I'd been thrown by her height and the husky tone of her voice, rare in someone so young. She had almond-shaped eyes and freckles on the bridge of her nose, and her short red hair fell in wavy curls around her temples and the tips of her ears.

"Madoc questioned one of the scouts," she replied. "The wolf was young and not used to pain. We discovered that Uther is rounding up Vorse girls for recruitment. She wants to bolster her wolf pack, attack a Great Hall, and conquer a jarldom. The kidnapped girls either agree to kill in the name of Skroll or choose the fire and are burned alive. Most choose Skroll."

I closed my eyes and put two fingers to my heart. "Hel."

Ink nodded. "Hel, indeed."

"From here we head north, toward Lake Le Fay," Stefan said. "We rescue Torvi's sister and kill as many wolf-priests as we can, by stealth, by cunning, by whatever it takes. We don't quit until every one of Uther's damn wolves is dead and burned to ash."

Gyda faced Stefan and put her fist to her heart. "I had every reason to hate Uther before she burned my friend's Hall and took her *Vite*-guzzling sister." She paused. "Our paths will cross again, and this time I will defeat the she-wolf. I'm going with you."

Stefan nodded, followed by Madoc, and then Ink.

Gyda looked at me. "Will you join us, Torvi? I would not like to leave you here to suffer your sorrow alone."

I held her gaze and hesitated.

I once asked Viggo how he'd obtained his two pink scars. He lowered his pipe, turned to me, and said, "Action is the surest way to defeat grief."

Whom he had grieved for to learn that wisdom, I didn't know, and never would now.

I leaned forward and pulled the knife from the leather sheath around Stefan's neck. "How long would it take you to teach Gyda and me the Amber Dance?" I ran the blade across the end of my thumb, and drops of blood oozed from my finger. It was sharp. Very sharp.

"A few months to learn the basics. Eight or nine weeks, if you prove to be fast learners." Stefan's gaze flickered from Gyda back to me. "This is a death mission. We three Bards made a pact to hunt the wolves. To the end. We have nothing to lose, and we take risks. I would not bring the two of you on such a journey."

Gyda merely shrugged and ran her fingers over her scalp. "I saw my death in a dream. I will not die, not at the hand of one of these wolves."

Ink took a step forward and placed slender fingers on Gyda's shoulder. "Dreams can lie."

Gyda laughed, a deep, soft chuckle. "True enough. But I will seek out Uther, regardless. She . . . has something I need." The druid paused. "And I want to get back that reckless fool sister of Torvi's, even if the brat does keep calling me a Pig Witch."

"And you?" Madoc glanced toward me.

My mother had said I would spend my life in the Ranger Hills and never leave. But she was dead, and I was about to prove her wrong.

I put my palm on my sternum, where my future knife would rest. "*Fortune favors brave women*. I will not spend the rest of my life hiding out here in this shepherd's hut, alone. If you Bards are going to hunt down Uther and the wolves, then yes, I will come with you. I will rescue Morgunn or die trying."

I moved my palm to my heart and felt the deep, hard pulse that craved vengeance. This ache would not be satisfied until a pile of wolf-priest corpses lay at my feet. I knew what this meant and where this feeling would take me.

"I may be a softhearted farm girl who's never traveled beyond the Middlelands, but I want wolf blood, a river of it," I said.

Madoc bowed his head and put his hand on his Butcher blade. "Your wish is my command."

EIGHT

We left at night.

The Bards had been hunting wolves for three weeks straight and needed rest. They'd slept through the day, bodies huddled together on the floor by the hearth. Gyda and I moved quietly around them.

I found Viggo's leather bag under the bed in the loft. He'd often taken it with him when he camped out with the sheep on the hills. I gathered extra clothing, nettle tea, two dull kitchen knives, flint, steel, and char cloth. I rolled Viggo's extra tunic into a bundle and slipped this in as well—I could use it as a pillow during the nights ahead, sleeping beside the fire. This is what I'd told myself, at least, when I made room for it.

I thought of Olli from the *Blood Frost Saga* as I packed my things. She was eleven when she set off on her own for the Skal Mountains, on a quest to find her sister, Eela, who had fled north after stealing a magical sword from a dying Elsh hedge-fighter.

I said my farewell to Viggo's hut. I ran my fingers over the hand-carved bench, the soft river stones of the hearth, the downy sheepskins that lay everywhere, giving the place a warm, snug feel.

Who knows when I will return.

The thought of the shepherd's home sitting empty as the years passed, rotting under wind and rain and snow until it finally collapsed in a sad heap of decayed timber—

Hel. It made my heart ache.

I woke the Bards at twilight. They each jerked when I touched them, quick hands to sharp knives. I imagined I would do this as well when I'd been on the road awhile.

We sat outside on the grass, eating dried sausage and hard-boiled eggs as the sun set, the song of the night birds trilling in the background.

"*The gloaming.*" Madoc waved a hand over the horizon. "That is what they call the end of twilight in Elshland."

His eyes were alert and clear, and his smile was easy and relaxed. The long rest had done him good.

"The gloaming," I repeated. "It's a fitting word—pretty, but melancholy."

I stood and swung Viggo's leather pack over my shoulder. It settled into the side of my torso in a comforting way. I'd given Gyda my cloak and wrapped Viggo's around my own shoulders—I was just tall enough to keep the hem from dragging on the ground.

The Bards finished eating and rose as one, three graceful

shadows under a darkening sky. I turned and closed the door to Viggo's hut one last time, my palm lingering on the handle.

"You will return," Ink said, moving to stand near me.

I glanced toward her. "Life shifts with the wind, and only death is certain."

Ink nodded, delicate chin moving under her drawn hood. "Say a prayer to Stray, then."

I moved two fingers to my heart. I, unlike Olli, from the *Blood Frost Saga,* would be back again someday.

Let it be so, Stray.

I heard a clucking noise and looked up—the chickens were roosting on the roof. They'd be fine on their own if a fox didn't eat them, and they could forage for bugs until winter. It was the best I could do.

I pointed north. "We can follow this stream for a while and then move onto the sheep trails for a few miles until we reach the Cloven Tell Valley. From there we can drop down onto the Stretch if we wish—we can move faster this way, though it does carry a certain amount of risk."

The main road through the Middlelands was known locally as the Stretch. It ran from the foot of Wolf Peak in the Skal Mountains to the city of Dongor in the south. Most of the major villages in the region lay near or on this road.

"The wolves fear no one and invite confrontation." Stefan scanned the dark hills, eyes narrowed. "Still, they don't often take the Stretch—makes them too easy a target for the Quicks' arrows. Lake Le Fay is some fifty miles from here, but they will use footpaths to get there."

Gyda nodded. "They are wolves. They slink down dark trails like beasts—they don't walk the open roads. They use the Stretch only when they attack a village."

Stefan looked at Gyda, eyebrows raised.

"Gyda followed Uther and the wolves for several days," I said, "before she came to live with Morgunn and me."

"Why would you follow a band of wolf-priests?" Madoc tilted his head, eyes on the druid. "Have you sworn to hunt them, like the Quicks?"

Gyda adjusted her cloak and gave Madoc another of her sly looks. "I have my reasons."

Madoc smiled. "Keep your secrets, then, wizard."

"I'm no simple wizard, Bard. Druids have religion—we worship the goddess Dune, and she is kind and wise. We have order and law, myths and traditions. Wizards are rogues who worship only magic and themselves."

Stefan pointed a thumb at Gyda. "Lots of opinions, this one."

I laughed. "Only about magic, which is her right."

Gyda gave me a nod and then pulled her hood down low over her face.

I didn't glance back over my shoulder at Viggo's hut as we left. It felt unlucky.

We followed the stream north, mile after mile, the night stretching out before us. The sheep trails crisscrossed the hills, eventually splitting off to the east or ending at the Bro-cee Leon Forest. The paths had many twists and turns, but I'd walked them enough times with Viggo that I moved forward with ease.

Stefan and I led, followed by Madoc, then Ink. Gyda took the end. We were mostly silent, speaking rarely, five figures slipping over black hills.

Around midnight we crossed paths with a shepherd. He was bony and young, with startled brown eyes. He pushed a cart filled with combed wool. The moonlight showed a face and tunic streaked with dirt, and his cheek bled from a cut near his ear.

Despite the blood and the dirt, his wool looked clean and soft. He was headed south to sell at one of the Fleece Festivals, no doubt. Viggo would have been on this journey as well, if he'd lived.

The shepherd drew near to me as he passed, so close that his arm brushed mine. "*Go back to where you came from*," he whispered. "*The wolves have come.*"

My eyes met his. "The wolves are whom we are seeking."

"You had best make peace with your gods, then."

I watched him over my shoulder until he disappeared into the dark.

I walked more carefully after this, my gaze on the surrounding hills. The tops of the nearby trees rustled as a wind blew past, and I shivered and pulled my cloak tighter around my shoulders.

Ominous warnings, be damned. Ominous winds, be damned. I wouldn't turn back now. I was all in, to the end.

We paused at dawn to nibble on cheese and tart green spring apples picked from a nearby tree. We'd eat the same for our midday meal.

A few more miles of brisk walking and we came to a halt at the top of a hill. I stood at the edge and looked out over the lower valley. We were fifteen miles from my steading, on Tather land—I'd been here the year before. Mother, Morgunn, and I had been invited to Tather Hall to celebrate the festival of the Wild Hunt.

I smiled at the memory. It had been a pleasant visit. The brawny, red-haired Tather sons were brave, jovial, and lively, and their Hall was filled with people from across the Middle-lands. Morgunn spent most of the celebration drunk beside the hearth, tucked gently between two Tather brothers twice her size.

I pictured my sister, hands tied, fingers numb, wrists scraped raw, stumbling behind a shaggy-cloaked wolf with bulging eyes.

I put my palm to chest and pressed in, as if I could hold the shards of my heart together by sheer force.

At least she lives.

I lifted my hand to shield the sun. The Stretch cut through the valley, wide and arrow-straight. I counted five villages spread across the lush, grassy plain and then glimpsed a few more hidden in patches of woodland. They were too small to have names—just hamlets really, a few rows of stone huts, with fields and mead-ows leading up almost to the doorsteps.

"Let's explore." I gestured toward the valley. "If the wolves are hiding nearby, the villagers will know."

Stefan nodded. "Just keep your eyes wide open, everyone."

We dropped down off the sheep trails and onto the main road. The Stretch was paved with stone, a remnant of the Raven War, when the Truscans from across the sea tried to conquer Vorse-land. They did not succeed, either with the land or the people. The Stretch was their last, doomed effort to clobber the Vorse into submission and civilization, stone by stone. They built the road for their army to travel in ease, and it was their downfall—roads are civilized, and the Vorse are not. The Stretch gave them a target. Vorse warriors from every jarldom united for this one brief time in our history, and they picked off the Truscans, one by one, then ten by ten, then fifty by fifty, then army by army, until the road was littered with corpses from the Skal Moun-tains to the Fremish border.

Aslaug had often compared the Vorse to the spotted horses of Riffa. It was said the Riffa horses had never been tamed, not throughout all the centuries since time began. Wild to the heart, wild to the bone.

I was proud to be Vorse. Or half Vorse, at least. I enjoyed the beat of my Vorse heel on the old Truscan stone of the Stretch. I felt it connecting me to my ancestors, to all the Vorse who had come before and fought and died to keep this land our own.

The Stretch was more dangerous than the sheep trails, but it didn't feel it, with miles of green trees arching over the path and shaggy cows grazing behind short stone walls. The sun was out, bright and strong, cutting through thick white clouds. Madoc walked in front. He often stopped and glanced around, eyes on the hills. Locks of dark hair clung to his throat, his skin damp in the sun's heat. It seemed to gentle him somehow.

Stefan and Gyda strode side by side, and I often heard the cheerful sound of their muted laughter. I walked beside Ink. She had become less shy as the morning wore on, and she spoke to me easily and warmly. I liked her thin, loping legs, her wide smile, her husky voice with its soft, pleasant tone that made listening a pleasure. We talked of small things: the types of trees we passed, the birds in flight above us, the names of mushrooms that grew along the road, our families, past and present.

"My father returned to the sea," I replied when she inquired about my parents. "Despite his promise. He was always a sailor at heart. The snow sickness took my mother this spring."

Ink nodded. "My mother is also gone."

"How did she die?"

"She was taken prisoner by Strega pirates when I was a child. She married one of the Pig Witch sorcerers, gave him four daughters, and bided her time. He let his guard down on the day his first son was born, and she gutted him like one of their pigs. She returned to Elshland, and to me, but eventually grew heartsick for her Strega children and her dead Pig Witch husband. She wasted away over the winter, and I buried her on a hill that overlooked the sea."

"Is that when you took to wandering?"

Ink's footsteps halted, and her eyes met mine. "Yes."

"Does it get easier?"

"Some. Especially if you keep moving." She paused. "You lost more than your mother, though. I believe you lost the shepherd who used to live in the hut we stayed in."

I nodded.

"And now the wolf-priests have taken your sister."

I nodded again.

Ink gave me a quick, sad smile. "Life is still worth living. It still is."

We walked on. I let myself think of Viggo over the next mile. I didn't stop the memories until my heart felt as if it had been knifed, blood spilling down my ribs.

We reached the first hamlet around noon. I saw girls picking berries in the hedgerow as we neared and a few boys chasing sheep. I saw mothers lullaby-ing infants, and a young farmer in a freshly tilled field, strong muscles sweating in the sun.

We received a few stares but were ignored until an older woman with faded brown hair set aside her butter churn and rose to her feet as we passed. She had a reckless, haughty look in her eyes—she'd outlived her fear of death and wasn't afraid of much anymore. She stopped in front of me, reached up, put her finger on my chin, and tilted my head down to look me in the eye.

"What are you doing in our village, girl?"

"Tracking wolves."

"The Quicks have driven them out of the Middlelands."

I shook my head. "Not all. One of the packs is still here, and rumor has it they plan to set up camp on the banks of Lake Le Fay."

The old woman turned and nodded at something off to the right. "See that tree, the tall one?"

We all tilted our heads up, scanning the length of a giant red pine, wide copper trunk framed by jade-green needles that twitched gently in the breeze.

"A red pine," Madoc said. "They are handsome trees. One of the largest in Vorseland."

"One of the largest anywhere," Stefan added.

"It's said their needles whisper the last words of the dying." Ink turned her head, listening.

I shivered in the bright sun. The tree's rustle did sound raspy and unearthly. Mother's voice had sounded this way on that last night.

"There is a watcher up there." The old woman flicked her chin toward the tree again. "Everyone under the age of eighty or over the age of ten takes a shift, night and day. We haven't survived this long, living on the Stretch, without learning when to run and hide. If this pack were hiding in our part of Cloven

Tell, we would know. We've seen smoke, but the wolves haven't come sniffing around here. Not yet."

The woman snapped her arm out and grabbed a strand of my hair between her worn, wrinkled fingers. She pulled it hard. "Wolves and witches. All wicked, all foul." She let go of my hair, and her gaze fell on Gyda, on her golden-stubbled skull. "Do you think you're better than the wolves, Pig Witch? Do you think you have the right to hunt them?"

"I'm no Strega, old one. I'm a druid."

"Wolf, witch, druid, Drake . . . what does it matter? All wicked, all foul." She put her gnarled hands on her lower back and moaned. When she straightened, she turned her cunning gaze on Stefan.

"I've seen no wolves, but the watchers have spied a pack of Drakes moving through the Middlelands, skulking down the Stretch. I'd stay away if I were you."

She sat down again with a great, heavy sigh, done with our talk. But for all her curt words, the woman gave us a drink of sweet, fresh milk before we left and wished us luck on our hunt.

We ate our supper at the foot of a small hill, next to a thin stream, a half mile off the Stretch. An old oak tree grew nearby, its thick limbs covered in soft green moss.

Stefan had snared a rabbit earlier, and it was sizzling in the black stewpot he carried with him, handle tied to his pack. Madoc slipped in a handful of dried herbs, a pinch of flaked

Fremish salt, and two shots of *Vite* from a flask in his pocket. The Butcher Bards ate well on the road.

Afterward, we washed our bowls in the cold stream and then curled up against the oak's large, curving roots, rubbing our full bellies and sipping *Vite*.

Ink and Stefan began to teach Gyda a game played with black-edged Butcher cards. I watched Madoc tense, off and on, in response to noises I didn't hear. He was on guard, and I felt better for having him near.

He reached up suddenly and took one of my locks between two fingers. "Your hair curls in fat ringlets like an Elsh Highlander's, but it's as night-black as an Elver's."

"Aye," I said, letting my word purr through my mouth in the Elsh accent.

Madoc let the lock drop, his finger grazing my cheek as he pulled his hand away. He offered me his pipe, and I took a long puff.

Gyda was on my left, Viggo's pipe to her lips. Stefan and Ink each smoked their own, white curls drifting between branches.

"We are still in the lush part of the Middlelands," Madoc said. "Have you traveled much farther north?"

"No. This is the farthest I've been from our family steading."

Madoc shook his head in a way that was both slightly scornful and rather melancholy.

"It wasn't by choice," I said. "Not everyone can roam, Madoc. I had a life on that farm, and I made the best of it. And when my life shifted and pushed me toward the open road, I embraced it."

I prickled at any hint that I was soft, that I was fearful, that I was less than Vorse.

Madoc put his hand on my shoulder. "Fair enough, Torvi. You are right."

"What is Vorseland like outside the Middlelands?" I asked. "I've always wanted to see it for myself."

"Depends. Up north, it's fairly wild. Instead of soft, rolling hills and grassy meadows, the landscape shifts to deep black lakes and deep, dark forests."

I took a puff from his pipe. It was no shepherd's kettle-leaf—the smoke tasted sweet and smelled autumnal—freshly harvested wheat, crisp air, clean wool, ripe apples. "What is this?"

"Brickle-leaf. It grows only on the high hills of Elshland. They dry the leaves in fall, near the red-gold fields of elf berries, and it takes on the taste of the fruit."

Ink leaned toward me and offered a sip of *Vite* from a flask. Her freckles shone in the pink-tinted evening light, speckling her long, thin arms and long, narrow nose. I took a drink and handed the flask back to her with a nod of thanks.

Gyda held out her palm, and Ink passed her the liquor. "The old woman in that hamlet spoke of a band of Drakes," she said. "What do you know of these mystics, storyteller?"

Ink flashed the druid a quick smile. "The Drakes are prophets from Creet, an island farther south than Iber. They can read the stars and find your fate in their glow. It is men, mostly, who have the gift. Or this is whom they are willing to teach, at least. Their adepts take a vow of celibacy, so they are unable to pass on their arts to their children." She took a breath through soft lips and then let it out again. "As you know, the Drakes often travel to Vorseland looking for fresh blood—clever Vorse boys they can train in their art. They have red cloaks and scarlet-dyed beards. If they come upon us, we can't refuse them our fire. It's unlucky and possibly dangerous."

Ink then proceeded to tell us a tale about Drakes, called *Nimway's Blade*. One balmy summer two of the red-cloaked mystics were summoned to a jarl's Hall to read the sand and stars for the jarl's beloved thirteen-year-old daughter, Nimway, as a name-day gift. The two Drakes divined that Nimway was the true daughter of a Boar Island Strega and would one day take up arms against the jarl. The jarl accused his wife of adultery and sentenced her to death by hanging. Before the sentence could be carried out, Nimway sneaked into the jarl's chamber as he slept, then beheaded him with his own double-headed battle-ax.

"You can see why the Drakes are treated with suspicion," Ink said when she'd finished the tale. "People seem to desire divination almost as much as they fear it."

Stefan crossed his arms and leaned back against the moss-covered oak. "A thankless task, prophecy. No wonder the Pig People are hostile and unfriendly, as a rule. Thank the gods Gyda exhibits none of these traits."

Gyda groaned loudly. "I am no Pig Witch, you ignorant rat bastard of a Butcher Bard. Say that one more time and I'll gut you and read your entrails."

Stefan burst into laughter, his eyes dancing. "You threaten better than anyone I know, druid. You make an art of it."

This made us all laugh, Gyda included.

My friend was both good-natured and fierce, quick to anger and quick to forget. Mischievous temperaments such as Stefan's couldn't resist provoking her.

My sister could never resist it, either.

Morgunn and I had never been apart, not even for a night, and I missed her. I missed the delicate salty smell of her skin and the warmth of her arms around me at night, as we slept beside the fire.

I said a prayer to Stray to keep her safe. Mother had always said that Morgunn was the brave one, the fighter, the survivor, the warrior, the true Vorse.

But when Stefan asked if Gyda and I were ready to learn the steps of the Amber Dance—the twelve ways of the knife, the twelve ways to cut and kill—I said yes.

In the last handful of decades, small schools had sprung up across Vorseland, teaching the steps of the Seventh Degree to any Vorse girl or woman who desired to learn. The schools were called Ovies, in tribute to the Boneless Mercy who had first taught the Seventh Degree to the legendary Frey. It was a training sequence that was best done with an ax or other large weapon, whereas the Elsh steps were for daggers and smaller blades.

"Hold the knife like this, Gyda, tip forward, edge pointed down." After a scornful glance at the two short, fat shepherd knives I'd take from Viggo's hut, Stefan lent Gyda his sleek Butcher blade. "Doing this allows you to dart in quick and low."

The druid stood in the shadow of the twisted oak tree, the bright sun setting slowly behind her. She moved easily through each fighting stance—she was a swift study. Or she had a good teacher. Both, perhaps.

I watched the two of them for a while, smiling as they exchanged barbs back and forth. Stefan referred to Gyda as a "damned druid," and she called him a "Butcher Bard bully," and both were thoroughly enjoying themselves.

"Some Butcher Bards throw their knives," Madoc said, handing me his dagger with a flick of his wrist. "This has value, since it can be done at a distance, like archery. But you can lose your knife that way, and you won't find another blade this sharp until you visit a Night Wild. So we practice close fighting."

He moved behind me, slid his arm across my belly, and then pulled it back, snap. "Quick moves, quiet blades—this is the way of the Bards."

We began in earnest. First the steps, then the sequences— lunge, sweep, jump, on and on—until we finished the first cycle of the Amber Dance.

"Dance the dance of the knife," Ink yelled out, encouraging us between puffs of her pipe. "Dance the dance of the blade."

We practiced the Amber Dance until the gloaming streaked

the sky with bright stripes of copper and red. There were actually eighteen cycles in all, but only the most dedicated Butcher Bards could perform the last six, and only after years of study.

Ink soon put down her pipe and joined us. For all her height, the storyteller excelled at the knife jigs. Where she was long and graceful, Stefan was short and fast, infusing his cycles with his easy good humor—he grinned each time he completed a perfect sequence, eyes gleaming, black curls tousled.

Madoc, on the other hand, made the knife dance look like art.

"It's cycle thirteen," Ink announced as Madoc leaped high and then landed low and light. "Thirteen is one of the trickiest to master—it's the sequence devoted to shadow-kills. This is why Madoc excels at slaying Uther's scouts."

Stefan gestured to Ink. "Stop watching Madoc flaunt his skill. I want to show this druid how to slit a neck, quick and clean."

Ink nodded. "Yes, they should both learn." She unclasped her cloak and then knelt in the soft grass.

Stefan gently lifted Ink's chin with his palm and then took Gyda's hand. "Careful now, you don't want to actually cut our poor storyteller. With your left hand, feel for the pulse, at the point where it's strongest, and with your right—"

Gyda pulled the six-inch piece of steel across Ink's throat, a few inches from her skin.

Stefan laughed. "We'll make a Butcher Bard of you yet. Torvi, your turn."

I took the knife. I put my fingers to Ink's strong, thin neck and pressed in softly, feeling for the beat of her blood.

I sliced the knife through the air, hard and swift.

"Good," Stefan said. "Though a stab to the neck is as good as a slice, and often easier to accomplish." He helped Ink to her feet and clapped her on the back. "But Uther's wolves aren't going to kneel down and just let you slit their throat as amiably as our red-haired poet here."

"Aye," Ink said. "And the best thing is to *not* use your knife. Your enemy's eyes will be drawn to it, so flash it about to distract them and then knee them in the stomach. When they're down on the ground, rolling in pain, *then* you open their necks."

"Spoken like a true Butcher Bard," Madoc said with a laugh. He'd finished the cycles and was catching his breath, one hand slowing filling his pipe as his gaze scanned the nearby hills.

We practiced until it was full dark and then halted so we could raise the tents—true Elsh roamers did not sleep in the open air. The Bards' tents were simple things of strong, waxed wool, rolled into bundles and easily carried. They would keep the wind out, and the rain as well.

Before bed, Madoc and I wandered downstream for a short night-walk. The beck was a tributary of the Sin, a main river that ran north to south, weaving through the Ranger Hills. I stopped at a bend in the stream and knelt on the banks. I cupped my hands, splashed cold river water onto my cheeks, and drank deeply, smiling as it cooled my mouth and throat, dry after the knife training.

The Bard sat down beside me, dragging his fingers through the water. The two of us listened to the stream chuckle and gurgle, flowing on, oblivious.

"Torvi?" he asked.

"Yes?"

"I'm glad you joined us."

I met his gaze. "Why? I have nothing to offer. I can't fight. I have no skills in archery or stealth or battle. I don't even know a bit of magic, like Gyda."

"I enjoy your company, is all."

I nodded and then smiled again.

Madoc fetched a black jug from his pack and passed it to me. "Moongold cider. It's made from apples and honey, by the light of a full moon, and left to ferment until it's strong as Hel."

I took a long drink, savoring the liquor as it slid down my throat.

"Careful," Madoc said. "It's stronger than you think."

"I've never tasted anything like it." I handed the jug back to Madoc, and he drank deeply. "It's better than our *Vite*, even. It tastes like . . . moonlight. My sister, Morgunn, would have loved its sweet, fiery taste."

"The Bards hold an apple festival every fall," Madoc said softly. He gave me the jug again, and I took another drink. "Each year the clans rejoin in an ancient apple grove near Whitby-on-the-Sea. We pick fruit and brew hard cider and feast and drink. Afterward, the Bards who own Iber horses travel to Elshland and stash the cider in nooks and crannies up and down both coasts, as well as a few secret spots in Vorseland and Frem. The liquor grows better with age. When this jug runs out, we should be able to get more from one of the Middleland Butcher Bard caves."

"You have caves with secret stashes of cider?" I raised my eyebrows. "That is . . . excellent."

We drank in silence until we were both flushed and smiling, and then we rose and returned to the camp.

Stefan generously lent his tent to Gyda and me and shared with Ink. We said our good-nights, and then the druid and I crawled through the wool flap and cuddled into each other, pulling our cloaks in tight.

Madoc would take the first watch, then Ink, then Stefan. They would let us two newcomers sleep through the night, until we'd gotten used to life on the road.

An arctic fox cried somewhere off in the distance. It was a sad, lonely sound. I stayed awake for some time. I didn't hear the wolves howling, but I knew Uther was close. A scent of something evil was in the air, like cold ash and rotten meat.

I fetched Viggo's tunic from my pack. I placed it under my head to keep my cheek from the cold ground, and it gave me some comfort.

Gyda's body was strong and warm next to mine, her breaths soft and steady. I took comfort in this as well.

NINE

❖

————————————

"Torvi. *Wake up. Quick, now.*"

I opened my eyes. It was dark still. Not yet midnight, I guessed. I shook off my dreams and sat up.

Madoc crouched at the entrance of my tent. He put a finger to his lips. "*Something's afoot. Rouse Gyda.*"

I shook the druid. She jerked awake, instantly alert. We crawled out of the tent. Ink and Stefan were already up, knives in hand, eyes on the far hills.

"Madoc spotted a small camp a half mile off," Ink said softly. "Might be a few of the wolves. Keep your shepherd's knife handy, Torvi. It won't be as sharp as our Butcher blades, but it's better than nothing."

Stefan gestured to the tents. "Let's pack up camp and put out the fire."

The Bards broke down the tents in moments, swift and quiet.

"Stay behind us," Madoc said, eyes on mine. "This is a scouting mission only."

We loped along behind the Bards, single file, Stefan in front,

Gyda at the end. The moon was bright, and we moved quickly. We crossed a wide meadow and then a small gully, heading toward the faint light of a distant fire.

We entered a small woodland of gentle oak trees. Three tents sat in a clearing near the middle of the copse, a circle of young oaks on three sides. We stayed outside the fire's reach, in the shadows.

The air smelled of dew and trees and soil . . . and something else. Something sickly sweet, like rotten fruit.

I leaned over, hands on my knees, and tried to catch my breath—I was hearty and hale, my life spent climbing hills, but the Bards ran like deer.

Was Morgunn in one of these tents, tied and gagged? The thought sent relief rippling through me, followed quickly by fear.

I moved toward Madoc. Something shattered under my heel, and I flinched. I lifted my foot and saw a broken glass vial leaking an orange liquid onto the ground. Yew berry poison.

To my left, I heard Ink step on another vial, and then Gyda, right beside me.

So this was the origin of the sweet smell.

Stefan made a quick gesture with his hand. The Bards dropped into a crouch—

"You're no wolves."

The voice came from the trees above. I heard rustling, and then—

"We set out bait to catch us some wolf-priests. Looks like we caught some Butcher Bards instead."

The Bards moved into the first position of the Amber Dance, blades drawn. Gyda and I fell back, hugging the shadows. We weren't yet ready for open battle and knew it.

Hear me, Stray, I prayed. *Don't let me die at the foot of these oak trees tonight. I just started my journey. I haven't found my sister. I've done nothing yet, nothing at all—*

"We're hunting," Stefan called out, keeping his voice soft. "A pack of wolves killed our companions."

Madoc moved closer to me. "This might be a trick," he whispered. "Use your knife, Torvi. Don't be afraid."

I nodded.

More rustling—

Three small shadows dropped from the trees.

Children. They were just children. Beside me, Ink breathed a sigh of relief, and Stefan laughed.

Two boys and one girl, all three wiry and strong, with long white-blond hair and sharp blue eyes, none older than twelve. They wore matching green tunics and matching fierce expressions. Each had a full quiver and a well-crafted bow. They sized us up, head to toe, and then promptly began talking over one another.

"We wanted to fight the wolves—"

"We figured the Quicks shouldn't get all the glory—"

"We are archers, too, just as good as the Quicks, nearly—"

"We are very troublesome, so our mother sent us on the road with our father—"

"He owns the best archery stall at the Cutross Night Wild—"

"He thinks we're all fast asleep in bed—"

"We got ourselves some poison and took to this copse to lure them in—"

"We thought they would see the fire on their way to the Night Wild and then be drawn closer once they smelled the yew berry—"

"We were going to put our arrows through their villainous necks—"

Madoc let out a low groan and held up both hands. "One at a time, one at a time. What are your names?"

"Ingrid."

"Ingvar."

"Ivor."

"Everyone just calls us the Arrows, for short, and because they can't tell us apart," Ingrid added.

"You say your father doesn't know where you are?" Madoc glanced at Ink. "How far is Cutross from here?"

She shrugged. "A few miles."

Madoc turned back to the children. "So while the Night Wild is raging in Cutross, you three sneaked away from your father's archery stall to fight wolves?"

"Yes. We are skilled archers."

"Vorseland needs us."

"Father won't let us join the Quicks, so we have to prove to him we're worthy."

The three Butcher Bards exchanged a look, and Stefan laughed again. "Change of plans. It appears we are going to a Night Wild tonight—we need to return these three rascals to their poor father." He turned to Gyda and me. "You two need better blades, in any case."

Madoc crossed his arms and stared down the three siblings. "Pack up the tents and put out the fire. We're taking you back to the market."

The Arrows roared in protest, waving their bows in the air.

"You can't tell us what to do—"

"We can take care of ourselves—"

"We are skilled archers—"

"We can slay the wolves, just give us a chance—"

"No one tells the Quicks what to do or drags them back to their father—"

Gyda's mouth twitched. I didn't dare meet her gaze, or we would both burst into laughter. These charming ruffians, with their bravery and scrappy innocence . . . I had a high tolerance for mischief, especially in children, and especially when accompanied by such valor.

Madoc groaned again. "Look, Arrows. If you let us return you to the Night Wild, I will tell your father that you rescued us from a band of woodland thieves, using nothing but your quick wits and your skill at archery."

That did the trick.

The Arrows discussed the offer quietly among themselves for a few moments, and then Ingrid turned to face us.

"We will go back to the Night Wild," she said. "But if we meet any wolves on the way, you will let us fight them."

Madoc fingered his dagger, thumb rubbing the hilt. "Deal."

TEN

W*e cut across open meadows and through dark ravines,* over rolling hills and flat, tilled farmland. The Arrows moved easily and were nearly as quiet as the Bards.

I expected the children to talk all the way to the outskirts of Cutross, but they were focused and silent, eyes on the shadows. They took wolf-hunting seriously.

We were forced to slow our pace slightly as we picked our way across a muddy field. Stefan glanced over his shoulder at Gyda and me. "Is this your first Night Wild?" he asked quietly.

We both nodded.

"You've never been to a Night Wild?" Ingrid looked at me with big blue eyes full of pity. "This is the saddest thing I've ever heard."

"The Night Wilds make life worth living," added one of her brothers, "along with archery and killing wolves."

"I'd be ashamed if I were as old as you two and had never been to a Night Wild," the last boy chimed in helpfully.

Gyda just laughed, soft, whispery peals, and I grinned.

"The Wilds are held all summer along the Stretch," Ingrid said in a voice that was charmingly arrogant and condescending. "Many traders believe that buying and selling at night brings good luck and goodwill from the gods. There are jugglers, singers, actors, storytellers, mystics, and magicians. There are exotic fruits, and cloaks edged in magical golden threads, and necklaces woven from the virginal tresses of Gothi nuns. You will find everything your heart desires and many more things besides."

Morgunn had often expressed a desire to see a Night Wild— she used to sit up late by the fire, her voice low and gentle, almost reverential, listing the stalls she'd like to visit, the sellers and goods she'd heard tell of, the food, the entertainers, the mead, the *Vite*, the wine.

Gyda put a hand on my arm. "I miss that little imp," she said, reading my thoughts. "I think of her often."

My gaze met hers, and I saw my heartache echoed in her eyes. She hadn't known Morgunn long, but she felt some of my pain. Morgunn was easy to like—she was Vorse to the heart, to the bone, like a character in a fireside tale, like Olli from the *Blood Frost Saga*, daring and brave, with just enough mischief to take the edge off.

To my left, I saw Madoc shake his head in warning. "Remember, everyone. We need to stay on guard. The market will be distracting, and there might be wolves skulking in the shadows. Uther will keep the bulk of the priests with her, but she may send half a dozen scouts."

Stefan threw his arm around the Bard's shoulders. "We will, Madoc. We will. And we shall slit the throat of any wolf who crosses our path. But let's also try to enjoy ourselves, no?"

"*Heltar,*" I whispered.

The others echoed me, the Bards, the druid, and the Arrows. "*Heltar.*"

The last mile to Cutross passed through a patch of ancient forest that teemed with bright bluebells in the moonlight, end to end, like something out of a fairy tale.

We heard howling as we neared the final stretch of flowers. Stefan made a gesture, and we all halted, listening.

"They're somewhere in the western hills," the Bard said. "A mile away, perhaps more. Sound carries easily on these night breezes. We will rest here until we are sure the howling is moving farther away, rather than closer."

Madoc fetched the black jug of moongold cider from his pack and passed it to me while we waited.

"Let us have some," whispered the Arrows.

"*Quiet.*" Madoc put his fingers to his lips and then handed them the jug. "One drink each. That's it."

Gyda pried the jug away from the Arrows after they'd each had their one sip. She took a long drink, swiped her hand across her mouth, and then smiled widely. "It tastes creamy and cool and lush . . . like moonlight."

"Why do we get only one sip of moongold?" Ingrid whispered loudly. "That's for babies. Can't we have another?"

"No," Madoc said gently. He turned to me. "How much coin do you have, Torvi?"

I'd brought the small bit of gold from last year's wool sale and added Viggo's spare klines as well. It wasn't much. "Enough to obtain two sharp Butcher Bard knives tonight, I hope."

Madoc took a sip of the moonlight liquor and then handed the jug to Stefan. "I admire the Vorse for carrying on with the markets despite the wolf attacks. They will have posted guards to watch for signs of trouble. Still—"

Gyda rubbed her skull with the palm of her hand and pulled her cloak tighter around her shoulders to ward off the midnight chill. "Do you truly think Uther will be at the market tonight?"

Madoc shrugged. "Uther would be a fool to let her wolves roam the Night Wild. But who can say what she will do, especially if she's high on poison. The only predictable thing about wolf-priests is that they are ever unpredictable. And they will be drawn to the bonfire flames, if nothing else—"

The howling came again, but it was fainter this time.

Stefan nodded. "They are moving east. Good."

The fire welcomed us long before we reached the edge of the Wild, a hundred torches gleaming like orange clusters of stars.

The smell of roasting meat and spiced mead floated in on the breeze . . . and a pungent, earthly smell I couldn't place.

"Burning trance sage," Ink said after watching me sniff the air. "When breathed in, it makes a person feel peaceful and languid."

Tents sprawled through the woodland, brightly dyed wool stretched tight over wooden frames, the colors dazzling in the firelight. I counted dozens of stalls as we passed, the rows radiating out from an open meadow at the heart of the market.

We made for the weapon stalls, crossing through the central field of the Night Wild. It was marked by a bonfire the size and breadth of an Elver tower from the sagas—the flames blazed up thirty, forty, feet into the sky. My companions and I stood watching the fire for a few moments before we moved on, letting our skin grow warm in its heat.

"It's wizard-touched," Ingrid said, nodding her chin at the fire.

"You can tell by the height and the silver-tipped flames," added her brother.

"The traders must have hired a passing sorcerer." The last Arrow looked at me, eyes sparkling. "You are going to have a good night."

We followed the Arrows to their father's stall—it was the largest in Weapons' Lane. Beautifully crafted bows hung throughout the tent, boasting a hundred types of polished wood.

Madoc marched the three sulking Arrows up to the tall, blond man behind the counter.

The Arrows' father looked down at the three young archers

and swore. "Where have you scoundrels been? You are supposed to be asleep in the caravan. I sent you to bed ages ago."

Madoc nodded gravely. "They were guarding a nearby patch of woodland. Your children rescued me and my companions from thieves and then escorted us back here to the market so that no harm could befall us on the way."

To the Bard's credit, he managed this with a straight face.

"Did they now?" the father asked with a great, booming laugh.

His laughter did nothing to dim the Arrows' matching expressions of defiance.

"We did save them, Father——"

"Without us, they would have been taken by wolves——"

"Without us, they would be dead, burned, bitten, stabbed——"

The stall owner whistled sharply, and the Arrows fell silent. He held out his hand to Madoc. "I'm Bjorn. Thank you for returning my lost demons."

Madoc smiled. "It was a pleasure."

"Can I offer you a reward?"

The Bard shook his head. "You're the one who should be rewarded. Raising these lively little archers must be no easy feat."

Bjorn laughed again. "Truth, Bard. Truth."

The three Arrows jumped on top of the stall counter and waved farewell as we walked away.

"I hope we meet them again someday," I said, watching them over my shoulder.

Stefan nodded. "We will if the gods are kind."

Gyda chuckled. "Little rascals."

Ink lowered her hood, and her red curls glowed in the fire-light. "In a few years, they will make excellent Quicks."

"Children like that are why I return to roam Vorseland every spring," Madoc said. "Fierce, brave, and mischievous—Vorse to the blood and to the bone."

We moved down a side path strung with garlands of wild-flowers. Half-naked men and women frolicked beside us, hold-ing torches high above their heads. They were dressed as Elsh forest sprites, their skin painted blue with woad, their clothing woven of bark and vines.

One leaned in close to me as I passed, her blue braids press-ing into my cheek. "*Let him go,*" she whispered. "*Free your heart and find another, my love.*"

"What did she say to you?" Gyda asked after the dancers had passed.

"She told me to release Viggo and take another lover."

Gyda wove her arm through mine. "Good advice, no doubt."

I nodded. "Easier said than done."

I'd felt close to Viggo when he and I were living in his hut. I often convinced myself he was merely off in the hills with the sheep and would return at any moment. But since taking to the road . . .

The shepherd was drifting away from me.

I had an intuition that the longer I wandered with these

Bards, the more Viggo would disappear from my memory . . . until suddenly he would vanish entirely, as if he'd never lived.

I worried the same would happen with Morgunn. The days would pass, and she would fade from my thoughts, fade from my heart, even as I drew closer to Lake Le Fay, even as I pursued her captors and tried to rescue her.

We stopped to watch four women dance on a low wooden stage. They were dressed as ravens, long, dark cloaks, black masks with black pointed beaks. A young girl stood in the corner, beating out a hypnotic rhythm on a drum that was twice her size.

The women danced like fire—nimble, flickering flames, arms raised, lithe bodies coiling together under a sky of butter-yellow stars.

"It's a dance of death," Stefan whispered as one of them knelt, head back, throat exposed.

Another dancer joined them. She climbed onto the shoulders of the tallest dancer while a third retrieved an ax from a corner of the stage.

"I recognize this. It's the story of Frey and the Boneless Mercies," I said.

Madoc leaned toward me, lips to my ear. "Watch the ending closely."

The final steps depicted the Mercies' battle with Logafell. It was a dance of the Seventh Degree, ax blades flashing. It was a dance of pain, a Boneless Mercy falling into a crumpled mass of long hair and dark cloak on a corner of the stage.

The drumbeats swelled. The young girl struck the drum with two mallets now, louder . . . louder . . .

One of the raven-cloaked dancers threw a dagger, and the giant fell. The two dancers landed hard on the stage with a thud that made my heart shake.

The drum went silent. No one in the audience spoke or moved for several long moments after the performance finished.

"It was glorious," I said to the performers when they took their bows at last. I placed two klines on the stage, my heart full.

The Bards kept one hand on their daggers as we strolled down another row of stalls. Stefan and Ink were growing more and more relaxed, lulled by the endless wonder and beauty of the Night Wild, as well as the trance sage. Madoc remained alert, eyes scanning the crowd.

He caught me watching him and pointed upward. I followed his arm, squinting in the dark. I saw a flicker of movement—

"There are guards in the trees," I said. Men and women watched from above, bows in hand, black-clad limbs nearly hidden by leaves.

Madoc nodded. "The market is being watched, and closely. It puts my mind at ease, somewhat."

Gyda turned to us, having overheard our conversation. "I'm comforted that the traders hired a wizard—that central bonfire is not just a tower of pretty, silver-edged flames. It's a sort of peace spell, I think, keeping out all those of a violent mind . . . or sedating them at least, aided by the trance sage."

I slowed my pace so that I could walk beside Ink. "My mother used to tell me a story about a Night Wild in the Borders," I said to the storyteller. "They held a contest of magic between an eighteen-year-old Pig Witch and a young, itinerant Fremish wizard. It started with flames and smoke and ended in a skin-fight— both mystics brawling in the dirt like a couple of spoiled Vorse children."

"'The Pig and the Prophet.'" Ink's green eyes danced. "Listeners still request that tale. Rumor has it that the Strega and the Fremish wizard later became lovers and raised a large pack of magically gifted children on an unmapped southern island."

"I can see losing your heart to a Frem magician, but a Pig Witch?" Stefan shook his head. "Their magic of swine and sacrifice and entrails . . . it makes my blood run cold."

"Agreed," Gyda said.

"And yet my mother loved a Strega, all the same." Ink lowered her gaze. "Loved and hated. Two sides of the same coin."

Stefan reached out and rested his hand on the storyteller's arm. "Enough of the past. Tonight we forget. Tonight we seize life by the horns. Tonight we grow wild."

"Truth," Ink said with a laugh. "Truth, brother Bard."

I saw kinship spark between the two Elsh artists, deep and genuine, and I envied it. I'd felt this kinship in the past, with Morgunn and Viggo.

I'd grown attached to the three Bards. There was a camaraderie swiftly growing between us. I admired them, especially the cheerful Stefan, with his dark, lively eyes and his amiable temperament and his gentle voice. He and Gyda exchanged quiet jokes and frequent laughter, and it brought me joy.

My heart lay buried on my steading, with a gray-eyed shepherd, but Gyda was free to love.

We entered the lane of food stalls and sampled fruit featuring every color under the sun—white, black, blue, purple, green, red, yellow. Ink and I shared a brightly striped fig—it hailed from an island so far away that even she, the storyteller, had never heard of it.

Ink bought sweet butter ale from two comely sisters, and Stefan purchased a red-hued reverie potion from a young Finn mystic clad in a white wool dress and a deer-skull mask. We all took turns sipping from the ceramic bottles as we walked, though Madoc's gaze remained fixed on the shadows.

"He doesn't seem to be enjoying this market," I said to Stefan when Madoc paused at a stall to inspect a wool cloak. "I don't believe it's the risk of wolves—he strikes me as a person more likely to court danger than run from it."

Stefan nodded. "Aye. He does have another reason. It's a sad story."

"Go on," I said. "Let's hear Madoc's sorrowful tale, if you're free to tell it."

The Elsh were not like the Vorse. They often discussed their past—they held no superstitions about it being unlucky.

Stefan took out his pipe and began to fill it with brickle-leaf. "Madoc was abandoned as an infant. Left at a Night Wild in Elshland. An old herb witch found him starving in an empty tent, half dead in the cold—she nursed him back to health with her earth magic."

"Madoc told you this willingly?" I asked.

"I had to get him drunk first. Very, very drunk. The healer died when Madoc was still a boy, and he wandered from camp to camp, never belonging anywhere, until he joined our band of Butcher Bards. We were his first real family . . . until Uther slaughtered our troupe as they slept peacefully by the fire." Stefan paused. "No one wants revenge on these wolves more than he does."

Madoc returned, and we walked on. The night began to slip and blur, images drifting in and out like clouds passing through the sky.

I saw two young men selling brightly dyed fabrics, billowing waves of purple, red, yellow, and blue silk that rippled in the night breeze. I drew near their stall, and the cool, sleek cloth draped itself over my body, caressing my skin.

I saw Elsh hedge witches standing guard over black cauldrons of bubbling brews, dried animals and dried herbs hanging from a cobweb of strings across the ceiling of their open tents. They called out their wares with melancholy songs—

"Cure your heart, cure your head, bring to life the fully dead. Who will buy? Who will buy?"

I saw several fortune-tellers, the most memorable being a thin, angular man with long, dark hair that reached to the floor of his striped tent. A blond-haired child stood beside him, leaning against his knee, whispering in his ear as he flipped circular white cards for the young woman who looked on, eyes wide.

I saw contortionists and tumblers—some were children no older than twelve or thirteen. They flipped and danced and twisted, bodies bending like willows. We stopped and watched them for some time, dazzled by their skill.

I saw a band of brigand musicians lurking under the branches of an oak tree, all dressed in tight-fitting black tunics, holding wooden flutes to their chests. They stared at me boldly, their narrowed eyes shifting from my face to the leather coin pouch at my waist. I started to walk toward them, but Ink took my arm.

"They are thieves as well as artists—as likely to give you a song as steal your coin. Both at the same time, usually."

"It would almost be worth having my coins stolen just to hear one of their melodies," I whispered.

The brigand musicians were spoken of in the sagas. Little was known about them, outside of their ability to appear in summer at the Night Wilds, then disappear again come autumn. Their songs were said to haunt their listeners the rest of their lives, the notes rippling through important events, echoing through dreams.

Stefan looked at me over his shoulder. "Save your coin. You and Gyda need blades. If we slay Uther and survive, there will be time to buy magic songs down the road."

Madoc nodded. "There will be all the time in the world."

We circled past the central bonfire again to return to Weapons' Lane and take the side path to the dagger stalls. A group of Long Death fanatics was preaching on one side of the field, naked except for their long hair, bodies powdered gray with ash. They took turns shouting out the attributes of their goddess, Klaw.

Ink nodded toward the group. "The Long Death followers appeared in Vorseland two years ago. Rumor has it they come from the dark moors of southern Frem. Klaw's worshippers claim she gives her true believers everlasting life."

"Does she?" I asked.

Ink shrugged. "I doubt it. Though something is worrisome in how quickly Klaw's followers are growing in number."

We turned to the left and slipped past a series of stalls devoted to brutish wooden clubs and hedge axes before finding the lane selling smaller blades—tiny, sophisticated Fremish knives and Elshland daggers.

I purchased two fine Butcher Bard blades at a knife stall recommended by Madoc. It was run by two broad-shouldered brothers with soft voices and wise eyes.

I lifted my hair so Madoc could tie the knife around my neck. The dagger felt good as it nestled into my sternum, as if it had always wanted to be there.

Gyda smiled when I tied the leather straps of the second hilt around her neck. "Thank you, Torvi," she said. "I will think of you every time I slit a wolf's neck with this delightful blade."

And just like that, we became Butcher Bards.

Ink spotted a fellow storyteller selling his stories near the last weapon stall and introduced herself. Storytellers always greeted one another—they exchanged news, rumors, and new tales. It was a convivial profession.

While we waited for Ink, I noticed a Bone Woman in a white tent near a dead juniper tree. She was beautiful, blue eyes and red hair. She wore a white fur cloak, which opened to reveal a strip of pale skin down the middle of her body. She sat by a small fire, a pile of scattered skeletons nearby, some human, some not.

"It's said that if one gazes into her bone-flames, they can hear, feel, and taste all the pleasures of the world," Madoc said. "A steaming bath, a cool wind under a hot sky, fire-roasted meat, ice-cold Ecstasy *Vite*, a lover's touch, a lover's sighs."

I moved forward to enter the Bone Woman's tent—I still had a few copper klines. Madoc reached out and pulled me back, gentle hand on my elbow. "The bone-flames show an illusion," he said. "Search for the true things. The pleasure will last longer."

Stefan chuckled. "And they can all be found here at the Night Wild, from the bath to the *Vite* to the lover's touch."

Ink rejoined us, and we followed Stefan as he ducked between two stalls and moved down a narrow side lane, toward the main theatrical stages. We soon came upon a group of young

Whistlers advertising their wares, lips pursed, low, eerie notes in perfect harmony. All six were tall and thin, with white hair and dark eyes.

"Siblings, most likely," Stefan said with a nod toward the group. "They say the gift runs in families."

"What are they selling?" Gyda asked.

"Their whistles are spells that you set out on the air." Ink made a sweeping gesture with her long-fingered hand. "They are expensive and can be used only once . . . But the magic is beautiful and unusual. If, say, you're lost in one of the Endless Forests, you can use one of their whistles to summon a yellow-horned owl, and she will guide you out of the dark woods. Or if a loved one dies in a faraway land, you can buy a whistle that will sing down a Kell Wraith from the sky. The bird will whisper the person's dying thoughts in your ear. Once heard, the notes of the whistle's song will stay with you until you use it, after which it disappears forever."

Madoc nodded. "It is an elegant magic. An old magic."

Gyda turned and approached the tallest of the Whistlers. They exchanged a few words. Gyda slid the small gold ring from the third finger of her left hand and handed it to the girl, who took it gently between two fingers and slipped it into a pocket of her tunic.

The Whistlers began to sing—at least, their lips stayed pursed, their expressions intent and focused. But I heard no notes and no song.

The druid returned to us a few moments later, eyes wide. "I gave them my mother's marriage ring." She paused. "I hope it was worth it. It felt right that I make this trade."

"I heard nothing," I said. "They whistled nothing but silence."

"The notes went into here." Gyda put her fist to her chest, to the right of her Butcher Bard dagger. "I can feel them inside me, fluttering softly like flower petals in a gentle summer breeze."

She took my hand and placed it on her heart, but I could feel nothing but her blood-beat.

I spotted more guards as we walked, both on the pathways and up in the trees. I saw no wolves—no wild-haired, half-starved girls, no shaggy wolf-pelt cloaks. Stefan had been right. Uther was no fool. It was much easier to attack a sleeping village than a heavily guarded market.

Madoc took the last sip of the reverie potion when Stefan offered and then returned his knife to his sheath and brought out his pipe.

We reached the main stages and spied an empty platform between two twisted oak trees. Stefan and Madoc exchanged glances, and then Stefan climbed the steps, lowered the hood of his cloak, and began to sing.

His voice was exquisite, captivating, just as I suspected it would be. It was soft but clear, able to carry past the stage and through the trees. He sang with his chin lifted, head tilted slightly back, chest out, hands at his sides.

I recognized the lyrics—they were from the *Sea and Ash*

Saga. The song told the story of Midnight, of how she was raised by a group of Winter Elvers, and how she led a Vorse army into battle when just thirteen and won herself a crown.

A crowd soon gathered and stood *savalikk* around us. We all breathed in unison as we listened, dozens of us, ribs in, ribs out, in rhythm with the song.

The earthy smell of trance sage floated by. It was burning in a copper thurible near the stage, its chains strung from the limb of a tree.

Madoc joined Stefan on the second verse, his deep voice pulling low notes that resonated perfectly with Stefan's higher tones. Together they sang the next fourteen verses, and no one in the crowd, from the oldest woman to the youngest child, moved.

Afterward, Ink took the stage. She was shy at first—she hid her flushed cheeks under her hood, and her usual graceful limbs moved awkwardly about the platform. But once she sat down and folded her long legs into the storyteller pose, she became calm and confident, almost regal.

She told the story of "The Pig and the Prophet." It was a marvelous tale, one of swirling cloaks and ancient curses, of plumes of white smoke and tears of blood, of screams and chants and howls. Ink's voice grew louder as she moved toward the climactic ending—both sorcerers wrestling in the mud until, filthy and exhausted, they began to laugh and the battle was called a draw.

Ink's voice was husky, in contrast to Stefan's and Madoc's, which were bright and clear. But her words carried as well as their notes, and the throaty quality seemed to add depth to the story.

She next told the tale of Esca's sword. Gyda drew near me as Ink began, and her eyes grew bright.

Esca was the son of a Vorse shepherd and a traveling mystic who had trained with the Orate Healers. He was born at high noon in high summer, and he bore a snakelike mark in his right eye—a slash of jade green slithering through deep brown.

When he was a boy of fourteen, Esca was running through the Ranger Hills, chasing sheep, when he chanced upon the mysterious Lake Monmouth, with its red sand and black waters. On the banks of the lake lay a beautiful female warrior, sword clutched to her chest. She died in his arms, bleeding out through a wound in her side. Esca built a pyre and sent the warrior to Holhalla. Before he placed her on the fire, he took her sword, Wrath. Later he would discover that it was one of three magical swords in Vorseland. With the sword strapped across his back, Esca left his sheep and set off to see the world.

Esca had many wonderful, dangerous adventures. One day, years later, after he'd won his northern jarldom, he threw a feast to celebrate the birth of his eleventh grandchild. The god Obin attended, dressed as a rangy beggar, a raven on his shoulder. At the end of the feast, Obin stole Esca's sword and plunged it into the ancient ash tree in the center of the Hall. He announced that whoever could pull the sword would inherit the jarldom.

Obin discarded his beggar's cloaks and called Esca to his side. Together they ascended into Holhalla, their bodies dissolving into smoke and rising into the sky.

Each of Esca's sons and daughters tried to pull the sword, but none could budge it from the tree. Wars ensued. Sibling fought sibling until the jarldom lay in ruin, until all of Esca's heirs had either died in battle or disappeared in the night. The jarldom was abandoned and soon forgotten. It lay hidden in the vast Green Wild Forest, patiently awaiting its next ruler.

The story of Esca stirred me—my skin prickled, and my blood throbbed. I thought of the night outside Viggo's hut when Gyda revealed her quest to Morgunn and me, her desire to find Esca's sword. We'd raised our fists to our hearts and cheered.

It suddenly felt possible—this quest, this sword, attaining this jarldom. It felt as real as the breath in my lungs, as real as the lilac-gray smoke from the nearby fire, as real as the pervasive, gentle witchy feeling that dominated the Night Wild.

The peaceful, easy life in Viggo's hill hut—

That had been the dream.

The open road, Gyda's quest, Uther, the wolves, my kidnapped sister . . . this was real.

"You would make a good jarl," I whispered to my friend, my cheek next to hers. You deserve to pull Esca's sword."

"So do you." Gyda pulled away from me and met my gaze. "Truly."

I started to shake my head, but she held up her hand. "I know there is bad blood between you and your mother. She believed you were weak and un-Vorse. But heroes come in all shapes and sizes, Torvi. Vorseland would do well to have a jarl who is as softhearted as she is brave."

I bowed my head and accepted her praise.

The audience placed coins on the edge of the stage as payment for the Bards' entertainment, as was the practice. Stefan grinned as he deftly gathered the coins, dividing them equally among himself, Ink, and Madoc.

"If anyone wants to buy another whistle or see the Bone Woman, we have more than enough," Stefan said with a laugh. He slipped the klines into the leather pouch he wore at his waist, and then he rose slowly to his feet, his eyes on something in the distance. The grin faded from his face.

"What is it?" I asked, following his gaze, my hand reaching for my new blade. "Did you spot a wolf?"

"No." He flicked his chin toward a nearby tent. "It's the Drakes."

Three of them stood underneath a yellow tent in a dark corner of the market, near the river. Red cloaks and forked red beards.

"I don't know why," Gyda said in a low voice, "but the sight of them sends a shiver down my spine."

"Yes," Stefan replied, rubbing his palms down his forearms. "I feel as if someone just stepped on my grave."

He began to walk toward the three mystics, all the same.

ELEVEN

✳

The youngest of the Drakes was my age, with dark hair and green eyes. The other two men were closer to fifty, both similar in appearance, handsome, with regular features and thick white hair that contrasted sharply with their red beards and red cloaks. The taller had pointed ears like mine, like an Elver's.

"Come, Bards," the young one called out. "We will read the sand for you. We will read the stars."

"We can't afford your price," Madoc said with a shake of his head. "Not even with our recent earnings."

Stefan crossed his arms and laughed. "Besides, what can you tell us, Drakes, that we would want to know?"

The young Drake moved his red cloak back behind his shoulders, tilted his head, and stared at the Bard. "We can tell you how to kill the Skroll worshipper, the Fremish bishop, the leader of the poison-drinking wolves."

"Uther," the two older Drakes added in unison.

Stefan looked startled for a moment but then let out a low chuckle. "We know how to kill her, Drakes. Stick a knife in her heart and she'll die like any other beast."

The younger Drake eyed Stefan coolly. "Continue on this path and you will all be slain, one by one, before you get a chance to take that blade of yours and slice open the wolf-queen."

Madoc moved forward. "And how do you know this, Drake?"

"I can see it in the stars shining above you—the gods favor this Uther, and she will not be easy to kill."

We were all silent for a few moments, the sounds of the Night Wild echoing in the distance, the scent of trance sage floating through the air.

The Drake with the pointed ears shifted slightly. "There is a druid with you—I see her there, behind the tall, red-haired storyteller."

Gyda lowered the hood of her cloak, letting the torchlight shine across her stubbled skull.

"We accept women now," the Drake said, "and have for the last hundred years, though few welcome our offer. Will you travel with us, druid, and learn our ways?"

The young Drake held up his hand, three fingers raised. "Three years is all we ask. At the end of this time, you may stay or go as you wish. We will provide you with safety, as well as the mental stimulation of our training, and the comfort and support of three mentors. All we wish in return is to continue to share our art so that it does not die and become lost to memory, like the songs of the Finch Folk in Elshland, or the metal-work of the Iron Foxes in the Far North."

Gyda glanced up at the night sky, then met the young Drake's gaze. "I will never join you."

The Drake stepped toward Gyda. He was slim and graceful, his dark, curly hair pulled back in a leather tie. He placed his thumb on Gyda's forehead, in the spot the mystics refer to as the third eye. "Esca's sword will not be wielded by a Boar Island wizard, not now, not ever. You'd be wise to come with us, druid. It is a better path. I see the potential in you to become a Hierophant, which is the highest rank among our people—they are lifelong scholars and respected leaders."

"If I cared about magical orders, Drake, I would have stayed on the Boar Islands. I will find that sword, despite what you say. The gods called me to this quest, and I won't disappoint them."

"*Heltar.*" I moved to stand next to Gyda and gazed at the Drakes. "None of us will pay your price. You had better try your offer on another band of travelers. We are not as desperate as some."

The green-eyed Drake turned. He stared into me, to the heart, to the blood, to the bone.

"Your father is the son of a Sea Witch," he said. "He was born in the Merrows, and sea magic is in your blood. We could teach you how to access this power. If you don't learn it soon, it could turn wild inside you and pull you into darkness."

"How the Hel do you know this?"

"Because your eyes turn violet in the moonlight, and because you smell like a Sea Witch, though you don't have the green hair. If your mother was the witch, you would have been raised in the Merrows, so I concluded that it was your father."

I raised my eyebrows. "I smell like a witch?"

The young Drake took my hand and pressed my wrist to his nose. "You smell of Fremish salt and the faint pine-resin scent of magic."

I glanced at Ink, and she gave a small nod. She'd known I was a Sea Witch as well.

So Morgunn and I were half witches, as well as half Elsh.

Witch.

I put two fingers to my heart and closed my eyes. I could feel my life path opening before me, a hundred new turns, a thousand new twists.

"Thank you for the offer to teach me your art," I said to the Drake, "and for telling me the true nature of my father's origins. But I have a sister who needs rescuing."

He nodded.

I held his gaze. "Out of curiosity, what path did you see for me if I'd chosen to join you?"

He stroked his chin with one thumb and gazed at me for a moment. "You would become one of the Bateleurs. They are storytellers and artistic magicians. The three of us are Chevaliers." He waved a hand at the other two Drakes. "We are travelers who recruit new members to our art. The Bateleurs are entertainers who live a life of song, dance, feasting, and revelry."

The Drake paused for a moment. He glanced up at the stars, then turned back to me. "I am, on occasion, rather envious of them."

I smiled at the thought of lively Drake Bateleurs carousing mysterious Halls in the mystics' ancient Creet villas.

The Drake echoed my smile, and it made his eyes soften. He suddenly looked rather sweet and very young.

"If you ever find yourself lost," he added, "without purpose or plan, visit us. It might prove useful." He reached into the dark recesses of his cloak and pulled out a small red soapstone carving of a cloaked man with a forked beard. "Follow the Stretch as far south as it will go and then head east until you reach the Quell Sea. Catch one of the striped ships to the Iber island of Santor. Show this figure to any of the healers at the Hall of Potions and they will tell you how to find us on Creet."

He handed me the carving. I gripped it in my fist, fingers closing around the cold stone. "Thank you," I replied, and meant it.

Madoc gave the young Drake a slight nod. "That's enough prophecies and truths for one evening. Farewell, mystics. Best of luck in finding someone to take you up on your offer."

He turned to go, but Stefan put a hand out to stop him. "Wait." The Bard moved deeper into the yellow tent. "Three years, you say? That's not so very long."

Madoc swore and grabbed Stefan's arm. "What the Hel are you doing?"

"I have a feeling here, in my gut." Stefan put his fist to his lower torso and pounded his hand against his hard belly. "I want to leave behind the Bard life for a while. I've felt it coming on for a while . . . a change, a fork in my path. I'm meant to go with the Drakes. Do you remember the older woman in the hamlet? She looked at me when she mentioned these mystics. She knew it as well. She could see it in my path."

I saw Gyda stiffen.

"No," Madoc said softly. "Please, Stefan. No."

Ink stepped between the two Bards, and her eyes met Stefan's. "He means it, Madoc. It's written all over his face."

The Drake with the pointed ears fetched something from a dark corner of the tent and then returned. He held out a heavy-looking black cloth bag toward Stefan, its sides bulging with strange angles and shapes. "Reach inside, Bard, and take the first object you find."

Stefan slid his hand into the sack and then pulled it out again. He opened his palm. It held a black metal ball the size of a small apple—one side of the sphere depicted a yellow star, the other, an hourglass.

"Yes," the mystic said. "The Bard is meant to join us, as I thought. He will become one of the Fools—freethinking Drakes who travel the world in search of knowledge."

The young Drake nodded. "The deal is struck. It is done."

I shivered and sniffed the air . . . There was a scent rising above the trance sage, something deep and resinous, like labdanum and woodsy Iber vanilla.

Magic.

Drake magic.

Gyda's eyes met mine. She smelled the magic as well. I took her arm, and she leaned against me.

The young Drake made a sweeping motion with his hand, and his red cloak swirled. "We will now read the sand and stars for you. Come." With a quick jerk of his wrists, he unrolled a large circular carpet. "Stand here, at one end."

We stepped up, our toes meeting the edge. I was close enough to the young Drake that our hips touched. He smelled of sunshine and frankincense and magic.

It was a beautiful carpet, intricately woven with small, perfect threads of white, orange, black, and blue. It depicted four dark male silhouettes standing among tall white dunes, blue sky with an orange sun.

The image felt strangely familiar, as if I'd seen it long ago, as a child.

One of the white-haired Drakes reached forward and took Stefan's knife from its sheath. Stefan's eyebrows rose. I'd learned that this was considered rude among the Bards, equivalent to touching a person's hair without her permission, or stroking her cheek.

The Drake began to whisper words in a tongue I didn't recognize. His voice started out soft, reminiscent of the Elsh accent purr, but ended husky and guttural, like Vorse from the Far North, past the Skals.

The mystic pushed up the sleeve of his tunic and slashed the skin of his inner forearm with Stefan's blade, a thin, straight cut. He held out his hand and made a fist.

The blood began to drip onto the carpet. Slowly. Very slowly. Each bead seemed to take longer, and move slower, than the one before.

We all watched, entranced.

"It's lovely," I whispered. "Like glistening red beads."

"Yes," Ink said. "Like vivid imp apples in the autumn."

The blood splashed onto woven thread. Drop, drop, drop.

My mind began to float, thoughts drifting in and out with each glisten, each splash of blood. I blinked and put my hand to my forehead.

"Too much trance sage," Gyda whispered with a shake of her head. "Too much reverie potion."

Drop, drop, drop . . .

It began to rain stars.

They fell from the roof of the tent, softly, slowly, bigger than snowflakes, as yellow as the sun. I reached out my hand, and the stars settled onto my palm, numerous rays ending in thin, narrow points.

Madoc put out his hand as well, fingers splayed. "They are as light as leaves," he said, "but as silky as a butterfly's wing."

Stefan and Gyda simply laughed with delight.

The stars fell, on and on, ethereal waves of them, until we were covered, stars in our hair, stars in our cloaks, stars on our skin, stars in our thoughts.

The young Drake took a step back and handed the knife to one of the older Drakes. The white-haired mystic began to whisper in the same shushing, guttural tones. He pushed back his sleeve, revealing a strong, tanned arm—

A flash of blade across brown skin—

His blood dripped down, drop by drop, slowly, beautifully . . .

The stars switched to sand. Soft, fine, white grains began to mist down from the corners of the tent's ceiling.

It rained sand as it had rained stars, though the gentle deluge was just beyond our reach. Small dunes began to form in the corners of the tent, and still it came down. I stretched out my arm and let it blanket the ends of my fingers, as tender as a lover's kiss.

The young Drake pursed his lips and blew.

The sand and stars whirled up into a great cloud, a churning wave of white and gold. It spun a few feet above our heads and then flew out into the night, disappearing into the dark.

Of all the sights at the Night Wild, this was the most magical, the most stunning.

The young Drake picked up a carved wooden staff from where it leaned against the tent frame. He pointed his staff at the carpet. "Now we can truly begin. Gather around."

Five items stood on the carpet: a soapstone carving of a tree, a wooden statue of a bear, a metal arrow, a pin in the shape of a small red bird, and a black twisted juniper branch.

The Drake moved his staff to the soapstone tree. "You must travel from here to the Brocee Leon Forest." The staff switched to the arrow. "You will track down a young Quick named Sven du Lac." The staff moved to the red bird. "She leads a band of archers knows as the Red Sparrows. They will help you kill this Fremish bishop—the one named Uther."

The Drake placed the staff on the carpet and picked up the bear in one hand and the branch in the other. He turned toward me, his red cloak billowing around him. "When the time comes, do not enter Uther's tent alone. Leave her to Sven."

I stared at him and said nothing.

"Do you hear me, Torvi, daughter of Igraine? Your sister will be in Uther's tent, but you will not try to rescue her yourself. Understood?"

How he knew my name, or my mother's name, I did not know. "Yes," I said. "I understand."

"*Veray, veray*," he replied.

This was an antiquated word meaning "yes, good, rightness, truth." It was no longer common in Vorseland, but it was still in use among travelers who had learned our language in distant lands.

The young Drake turned to Gyda. "You have a question for Uther, and she has an answer. You will need to slay all her wolves before she will talk."

Gyda nodded slowly.

The three mystics then drew together, a sea of red. When they parted again, the young Drake held a scarlet cloak in his arms. He held it out to Stefan. "It's time. We leave tonight for the Skal Mountains—we have business there. Say your farewells."

He paused. "Remember, you will return to your companions in three years if you choose, your tongue suffused with the language of our people and all that this entails."

The Drakes moved backward into the shadows of the tent to give us space.

Madoc began to weep, tears sliding down his cheeks. Ink went to him and put her palm to his heart. He clutched it in his own, and they both turned to look at Stefan.

"I am sorry that I won't be there to help you slay Uther and her beasts." Stefan reached forward and took Madoc in his arms. "I know you will see it through. I know I can count on you."

Madoc wept softly against Stefan's shoulder while Ink held them both in her arms. Gyda and I stood quietly by. We'd known the good-natured singer for only a short time—we hadn't earned this warm parting, as much as we both wanted to partake of it.

Ink and Madoc suddenly released Stefan, spun on their heels, and walked off into the night without another word.

Stefan came to me then. He gripped my right forearm in his hand, leaned forward, and whispered in my ear. "I trust these Drakes," he said. "Abide by their warning, Torvi."

I nodded.

"Madoc will help you find your sister. Trust in him as well."

I nodded.

"I'm content in my choice and feel that it is the right one. Remind my fellow Bards of this often."

I nodded.

He turned to Gyda. He slid his fingers around the back of her neck and cupped her skull. She gripped his tunic in her fists and pulled him to her. They kissed, slowly, languidly.

"Stick close to Ink and Madoc, and keep one another company until I return." Stefan kissed Gyda under her strong jaw and across her neck. "I will come back to you all," he said. "I will find you if I have to hunt you down across all of Elshland, all of Vorseland, all of anywhere, all of everywhere."

He released the druid. "Don't let Uther kill you. You can't die, any of you. I've lost enough."

"So have we all," I said.

We left him in the yellow tent, with the Drakes watching on from the shadows. Gyda took my arm, and we walked off into the night.

I glanced back over my shoulder after a few hundred yards, hoping for one last glimpse of Stefan, but the yellow tent was gone. A large yew stood in its place, its ancient, twisted limbs and gnarled branches indicating it had held that spot since the time of the sagas.

I shivered.

TWELVE

❧

"**E**ven the song of the night birds seems melancholy tonight," the storyteller said.

"Yes," I replied. "It sounds like weeping."

The four of us were making our way back to our camp in the curve of the Sin, our heads bowed, our steps slow.

It was near dawn. There was no light on the horizon, but I felt the sunrise in the air, in the sharp cold, in the ghostly stillness.

"Stefan has always been impulsive," Madoc said softly.

Ink reached into her pack and pulled out a resin-tipped fire stave—she'd purchased a large bundle at the Night Wild for lighting her pipe. She placed the edge of the stick on the still-burning coals from the evening fire, and it burst into flame.

"No," she answered, eyes on Madoc's, "it was more than that. There was an ache in his voice when he sang at the Night Wild. His soft, singer heart is broken. Emmelian and Isobel were like siblings to him." She paused. "You are fueled by vengeance, and that is how you will cure your sorrow. But Stefan is on another journey now, one of knowledge."

Ink lit her pipe and then offered it to Gyda.

The druid took a deep puff. "His path is the Eight of Coins."

Ink raised her eyebrows. "The Elsh Fortune Cards. Yes."

Gyda nodded. "Stefan will heal through the pursuit of knowledge and skill." She paused. "Damn that Bard. I already miss him."

I slid my arm around the druid's waist, and she pressed herself into my side.

"Stefan chose his own path," I said. "As we all must do in the end. And what is three years, after all? A small slice of life."

Gyda kissed my cheek and then took another puff of Ink's pipe. "Three years is a small sacrifice for the fulfillment of a quest. This is what matters in life. Finding a crusade and following it to the end. I'll forgive Stefan for his choice. Just . . . not yet."

The next day we headed northeast, toward the Brocee Leon.

There were seven Endless Forests in Vorseland. The Brocee Leon stretched through the Middlelands—like all of Vorseland's Endless Forests, it contained miles upon miles of unmapped trees beyond its dark borders, as well as secret roads, bands of Quicks, itinerant wizards and mystics, tree towns, and the gods knew what else.

The Green Wild Forest was the largest of the forests and the farthest north. The Myrk Forest, in the Borders, was the safest, for more bands of Quicks roamed that wood than any other.

There were four other Endless Forests, but the Middlelands' Brocee Leon was famous for being the darkest, the eeriest, and the most haunted.

If I could see only one of the seven in my life, this was the one I'd choose.

The landscape grew more barren as the day wore on. We were in the Middleland Moors—a treeless stretch of low, un-cultivated hills capped in a blanket of purple heather. It was beautiful in a way, though very different from the green, grassy steading where I'd grown up.

We stopped only for a quick meal of smoked fish and summer pears, eaten silently in a patch of heather, under a cloudy sky.

Madoc often looked over his shoulder as we walked. It pained him to leave Uther's trail. I felt it in his posture, saw it in his eyes.

"We need Sven and her Red Sparrows," I said the sixth time I saw him look back toward the Ranger Hills, far in the distance. "You know we do."

He halted and turned to face me. "And how was that information worth the price of losing Stefan?"

"He will learn a trade from these Drakes, one that might prove useful down the road, for him and for all of us." I put my hand on Madoc's shoulder. "You're upset about Stefan, and I miss Morgunn, but we need to sacrifice the urge for quick, sui-cidal vengeance and follow a new path. Do you want Stefan to return in a few years only to discover that we've all been killed on the shores of Lake Le Fay?" I paused. "Put away your rage for now, Bard. Let us go into the Endless Forest and see what adventure awaits us there."

He rested his hand on mine. "You are right. If you can walk away from the path toward your sister, then I can delay my revenge. I will bury my anger, and when I return to it, it will be all the stronger."

Madoc kept his word. He was serene for the rest of the day's walk, shoulders relaxed, gaze forward.

We set up camp in a low ravine at the edge of the Moors, beneath a scattering of skeletal trees climbing up the steep sides. It was a blustery night, the wind howling like wolves. I thought it might turn to rain, but the clouds stayed dry.

We practiced the steps of the Amber Dance before we ate, though we did it without joy, our movements slow and heavy.

We missed Stefan.

Sad thoughts circled my mind as I moved through the Amber cycles. *Aslaug, Father, Mother, Morgunn, Viggo, Stefan . . .*

Is life nothing but a series of events leading to heartache?

"We will head first to Tintagle," Ink announced as I helped her prepare supper—roan mushroom soup with wild garlic, dried herbs, and moongold cider. "Tintagle is one of the Brocee Leon tree towns. We can stop in the Wayward Sisters Tavern. One of the Pinket Trills will know if any Quicks have passed through recently, and where they are headed next."

I tasted the soup and added more Fremish salt. "Are the tree towns safe, Ink?" I was both eager to see Tintagle and uneasy about what I would find there. I'd heard many stories about the tree towns of the Endless Forests, and some of them were bloody, dark tales of travelers robbed and left for dead in the crooks of giant trees, or Stregas gutting fellow wanderers instead of pigs and selling their prophecies to wealthy merchants.

The storyteller paused and ran her long fingers through her short red curls. "Somewhat. They are built high in the oldest blood trees, as the name implies. It offers them protection, as they can't be attacked by marauding wolves, like villages in the Middlelands."

I nodded. "It reminds me of the Scorch Trees in the Merrows."

"Yes, though the blood trees do not emit warmth like the Scorch. That said, they don't shed their leaves come winter— the Brocee Leon maintains a perpetual state of cool, autumnal temperatures all year long."

Madoc appeared at my side. I let him stir the soup, his cheeks lingering over the warm steam. "Little can be grown on the forest floor but root vegetables, which is why the tree towns depend on trade," he added. "It's also why the citizens take pains to ensure their villages are as welcoming as possible— every twist and turn, every angle and curve, is lit with torches at night. Tintagle gleams like a Night Wild and shines like stars."

Ink took a puff from her pipe and let the smoke out slowly through her lips. "Tintagle and all the tree towns in Brocee Leon have pink-tinted glass in their windows, brought in via trade with Fremish caravans that pass through this forest on their way to Finnmark. The pale rose glass casts a strange light into the homes and gives them a magical air, as if crafted by the cheerful, lighthearted Fay that are said to live high in the alpine meadows of Frem."

Madoc glanced toward me and smiled. "Your first tree town. You will fall in love, I should think."

I nodded. "My first for many things."

The mushroom soup was earthy, savory, and filling. We followed it with slow, meditative pipe-smoking, our backs turned to the wind.

Ink removed her cloak and let her red curls toss in the breeze. "Has anyone heard the tale of the blue-tongued mage and the golden-eyed hedge-fighter?"

I shook my head. "No, and we could all use a story."

"Spin your yarn, poet," Gyda said with a laugh.

Ink crossed her legs and began.

"One cold winter's day during the second Witch War, a hedge-fighter appeared at Jarl Roth's Great Hall in Blue Vee. She was brawny and handsome, dressed in black leather and wool. Her hair had been snipped into ragged clumps close to her skull—she was in a nine-month mourning. Her blood companion had recently been killed during one of the Elshland monk battles, the spell-scripture Vicars having finally defeated the blood-drinking Clerics . . ."

Many rounds of *Vite* later, Ink finished her story. She bowed her head in acceptance of our thanks, and when she raised her eyes, they were fixed on Gyda. "My tale had a hidden price. I want to learn your Boar Island magic, druid."

Madoc nodded. "I second this."

I said nothing—I was curious to see how my friend would respond.

Gyda took a deep breath, let it out, and shrugged. She rose and reached into her pack. She pulled out a curved glass bottle filled with fine brick-red sand. "I acquired this at the Night Wild. It's from Riffa and is used in sand reading."

"Sand reading?" I raised my eyebrows.

"It's a variation on the sorcery performed by the Drakes . . . It's a form of palm reading. It's one of the first types of magic taught to druid children—the focus is on patience and empathy." She grinned at me. "Come, Torvi. You and Madoc stand here by the fire, facing each other. Ink, you will observe."

Madoc laughed softly for the first time since Stefan had left us. "I've always wanted to see druid magic."

"Get closer, you two," Gyda said. "Yes. Even closer."

Madoc and I now stood within inches of each other. I was so close I could smell him—mingled scents of pipe smoke, neroli, and cedar.

"Torvi, take Madoc's right wrist."

I wrapped my fingers around Madoc's warm skin. "What is a sand reading meant to do?"

"It will reveal the true feelings of the one who holds the sand."

"What if I don't want my true feelings revealed?" Madoc eyed the druid and frowned.

"Quiet, Madoc." Ink stood near my right shoulder, watching. "We're trying to learn something."

Gyda grinned at Madoc, then looked at me. "Turn Madoc's hand upright and pour the Riffa sand into his palm, as much as it will hold."

I took the bottle of sand from the druid with my free hand and poured the soft red silt into Madoc's palm.

"Now keep your fingers on his wrist, look into his eyes, and *hold*. Do not move. Keep your eyes locked on each other, and do not move."

I lifted my gaze.

Madoc and I stared at each other and held. The moments passed. We stayed silent and still. *Savalikk.*

It was an oddly intimate thing to look this deeply into someone.

My mother used to have a shaggy wolfhound named Lycan, who would stare longingly into her eyes each night before falling asleep. I'd always thought there was something rather vulnerable about it, and tender.

I blinked slowly, and Madoc did the same.

"Hold," Gyda repeated.

We held.

I remembered the nights I'd stayed in Viggo's loft, and how, spent and drowsy, we would fall asleep gazing into each other. Like my mother and her wolfhound.

The sand on Madoc's palm began to give off a steady, deep heat, as if from a dying fire. Madoc and I breathed in sharply when we felt the warmth.

The front of my neck began to flush, and my fingers grew hot where they touched the Bard's wrist.

"Do you feel the sand growing warm?" Gyda asked.

I nodded.

"Then close your eyes, Torvi."

I shut my eyes and let out a small sigh as the connection broke between me and the Bard.

Madoc.

I pictured him in my mind, his thick, dark hair, his expressive eyebrows, his thin lips, which turned up slightly at the corners even when he wasn't smiling.

The sand grew warmer still . . .

"Here come his memories, Torvi," Gyda whispered. "Keep your eyes closed, and pay attention."

A swift, heady blur of images flooded my mind, so strong I shuddered with it, my arms shaking, my spine twitching.

I saw every vivid, jagged ache of Madoc's life: his lonely childhood, the death of the wise woman who had raised him, the endless wandering, the brief flash of joy when he took up with Stefan's band of Bards, the grisly colors of their deaths, red blood and white bone on a jade-green field tucked into the curve of a blue stream.

I saw it all.

I dropped Madoc's wrist and put my hand to my chest. I gasped, clutching at my heart, my fingers cupping in like claws.

"Torvi?" he whispered. "What did you see?"

"Everything," I replied. "I felt . . . everything."

Madoc nodded. He tilted his hand and let the Riffa sand pour onto the ground. Our eyes met again, and then I took him in my arms.

We held each other close.

"And that is druid sand reading," Gyda said gently behind us.

THIRTEEN

❧

It took us four days to reach the border of the Brocee Leon Forest. Four endless days of the stark Middleland Moors, wide, moody skies with thick clouds and plum-colored heather as far as the eye could see.

At noon on the fourth day, the Moors came to a sudden end in a line of tall trees—a long, dark stretch of green cutting across the horizon.

From a sea of heather to a sea of trees.

I'd never seen the Quell Sea, though the thought of it stirred complex emotions inside me, from curiosity to a bitter sort of loathing—it had, after all, stolen my father.

We were on one of the small roads that snaked into the Endless Forest, a dirt path about four feet wide. Madoc and I came to a stop a quarter mile from the entrance, Ink and Gyda halting behind us.

It was a bright summer day. The birds were sweetly singing, and blue-and-yellow butterflies danced across our path. The wind picked up suddenly, a great gust that blew through the millions of Brocee Leon leaves. I put my palm to my heart—the rustling was thunderous, as if the forest were shouting.

"It sounds like crashing waves," Ink yelled over the noise. "During a winter storm."

Next to me, Madoc grasped the hilt of the Butcher blade that hung over his sternum. "It sounds like a thousand Winter Elvers dancing on the ice of Lake Root."

Gyda touched two fingers to her forehead, then moved them to her lips. "It sounds like the clamor of the gods."

"It sounds like the end of the world," I said. "And the beginning."

Ink scanned the surrounding countryside, a palm raised to her forehead to shield the sun. "Little wonder no hamlets are nearby—who could tolerate this unearthly noise each time the wind blew?"

It was colder inside the Brocee Leon, much colder, as if we'd transitioned from full summer into deep autumn. We pulled our cloaks around our shoulders and tugged up our hoods. The air was thick and smelled of rain and decay.

Once inside, we could no longer hear the wind, no longer hear the roar of the endless leaves. All was *savalikk*.

We tilted our heads, staring up. The blood trees had gray trunks and gray limbs, both of which dripped tentacles of dark green moss, cascading down from upper branches in great swaths.

"It reminds me of the Fremish tale of Persinetta," Ink said.

I put my hand on one of the wide trunks gingerly, as if petting a wild beast. "The lonely Sea Witch trapped in the forest tower lets down her long, green-tinged hair so that the Iber sailor can climb up and make love to her in the light of the full moon. It was one of Morgunn's favorite stories."

"Blood trees are also known as serpent trees or dragon trees," Ink said. "They bleed red." She snapped a small branch from a young tree, and crimson drops of sap bubbled up from the fresh wound.

Gyda touched the sap with her thumb. "Yes. The sap dries into an amber-hued resin—though it takes years to harden properly. We burn it on the Boar Islands during religious ceremonies. It produces a spicy, woody incense."

"We call it *dragon's tears* in Elshland," Madoc said.

The leaves of the blood trees were pale green with bright red veins—they were delicate and beautiful, though the dense, endless mass of them almost blocked out the sky. Scattered rays of sunlight slid down branches in thin, wispy streams and cast long shadows across the forest floor.

I picked up the severed branch and let the sap drip slowly onto the toe of my boot. "Dragon's tears . . . there's a song about it in the *Blood Frost Saga*. Olli takes shelter under a blood tree during a violent thunderstorm. Lightning strikes the tree while she sleeps, and she wakes up to find herself covered in its thick red sap. The song is a lament for the fallen tree—"

A forest cat hissed somewhere off to the right, and the four of us dropped into the first position of the Amber Dance, knives drawn.

"Stay on guard, Bards," Madoc said. "Watch the road, watch the trees. Who knows what lurks in these woods."

We moved down the dirt path, alert, hands on our hilts. Strands of moss caught at our tunics, brushed our arms, tickled our ears.

I began to notice a tug on my boots as I walked, a slight drag as if stepping through mud, though the forest floor was dry.

Gyda noticed it as well. "The forest is trying to grab hold of us," she whispered.

Ink looked at us over her shoulder. "There's an old Elshland tale that claims every ancient blood tree in the Brocee Leon was once a living creature—men, women, and children who had wandered too near an evil wizard's squalid, decaying Great Hall and been enchanted. Their legs grew into roots, their torsos into trunks, their skin into bark, their hair into leaves."

We all paused and looked up at the trees again. My eyes ran over thick trunks and graceful limbs, and I imagined I saw a child's soft brow, a woman's quizzical expression, and a young man's smile.

Some miles later, just as the streaks of sun began to turn pink with twilight, the forest path curved right and then forked at an old stone signpost.

Madoc, Ink, and Gyda reached for their pipes and began to

take small, lazy puffs while we all rested, though both the Bards stayed tense, eyes on the distance.

I'd heard several dark tales of the Brocee Leon—mostly of the Elsbeths, a band of cold-blooded thieves and brigands from the Skal Mountains who cut out travelers' hearts, roasted them on spits, and fed them to their children and their strange, saucer-eyed dogs.

I shivered, and Madoc flicked his gaze to mine. "Missing your little hill hut, Torvi?"

"Yes." I tapped the blade of my Butcher Bard knife on my thigh and thought of my mother. *Fortune favors brave women.* "Yes and no."

I suddenly longed to be back in the shepherd's hut in the hills again. *Crawling under a pile of furs, Viggo's strong arms pulling me into him, the wind whistling outside, the fire crackling below, Mother and Aslaug and Morgunn tucked safely into their beds back in the Hall, nothing to worry about, nothing to think about, no regrets, no decisions . . .*

Ink gestured with her chin at the carved stone post that pointed west, the word TINTAGLE etched into the length. "Hard to miss the path to the tree town. There's nowhere else to go."

The post had two other arms, one pointing east to FISHER IVES, and one pointing north to a place called HEART SEED . . . though no path led in either direction.

I glanced at Ink. "Are Fisher Ives and Heart Seed tree towns?"

She shrugged. "This signpost has stood here for centuries—what those places are, or what they were, few people know or remember. Regardless, the paths leading there are long gone. We Bards have only ever taken the road to Tintagle."

We reached the tree town shortly after nightfall. It shone like stars.

Fires blazed in countless braziers on a hundred smooth, curving stairways, each of which circled the giant trunk of an ancient blood tree.

Pink-hued windows dotted each building, as Ink had described. The homes themselves curved like the stairways, crescent moons around the trunks, with timbered roofs left open to the sky at the center, allowing the tree trunks to rise through the ceilings.

"It's rather ingenious." Madoc gestured up to the town. "The blood tree leaves shield the roofs from rain as securely as our Elshland shingles, but allow the smoke from the hearth fires to float upward through the open roof, keeping the insides of the dwellings clean, with plenty of fresh air."

We passed a few brightly lit homes that sat directly along the forest path, then came to a stop at the base of a stairway carved with several small images of frogs, toads, snakes, and rats. A wooden sign hung on the trunk of the tree it encircled—the words WAYWARD SISTERS TAVERN were painted in bold yellow letters.

This would be my first taste of true civilization since I'd last visited Trow all those weeks ago, before the snow sickness, before it was burned. Despite my apprehension about tree towns, I was looking forward to leaving the open road for a while and nestling into safe, settled civilization again.

I began to climb the steps, then returned to the bottom, gripped Gyda's arm, and pulled her up after me.

"I disapprove of heights," the druid said as I prodded her up the stairs.

"I won't let you fall, Pig Witch."

The Wayward Sisters Tavern was the largest building on the east side of Tintagle. My companions and I crossed a circular platform and then walked up seven more steps to the heavy front doors. I gave them a hard push with the palms of my hands.

Warmth hit me like a hot summer breeze. I stepped inside, followed by Ink, Gyda, and Madoc, and the doors shut behind us. A roaring fire burned in the central stone hearth, and the inn was as bright as sunlight. It was loud with chatter and thumping mugs and crackling logs. I could feel the noise humming in my rib cage, and it warmed me more than the fire.

Perhaps I will bring Morgunn to this tree town after we slay Uther and her wolves.

The two of us could return together. We could go anywhere, do anything. Traveling with the Butcher Bards had taught me this above all else—wandering with friends provided its own sense of safety, its own comfort, despite the perils of the open road and the risks that came from having no one place to call home.

The four of us strode toward the thick, smooth length of polished wood that marked the bar and elbowed our way to the front.

Two women were working the ale, filling wooden mugs from the large barrels behind them. They were twins, or perhaps sisters very close in age, about thirty years old, each with wide-set eyes that were such a unique shade of light brown they appeared almost golden. Both women had thick blond hair that hung in ringlets around their sweet, heart-shaped faces.

Ink nodded toward the golden-eyed women. "That's two of the Wayward Sisters—they are known collectively as the Pinket Trills. They took over this tavern from their mother and their five aunts some years ago. The women of the Pinket Trill family have run this inn as long as anyone can remember."

We ordered eight mugs of ale, two for each of us, as well as rye-flour flatbread, bowls of duck-and-barley soup, and sour cream porridge with honey for dessert. I led us to a half-empty table near the fire and smiled at two green-cloaked Sea Witches when they slid down to give us room. I unclasped my cloak, dropped my pack, and sat down on the bench with a contented sigh.

I eyed the witches as I took long swigs of the ice-cold ale. They were my family, in a sense.

The ale was the best I'd ever tasted, a toasted sweetness that balanced perfectly with the malted bitterness, fruit and floral notes mingling on the back of the tongue.

"The Pinket Trills are known for their skill in the fermented arts," Ink said. "It's rumored that they practice some sort of herbal sorcery."

Gyda laughed. "So that's why this ale tastes of magic."

I stopped staring at the Sea Witches and began to watch the other people as we ate, curious as to who they were and how they had also ended up at the Wayward Sisters Tavern. I was a wanderer now, and I felt a sort of kinship to all travelers who were on their own journeys, far from home.

The table nearest to ours held a family of seven mischievous-looking, curly-haired boys, all of whom were shouting and laughing while their handsome mother and father looked on with mild amusement. Another table held half a dozen traveling cobblers, easy to spot for their calloused, hardworking hands and their fine leather boots.

There was a table of five Boneless Mercies in the far corner, black cloaks blurring into the shadows. They were smiling, postures relaxed. Each time they drained a mug of ale, another blond Pinket Trill sister refilled it. Mercies drank for free in all taverns now, a tribute to Frey and her companions.

I saw a line of silver-haired Relic Hunters on a bench near the trunk of the blood tree—three young women and one girl no older than fourteen. The girl was the leader, despite her youth. When she spoke, all three women listened.

A Pinket Trill sister began to clear our plates. "Will you be staying the night?" she asked, one hand holding two brimming mugs of ale, the other resting on her soft hip. "Our rooms at the back are full, but you're welcome to sleep here on the floor by the fire. There's a pile of sheepskins in the corner if it gets cold." She gave me a smile, full lips and sparkling golden eyes.

I glanced around the table at my companions. Three quick nods. "Yes," I said. "We will stay. Happily."

The Sea Witches finished eating and introduced themselves. They were named Spruce and Cedar, sweet epithets that suited their sweet natures. They had the telltale green-hued hair of the Merrow women and smooth, unlined skin. It was difficult to guess their ages—they could have been anywhere between twenty and fifty.

I debated revealing to them that my father had come from the Merrows, but I decided I wasn't yet ready to claim my witch heritage.

Spruce and Cedar taught us songs from the Merrows. The melodies alternated between soft and haunting and light and jolly. The lyrics spoke of storms and spells and sailors and dreams.

When the witches tired of singing, Madoc rose and began an Elshland ballad of whimsy and adventure called "The Five Trolls of Troll Mountain." It required the audience to stand on benches and stomp their feet whenever he sang the word *troll*, which was often.

People drifted inside from the outdoor tables, and the room

was soon full from end to end and loud enough to wake the dead.

The Pinket Trills didn't mind our rowdiness—all five of them stopped working long enough to join in on Madoc's song and pound their heels with the rest of us.

"Stefan would have loved this," I whispered to Gyda between refrains.

She put her arm around my waist and pressed her lips to my temple. "I know," she replied. "So let's continue to be merry in his name."

Madoc sang many more songs—tree songs, sea songs, songs of heroism, songs of murder, songs of travel, songs from the sagas, songs of love and friendship and heartbreak. His deep voice echoed through the inn, the notes surrounding us, comforting us like a thick, warm quilt on a cold night.

His eyes grew wet when he sang "A Cloak, a Dagger, a Journey," about a mother who gave her only child to the Drakes to break a Pig Witch curse. Some of the native Vorse in the room flinched at Madoc's tears, but they said nothing. Madoc was Elsh.

I felt my heart stir, my blood grow warm, as I watched the Bard perform his art. Singing made Madoc even more beautiful. His skin glowed in the firelight, and his eyes were large and luminous.

The Bard took a seat beside me. It was Ink's turn. She walked to the center of the tavern.

The storyteller did not tell one of her quiet, *savalikk* tales—we were all too drunk for this—but one that featured a foolish hedge-fighter with a wooden sword. He wandered the pastoral Elshland countryside, seeking dragons, only to end up battling apple-cheeked milkmaids and spindly scarecrows instead. Like Madoc's first song, it required the listeners to participate, this time shouting out phrases at key moments, and we were all laughing helplessly by the end. Even the five Boneless Mercies chuckled from their shadowed corner.

The Sea Witches bought our table another round of ale, and then we bought a third, and on and on it went. The Pinket Trills kept the amber brew coming, and we kept pace with the Sea Witches.

By midnight we'd closed down the tavern—everyone else had gone, either to their rooms at the back of the inn or to their camps somewhere on the forest floor. The six of us stumbled over to the dying fire and fell into a heap. Gyda squeezed between the two Sea Witches, and I curled up between Madoc and Ink, my nose buried in the storyteller's curls, my back pressed against the singer's chest.

A night breeze swirled down from the sky above, rustling the ceiling of leaves—it was a soft, drowsy sound.

One of the Pinket Trills drew near, her arms loaded with furs. She leaned over and tucked me, Ink, and Madoc under two thick sheepskins.

"Do you know of Heart Seed and Fisher Ives?" I asked sleepily.

"The signpost to Tintagle points to these other towns, though no roads lead in their direction."

Her thick blond hair tickled my cheek as she pulled the pelt down my body. She straightened, met my gaze, and nodded. "There are dark rumors about that side of the forest. Storytellers stay in our inn often, and one who frequents us regularly is quite old—ninety if she is a day—but still as sharp as a tack. She tells a tale about Fisher Ives."

The Pinket Trill sister paused. Ink, Gyda, and the witches were asleep, but Madoc was awake—I felt his body shift next to mine, waiting to hear more.

"What is your name?" I asked her before she could speak again.

"There are five of us Pinket Trills," she answered. "All sisters. My birth name is Sunset, and my sisters are Evening, Noon, Dawn, and Midnight."

"Lovely," I said. "You're all lovely."

She smiled wide, ear to ear. "This old storyteller claims that Fisher Ives is the name of an abandoned tree town. A young Jade Fell outcast came to these woods two hundred years ago. The Jade Fell built herself a tower of black river stone in the middle of the village—each stone plucked from the banks of the Messina River, which flows through the center of the Brocee Leon. From her tower, the Jade Fell wove great spells, and her sorcery rippled through the forest and caused great harm. Thiss Brambles grew over the road to Fisher Ives until the path was entirely lost to the woods. People left the tree town, and it went to ruin. The witch was finally slain by a young female Quick—the brave archer shot an arrow through her black Jade Fell heart, and the witch fell from her tower. The storyteller went on to say that the trees then took their revenge on the witch. Their roots covered her corpse and broke all her bones in their tight knots and gnarls." She paused. "Though this might have been her own embellishment."

"I'll have to tell this story to Ink tomorrow," I replied softly. "She will be interested."

Sunset began to rub one of her tight blond curls between two fingers. "It's funny you should ask about Fisher Ives. We had a band of Quicks through here the other night, and their young leader claimed she had found the Fisher Ives tower. She and her companions were fetching supplies in Tintagel, planning to return and set up camp at its base."

I jerked fully awake at this. Madoc and I gently untangled our limbs from Ink, who slept on, oblivious.

"Was the Quick leader named Sven du Lac, by chance?" I rose to my feet, Madoc beside me.

Sunset nodded. "She was."

The Bard and I exchanged glances. "We came to the Brocee Leon to find Sven and her band of Red Sparrow Quicks," I said. "As advised to us by three Drakes at a Night Wild."

"We lost a companion to them to gain that information," Madoc added quietly.

Sunset tilted her head, and blond ringlets fell across her shoulder. "Why do you seek Sven du Lac? She's a tiny thing, comes up only to my shoulder, but they say she fears nothing and no one. She and her Sparrows have sworn to protect this corner of the forest, and all of us who live here are in her debt."

"We hope to acquire her help." I paused. "A horde of wolf-priests slew a band of Butcher Bards and then took my sister and burned down my family Hall."

Sunset reached out and grasped my shoulder. "I'm sorry for your loss. I've heard much of these Fremish wolves. I thought they'd been driven out of the Middlelands."

"There is one pack left, led by a bishop named Uther. We believe they have set up a temporary camp on Lake Le Fay."

Sunset reached into the pocket of her long tunic. She pulled out a small ceramic vial, removed the stopper, and dabbed its purple liquid on my wrists and then my throat. "Breathe in," she said.

I did. I smelled sharp gella seed, sweet sea-thorn berries, earthy Wild Carrot Oil, and a hint of herbal blue chamomile.

"It's an oracle perfume. I brew it myself in a little work-shop I built on the forest floor. My mother was an Alchemical Witch, and her mother before her. It's the reason our ale is so delicious." She smiled. "The oracle ingredients are rare and expensive on the open market, but I grow my own and distill them myself. I like to keep a vial of this scent on hand in case

I come across a traveler who seems to be on a quest of some sort."

Madoc leaned toward me and pressed the tip of his nose into the hollow of my throat. He took my hand, raised my wrist, and did it again. He breathed in deeply one last time and then pulled away.

"Torvi smells of . . . *victory*." He looked at Sunset. "How did you do that?"

She laughed. "The scent changes when it settles into a person's skin. I can't predict the result."

"*Hel*," Madoc replied. "You are a skilled witch."

Madoc's eyes met mine. "We are going to succeed. The four of us are going to find Sven du Lac, rescue your sister, and kill every last one of those poison-drinking dogs. That scent speaks the truth."

I nodded. I, too, had smelled victory in the oracle scent.

I'd also smelled sorrow and pain and loss and love.

Madoc slept in my arms that night.

The two of us had grown close since the sand reading. In a few moments, Gyda's druid magic had poured all of Madoc's pain, his wonder, his happiness, and his pride into my heart. There was a bond between us now—the thick, unbreakable kind that generally formed between two people only after several years, when they'd walked beside each other through all of life's joys and sorrows.

I enjoyed the feel of a man's limbs against mine again. It didn't lessen my heartache, but it did bring a primal sense of comfort.

FOURTEEN

❋

I woke to sunshine filtering down through green leaves and to the sound of children's laughter.

I sat up and rubbed my eyes. Two of the Pinket Trills were serving what looked to be barley porridge with butter and honey to the couple with the seven lively sons. It was a pleasant scene: the rowdy boys, the smell of warm, well-made food.

I glanced down at Madoc. He was smiling in his sleep. A thin ray of morning sun illuminated the freckles across his nose. It made him look younger.

The Sea Witches had departed at first light. They woke us gently to say farewell.

"Come visit us in the Merrows," Spruce said in her high, silvery voice. "We shall sing and drink and be merry."

"Yes," added Cedar. "Feast with us in the grand Scorch Trees, and meet the queen of the witches."

"I will," I promised as I kissed both on each cheek. "Someday I will."

Madoc and I shared the news of Sven du Lac with Gyda and

Ink over barley porridge and mugs of fresh, tart midsummer apple cider.

Ink took a large bite of her porridge, her wooden spoon dripping amber honey and melted butter, then looked at Madoc. "I thought it would take longer than this to track down these Quicks. Either the gods are smiling on us or the Drakes' magic is even stronger than I thought."

"Aye," Madoc said. "Though we still need to find this Fisher Ives tower."

Sunset appeared at our table, holding a brimming pitcher of cream.

"Did we die and reach Holhalla?" Gyda asked, glancing at the ceramic mug of snow-white dairy. "This place grows better by the hour."

Sunset laughed. "The Hoffs bring us fresh milk daily. They are a family of six cheerful, robust sisters—they run a large barn at the base of the trees on the far side of Tintagle. The cows feast on the tree moss as well as hay, and it gives the milk a sweet, earthy taste."

She poured the cream onto our second helping of porridge, then sat down beside us at the table. "The Fisher Ives tower, yes . . . You can't follow the sign at the crossroads. It now leads into a mile-long patch of Thiss Brambles. You need another path."

The Pinket Trill sister leaned into me, her round shoulder pressing against mine in a companionable way.

"Sven du Lac gladly revealed how to find the tower when I

asked—they are an open folk, those archers, not prone to secrets, especially after a few pints." She paused and took a bite of my porridge. "When that Jade Fell witch cast her spells, some of them echoed through the forest and caused certain sensitive trees to suffer a spell blight. You can follow this line of blighted trees east from Tintagle, back to her tower . . . like sailors follow the stars in the night sky."

Gyda finished her second helping of porridge and pushed the bowl away from her with a contented sigh. "What signs do the trees exhibit to indicate that they've been spell-blighted?"

Sunset took another bite of my porridge, cream dripping off the spoon. "There is an odd tree at the edge of the village, near the Hoff barn. You might start there." She rose from the table with a swish of blue linen and blond ringlets. "Keep an eye out for the Elsbeths and the Salvation monks. Good luck, Bards."

We walked slowly down the Wayward Sisters' long, curving staircase, green blood tree leaves stroking our arms and shoulders as we passed.

When my boots touched the forest floor, I turned and stared up at the tree town. Tintagle looked beautiful in the dappled forest daylight, all the comfortable dwellings tucked into fat tree limbs, curls of hearth smoke drifting up through open ceilings, the citizens going about their daily routines, the smell of freshly baked bread filling the air.

I hoped I would be back again someday.

"I could live here," Ink said, voicing my thoughts. "I can picture myself settling down, drinking and eating and telling stories every night in the Wayward. It would be a good life."

Madoc threw his arm around the red-haired Bard. "You'll never put down roots, storyteller. It's not in your blood, just as it's not in mine."

I eyed the Bards. "And is wandering in my blood as well?"

Madoc put his free arm around my shoulders. "Time will tell, Torvi."

Bellies full and spirits momentarily content, the four of us wandered slowly down the forest path to the edge of Tintagle, to the very last ancient blood tree with the very last house built around its fat trunk.

There, at its base, we found a long wooden barn encircled by a fence of woven tree branches. Shaggy Vorse cows grazed the forest floor, leisurely nibbling at moss between shafts of sunlight.

I leaned over the fence and petted a red cow with deep, gentle eyes.

"Forest cows," Madoc said. He reached out his hand and let the beast press its soft nose into his palm. "There should be a song about such lazy, pastoral creatures. Very few Vorse ballads mention cows—"

"Look." Gyda pointed down the path. "That is the single most menacing tree I've ever seen."

We all turned and followed her gaze. A patch of regal candle oaks stood in a small copse up ahead, pale blue-gray trunks and blue-green leaves. They were all healthy, strong, normal trees—

Except for one.

One of the trees was . . . wrong. Bent, twisted, its faded bark flaking in spots and showing pink wood beneath, like an open wound.

"It does, indeed, look blighted." My skin prickled, and I ran my palms down my arms.

"By the gods, it gives me an eerie feeling." Madoc put his hand to his dagger. "It looks like a hunched demon, leering over its shoulder."

The tree did appear to smirk, with a crescent pink wound forming an evil smile midway up the trunk.

My contented mood began to fade, replaced with raw, bleak dread.

We walked toward the blighted tree, slowly, warily. The oak's limbs looked taut, stretched, each pulled in the same eastward direction, almost as if against the tree's will.

"I'll climb." I grabbed the lowest branch, cringing as the bark crumbled beneath my palms like ash. I hoisted myself up, careful of the oozing pink wounds. I shuddered as my sleeve pressed into a line of sticky sap. I would need a bath after this.

The candle oaks were much shorter than their giant blood tree neighbors, but the blighted tree was still about a hundred yards tall. When I cleared the top several moments later, my muscles were shaking and my cloak and tunic were covered in blue blight dust.

I braced my legs against a branch and scanned the view.

There. The next blighted tree stood about a half mile ahead in the forest gloom, dead east. We were on the Fisher Ives path.

We followed the blighted candle oaks for five days, the landscape an unending stretch of moss, trees, and dreary shadows. We saw no homes, and the only people who crossed our paths in all that time were four young Mushroom Hunters, brothers by the look of them.

The Mushroom Hunters were forest roamers like the Quicks, though they hunted rare mushrooms instead of game. They carried their finds, both poisonous and edible, in finely woven linen sacks. Their mushrooms would be sold at Night Wilds across Vorseland, to mystics for potions and to the wealthy as a welcome addition to stews.

The journey passed slowly. The farther we traveled from Tintagle, the quieter we became. The Elsbeths were on everyone's minds. Madoc rarely spoke, his gaze always on the shadows.

"Who are the Salvation monks?" I asked after we'd all eaten a silent supper of Elsh stew—mead, wild greens, dried lamb sausage. "Sunset warned us about them before we left the Wayward Sisters Tavern."

Ink crossed her long legs and leaned back against the trunk of a young blood tree, pipe in hand. "Do you really want to know, Torvi?"

I hesitated. "Yes."

Madoc moved to sit next to me and handed me the jug of moongold cider. "They are hermits who hunt down travelers in the Endless Forests. They wear yellow cloaks and have tonsured scalps, like Elshland monks."

I settled closer to the Bard, until my hip touched his. "And what do they do to these travelers when they find them?"

"Slit their throats and then grind their bones into powder, which they use to make a delicate ceramic called boneware."

Gyda let out a puff of smoke and frowned. "Yes. I've heard of this. Human bones create a stunning white porcelain, unlike the bones of animals."

Ink nodded. "You will find boneware on jarls' tables through-out Vorseland. They know its origins but ask no questions when the hermits come selling their cups and plates in winter."

I dreamed of young men that night, yellow-cloaked and glis-tening with sweat as they hacked limbs from bodies and ground bones into a milky-white flour. I did not sleep well.

On the third day we veered near a main forest road and stum-bled upon the home of an herb witch. It was built into the hol-low trunk of an ancient blood tree, complete with two windows and a small wooden door, smoke rising out of an Elsh-style chimney. Ink, who had the best eyesight, spotted the small sign advertising POTIONS AND SALVES.

The witch answered promptly when we knocked. She was young, with straight red hair that reached her waist, and had a kind, heart-shaped face.

Madoc bought four mugs of bee tonic, and we drank them standing by the witch's front door. The tonic tasted of honey and vinegar and revived my spirits, which had been dampened by the forest's endless gloom and ceaseless thoughts of tonsured, knife-wielding monks.

The young witch watched Madoc as he sipped his drink, her eyes resting on the soft-looking skin at the top of his tunic. There was longing in her gaze.

I wondered how she had ended up in the middle of these woods. Had she been forced to leave her prior home? Or had she chosen to run away?

I wondered when she last had a lover, and how she bore the loneliness. I pitied her . . . until it occurred to me that selling potions from a hollow tree in the Brocee Leon was not so very different from living in a shepherd's hut in the Ranger Hills.

When I wasn't consumed with thoughts of Elsbeths and monks, I worried that we were wandering in circles, getting more and more lost. But when I climbed the next blighted tree and lodged myself in the high branches, the crooked limbs of the next spell-wounded oak would appear before me as if by magic. As if the tower wanted to be found.

We ate snared forest rabbit for our dinner. The Brocee Leon hares had fur of a reddish brown, and their flesh was a dark purple-gray, almost black . . . but the creatures tasted fine, especially when stewed in the Bards' cooking pot with a bit of mead, wild garlic, and freshly picked butter mushrooms.

We practiced the Amber Dance in the evenings, and the steps were beginning to feel more instinctual to me, more natural. I began to move quicker, with more grace.

I heard wolves howling on three of the nights—melancholy, lonely sounds that echoed through the forest's stillness. It was the wailing of real wolves, not wolf-priests. This is what I told myself, at least.

On the final night, the faint sound of chanting floated on the night breeze as we readied the tents. Deep male voices, strange rhythmic words.

We doused our fire.

Madoc joined me for the first watch. We sat side by side, watching the trees, not moving, not speaking. The hours passed slowly.

Every rustle of leaves, every snapped branch, every call of a night bird—

I tensed for a swarm of yellow-cloaked monks, bursting through the trees, moonbeams glinting off their blades.

Sweat slipped off my temples, down my cheeks, down my neck. I gripped my Butcher Bard knife in my clammy fist.

Yet, for all my fear . . .

I did not yearn to be back in Viggo's hut, safe in his bed, under his furs. I was precisely where I wanted to be, on the path to rescuing my sister, defending my companions from cut-throat, bone-grinding monks.

If I died, it would be a good death. A Vorse death.

Whereas my mother had died in her bed, coughing up blood, protecting no one.

"Stay strong, Torvi," Madoc whispered, lips by my ear, strange monk chants floating in on midnight winds. "Remember your training."

Ink and Gyda joined us eventually, both too unnerved by the chanting to sleep. The four of us waited out the night, together, in silence.

Dawn arrived, pink rays ripping up the night sky. The monks' chants faded with the sunrise. We'd survived the night.

Fortune favors brave women.

It was nearing sunset on the sixth day when I finally spotted the tower.

It rose up from a small clearing in the forest, a patch of bright green grass, the fast-moving Messina River curving around the tower like a soft blue ribbon.

The black column was a hundred feet tall, perhaps more—though it was still shorter than the giant blood trees. This hid it from view unless a person was quite close. From far away, it looked to be no more than a shadow between giant trunks.

We stood at the edge of the trees, in the dark, damp air of the forest. I saw no traces of the Quicks or their camp.

It was a risk to leave the woods for the bright light of the open meadow. There was no shelter, nowhere to hide.

I stepped forward slowly, eyes on the far trees, and my companions followed. Fresh, warm air hit my lungs, and I breathed in deep. I pushed up the sleeves of my tunic and stretched out my arms into the sunlight. It felt like a lover's caress after all that time in the gloom.

We circled the base of the tower slowly, hands on our knives, feet moving through soft, waving grass.

"It has no door." Madoc lifted his hand to shield his eyes from the sun. "There's no way into this tower except for those three large windows at the top. Only the birds can enter."

The Bard was right. I'd been distracted by the tower's height and the beautiful sheen of its black river stones as the sun spilled off their curves. I hadn't noticed there was no way to get inside.

"It's said that Mountain Witches can fly," Ink said, her gaze on the high windows. "I didn't think it was true."

"I've heard that as well." Gyda nodded. "We have several tales of the Jade Fells on the Boar Islands, and most end with the Mountain Witches transforming themselves into owls and other birds and taking to the air."

Ink glanced at the druid. "I hunger for all new stories, and I have not heard these. You must——"

"And how did a band of Elshland Butcher Bards find the Fisher Ives tower?"

Four figures stepped out from the edge of the trees, four arrows pointed at our throats.

We went *savalikk*. The Quicks walked toward us, bows raised.

My fingers itched to grasp the knife at my sternum, but I kept still. I'd have an arrow through my heart before I could pull the blade from its sheath.

The archer in front was fourteen or fifteen, short, with shaggy black hair and the wiry, muscled frame of a person who spends her days running. She brought her arrow to the hollow of my neck and then looked up at me with sharp green eyes.

"Hello, Sven du Lac," I said.

She scanned my frame slowly, almost lazily, and then laughed. "How do you know who I am?"

I gently pushed her arrow away from my neck with two fingers. "We were sent to find you."

Sven lowered her bow. "Sent by whom?"

"Three Drakes at a Night Wild."

She laughed again, a feathery, childlike sound. "And how did you know I would be here at this tower?"

Gyda stepped toward the Quick leader, grinning. She was charmed by the girl's easygoing merriment at our sudden appearance, as was I. "Like all intelligent travelers, we asked at the Wayward Sisters Tavern," she said.

Three more Quicks strode out of the trees to join the four before us. The tallest of them was carrying a small brown deer over her broad shoulders, like a goddess from the sagas.

"I'm Torvi," I said, "and this is Gyda, a druid from the Boar Islands. The dark-haired Bard is Madoc—he sings. The tall woman is Ink, a fellow Bard and storyteller."

Sven nodded but did not shake our hands. She kept her right fist on her bow.

"We are the Red Sparrows," she said as the Quicks lined up beside her. "There are several bands of Quicks in the Brocee Leon Forest, but we are the fastest, the most dedicated, and the most lighthearted."

A few archers behind her cheered at this, and several grinned. I counted five women and two men, none older than Gyda. The youngest was a dark-haired girl with a swirling blue tattoo on her left cheek—she was a Glee Starr from the southern Skyye Islands. It puzzled me how a girl from Skyye would end up roaming an Endless Forest with the Quicks . . . but then Gyda was a druid from the Boar Islands and I was a half Elsh, half Sea Witch from the Ranger Hills, and here we were, traveling with two Butcher Bards.

"I'm Teel," the Glee Starr girl said when she caught me staring.

"You will learn all their names in time." Sven reached into

a wool pack at her waist and retrieved flint, steel, and a char cloth. "But first, we eat."

———————

"So what do you want with me and the Red Sparrows?" Sven tilted her head, and her shaggy black hair shifted, revealing pointed ears—she looked Elver, like me, though I was much taller.

The Quicks sat in a crescent shape around the fire, Sven at the edge, a haunch of venison sizzling on a spit behind them. She had set up their camp near the edge of the woods, on the opposite side of the meadow from where we'd entered. They had built a stone firepit on the forest floor and were living in the ruins of the tree town, which was now just a scattering of buildings nearly hidden in the leaves, a handful of deer hides stretched across decaying walls. The Quicks preferred to sleep in trees, rather than in tents like the Butcher Bards.

I met du Lac's gaze. "We need you to help us slay a pack of wolf-priests."

I told the Quicks our story, of Uther's attack on the Butcher Bards, the burning of my home, the kidnapping of my sister, our trade with the Drakes, the loss of Stefan, and of the information we'd acquired at the Wayward Sisters Tavern and how we'd followed the blighted trees to the Fisher Ives tower.

The Quicks listened closely as I spoke, their arms wrapped casually around bent knees, bows on the ground nearby, close at hand.

Sven nodded when I finished, the ends of her dark hair touching her sharp cheekbones. "I understand your quest, Bard, and it is a worthy one. But why would I risk losing members of my band to join in your fight?"

"The Drakes seemed to think that you, of all other Quicks, would be the person to aid us."

Sven's eyes narrowed. "A band of wolf-priests attacked my village in the Middlelands three years ago. The leader killed my mother and three younger sisters and took me alive to join her pack, though I later escaped. The Drakes are no fools. They knew I would be tempted to avenge my family." She paused. "I will think on this."

I was silent for a moment and then looked over my shoulder at the tower, black against a midnight-blue sky. "I'm surprised you didn't set up camp inside that ominous black column. Though I suppose you Quicks don't like being confined."

"I get restless when I can't see the sky above me. We also haven't yet figured out how to get in." Sven shrugged small, hard shoulders. "You've been honest and open with us, and I will be honest in return. There is a rumor among us Quicks that this black tower contains a library—a library that holds several very rare books of magic. One of these books is the only known copy of *Skinn Lykill*. I'd like to get my hands on this tome. It's why we are here."

Ink lowered her hood and sat up straighter. She was shy with strangers and hadn't spoken much, but this sparked her interest. "*Skinn Lykill* . . . is that a grimoire?"

184

One of the Quicks caught the storyteller's gaze—he was lean and tall, with dark hair. He put his hand to his chest. "I'm Galath."

Ink gave him a nod, and he continued.

"*Skinn Lykill* is Old Vorse for 'skin key,' which is another name for a hide-covered book of spells—though this book contains only one enchantment, rather than several."

"And what kind of enchantment is it?" Ink leaned forward. She was intrigued, as was I.

"The book tells of the Rover King. He was abandoned as a Fremish boy in one of the Endless Forests—*Skinn Lykill* is the story of how he came to be raised by a band of Quicks."

Cheers erupted at this, and Galath smiled as he waited patiently for the archers to quiet back down. "This is the story of how the Rover King studied sorcery with an itinerant magician, and how he studied thievery with a company of crooks. It's the story of how he fought and slayed the Thing in the Deep to avenge his true love, and how he found the Eternal Cup, drank its contents, and became a god."

"It's said that only a true roamer can read *Skinn Lykill*." Sven reached forward and plucked Madoc's pipe from his lips. "May I have a smoke? It's been many months since I've tasted Elsh brickle-leaf."

"Take as much as you'd like."

Sven flashed Madoc a wide smile and then began to puff on his pipe, thin plumes of smoke flowing through her lips. "It's said that *Skinn Lykill* can be used to summon the Rover King and bring him to walk among us for the whole of one night, dusk to dawn."

"Yes," Teel whispered. The Glee Starr's dark eyes were soft and shining in the firelight, her tattoo a vivid blue. "And I've heard that the Rover King will grant each Quick who walks beside him a bow made from a branch of the drasil ash."

Galath nodded. "A bow from the Tree of Life, the Tree of the Gods—that would be something indeed. It's said a drasil bow grants the archer immortality."

Gyda eyed Sven for a moment, then leaned toward me and whispered in my ear.

When she finished, I turned to Sven du Lac. "If we help you get *Skinn Lykill*, will you help us kill Uther and her wolves?"

Sven tilted her head to the side, sharp green eyes on mine. "And how will you help me do this?"

"Gyda has agreed to try her druid magic on the tower."

Gyda held up a hand, palm facing out. "I'm not a true druid—I left in the middle of my training. But I've grasped the fundamentals of prayer, and balance, and the drift of the nature languages—the speech of trees, earth, and sky."

Sven didn't answer for a few moments. She sat staring at the flames, smoking Madoc's pipe. Finally, she rose to her feet and faced the Red Sparrows. "Well? Are you in, Sparrows?"

The Quicks grabbed their bows and raised their weapons as one.

I smiled. I admired these archers. They knew how to live.

They knew how to die.

Sven met my gaze. "There are just seven of us, but we each fight as well as three trained warriors. It will be enough to kill a pack of wolves. We will make this trade."

I sank my teeth into tender meat and sighed with pleasure.

"We believe the wolves are camped along Lake Le Fay," Madoc said between bites of venison and sips of *Vite*.

"Do you know how to reach the lake from here?" I ask Sven.

She wiped a spot of grease from her chin. "I know of a path that cuts through the forest—we can reach the lake in two days, maybe three."

My blood began to beat faster. I was this close to freeing Morgunn. Just a few days of travel—and one hellish wolf battle— stood between us now.

Sven reached out and touched the blade at my sternum. "Have the Bards taught you and the druid how to use your knives?"

I took my dagger in my fist. "Yes. We've been learning the Amber Dance and are picking it up fast. We won't hold you back during the fight."

Sven slipped a bite of meat between her lips and then followed it with a long drink of *Vite*. She turned and handed the flask to Gyda. "And what is your stake in all this, druid?"

Gyda took a sip of *Vite*, then another. "Uther captured me

and tried to burn me alive, along with one of your own. His name was Melient—we escaped the flames together. He was headed toward this forest to meet up with his fellow Quicks." Gyda looked up at the night sky and rubbed her hand across her stubbled blond hair. "I think of him often and wonder if he found his companions."

Sven du Lac reached forward and gently punched Gyda in the shoulder. "Then I have good news for you, druid. Melient is alive and well. He and his pack of Quicks are camped in the ruins of the abandoned tree town of Heart Seed, some seventy miles north of here. We met up with them in Tintagle."

Gyda tilted her head back and let out a roar of joy. She threw her arms around the Quick leader. "That is good news indeed."

"You should visit Melient when we are done killing wolves," Sven said after Gyda released her. "Head toward the tree town of Rowan-Ripp. Ask at the Pink Dragon Inn. They will tell you how to find him."

"I have other business to attend to after we slay Uther. But someday, when I'm free of quests . . . yes, I will go to him." Gyda drew a line in the air and crossed it at both ends. An Elsh life oath.

Madoc held out his palm, and Sven returned his pipe. He re-filled the bowl and lit it with one of Ink's fire staves. "If I survive this upcoming wolf battle, I will join you in finding this Quick, Gyda. The Pink Dragon Inn . . . I like the sound of this."

Ink nodded. "I will join you as well. I like these tree towns, and I like these Quicks."

I drew a line in the air and crossed it at both ends, as Gyda had done. "Help me rescue my sister, and I will follow you, druid. I will follow you to the ends of an Endless Forest."

❦

FIFTEEN

Gyda stood in a shaft of moonlight at the foot of the Fisher Ives tower, whispering strange words softly under her breath, fingers flickering in peculiar gestures.

"How goes it?" I asked gently. She'd been at it for some time, but I didn't want to rush her. The druid knew that breaking the tower's magic was all that stood between us and rescuing Morgunn.

I inched sideways, trying not to hover near her shoulder.

Gyda furrowed her brow and shook her head. Drops of sweat slid across her forehead, glistening in the moonlight. "This tower is tethered by some sort of archaic Mountain Witch magic. I've never encountered it before. It's uncivilized. Wild. More beast than human."

A shadow approached, and we both turned, expecting Sven.

"That tower will never reveal its secrets." This came from a deep voice laced with a rich Iber accent.

The shadow stepped into a moonbeam—a woman with close-cropped black hair, a thin waist, and wide shoulders. It was the

Quick from earlier, the one who had carried the deer over her shoulders.

"I'm Lionel." She nodded at the tower. "We've been trying to find a door for days. My father was the son of a Sea Witch, and I have the Merrow magic in my blood. I've tried all the prayer-spells he taught me, and a few more. Yet . . . nothing."

I turned to her. "My father was also the son of a Sea Witch."

She gazed at me for a moment, then reached forward and took my wrist. She pulled me deeper into the shaft of moon-light, lifted my chin with her thumb, and tilted my eyes toward the moon. "Indeed. Violet irises, like mine." She released me. "Hello, sister Sea Witch."

I smiled. "I suppose I can call myself a Sea Witch now, though I know nothing of their life, nothing of their magic."

"Have you visited the Merrows?"

"I have not, though I recently received an invitation from two Sea Witches, and I mean to go." I paused. "My father ran back to the sea, in the end. Despite all his promises."

Lionel nodded. "As did mine. They always do."

Gyda groaned. "Can you two go share your Sea Witch se-crets back in the trees? I need to focus."

I bowed my head in apology, and Lionel simply laughed. We turned and crossed the meadow, moving toward the woods.

Lionel pulled a flask of *Vite* from her pack and offered it to me. "You should take the famous prickly path through the Thiss Brambles, meet your father's family, climb the Scorch Trees. I visited a few years ago—I meant to stay a few days but didn't leave for months."

The *Vite* slipped down my throat and made my insides spark and burn. My worries about Gyda and the tower began to ease. "What kept you there?"

"The Merrows are a contented place. They exist outside time, almost. If life ever becomes too much to bear, Torvi, retreat to the Merrows. It will help you heal." Lionel looked at me and shrugged. "I left because I'm a roamer. I pray to the Rover King. I have to keep moving or my joy dries up like dew in the hot morning sun."

Lionel took my hand and pressed it to her heart. "The Sea Witches will show you how to pray and how to control what's in your blood. You will need it, sooner or later." She released my hand and wove her arm around my waist. "It's nice to have another witch around, if only for a little while. We thrive in each other's company."

I heard laughter and looked up. The rest of the Quicks had climbed the trees and were lounging in the abandoned tree homes, drinking *Vite* and playing a Vorse game of conquest called Jacobs. It used a large vellum map and small wooden pieces carved in the shapes of snakelike sea monsters, Iber horses, Arctic Syrens, wolves, and longboats.

I'd played Jacobs with the Tather sons in their Great Hall. I lost to Eric every time, but he smiled so sweetly when he took my last piece that I hardly cared.

Viggo and I had often whiled away the time with an older version of Jacobs, a Fremish game called Jaques. We would play it on long winter nights, next to the fire, stretched out on our bellies. He'd carved the pieces himself and drawn a map with charcoal on an empty sack used for wool.

Viggo.

I waited for the pain to begin, the ache, the heart sting. It was there, the blazing ember of pain that never left . . . But it had lessened slightly. It was no longer scorching, no longer howling. I could bear it.

I was healing.

Madoc leaped down from a nearby tree and landed gently, gracefully. He saw me and nodded.

"How did you do?" I asked.

"I won, naturally." He grinned. "I always win at Jacobs. I shall celebrate with my pipe. Join me?"

I took a few slow puffs when he offered, the sweet-smelling smoke weaving through the limbs of the beautiful Brocee Leon blood trees.

Ink and Sven soon joined us on the ground, both smiling. They had done well in their games.

"How goes it with the druid?" Sven gestured to Gyda, near the black tower.

I sighed. "Not well. She said the magic is archaic and wild."

We all turned and watched Gyda for a few moments, a dark shadow standing under a dark tower.

The druid threw up her arms and let out a deep, guttural scream. She turned and came toward us. "Lionel is right. There is no getting into this tower, not by magic—mountain, druid, Sea Witch, or otherwise. I've tried every spell I know." She paused and ran her fingers through her short hair. "I have one last hope of getting into that tower. We will have to fly."

Sven du Lac raised her eyebrows.

Ink turned to the Quick leader. "In the story 'Twilight Comes the End,' a kidnapped Gothi nun eats a Sly Barbaric Mushroom and floats out of her captor's prison tower, into the night sky, where she slides down the stars and lands safely on the ground in a patch of blue wildflowers."

Gyda nodded. "Precisely. If Sly Barbaric Mushrooms can get you out of a tower, perhaps they can also get you in."

Sven laughed, loud and long. "Ingenious, druid. Ingenious."

Gyda wiped sweat from her forehead, grinned, and then gestured to the forest. "Have you seen a patch of Sly in your rambles through these woods?"

"They are rare, but, yes, we have seen them." Sven pointed west. "A patch of them grows in a small hollow half a mile from here."

Lionel unclasped her cloak and handed it to me. "I run faster without it." She glanced around the group. "One for each of us?"

We nodded.

"Excellent. This will be a memorable night."

She took off into the dark trees and returned a short time later, six plump red-and-white mushrooms in her pack.

We each plucked one from her palm. Ink held her mushroom between two fingers and gazed at it fondly. Sven and Lionel grinned.

Gyda frowned. "I will defeat this magic if it kills me."

We chewed the earthy, bittersweet fungi as we strode back to the tower. Together we sank to the ground at the tower's base, near enough that we were touching—this was the custom when taking Sly Barbaric Mushrooms with a group. It was considered unlucky to eat the mushrooms alone.

I'd taken Sly with Viggo, not long after we'd first met. We'd stumbled upon a patch of them while following the sheep across the hills one summer afternoon. We each ate one after our dinner, outside under the stars, stretched out naked on his wool cloak.

It had been a night like this one: warm, placid breeze, cloudless sky, big moon.

I kicked off my boots and lay back in the grass, my cloak spread out beneath me, the tower spread out above.

I crossed my arms under my head and thought of the shepherd, every detail I could remember: the shape of his fingers, the length of his toes . . .

My body began to tingle, my muscles gently quivering in a pleasant way. I closed my eyes and imagined Viggo's lips kissing my stomach and the sides of my waist . . .

Someone whispered my name, and I opened my eyes.

Madoc. I smiled and put my fingers to his cheek.

Sven sat nearby, cross-legged, a dark glint in her eye.

"*She craves that book*," I whispered to the Bard. He nodded, cheek moving against my hand.

I reached out and touched Ink's inner arm. She lay on her back, gazing up, face intent, as if she were reading the sky.

The storyteller began to trace patterns in the stars with her fingers, chanting ancient Elsh words under her breath, her red curls swaying over her forehead and ears.

Gyda and Lionel sat with their backs to the tower, knees bent, sides touching. They were gravely playing a child's hand game called Fox, Bear, Fire, their expressions focused, lips drawn tight.

I laughed at their seriousness, and Madoc laughed as well. I felt his ribs shake next to mine.

I closed my eyes again and lay still for a moment, listening to the earth singing beneath me. Its voice was low, booming, as rich as Madoc's, as deep as forests, as wide as woods.

It was a song of heroes, of quests and adventure, of old sorrows and new love and endless battles and enduring peace.

"*Here we go*," I heard Sven whisper beside me.

"*Hear the song*," Ink said. "*Feel the beats.*"

I began to float, my body drifting upward until I was standing, arms out wide—

Cool night air, pushing my skin into my bones, the tips of my hair trembling . . .

I slid across the ground, heels raised, toes pressing into crisp grass and soft earth.

Up.

Up.

I slipped up the night sky, like the witch I was. I reached out my hand, and my fingernails scratched the stars.

The tower loomed to my left. I let my body brush against it as I rose higher and higher still. The moon swelled and drew closer to me. I held it in my arms, squeezing it against my heart while the stars kissed my toes.

I could sense the others more than see them—my eyes were full of moon and sky and black, black tower.

"Torvi."

Someone shouted my name, and I went toward the sound, letting my heart lead the way, letting the stars splash against my skin like bright drops of rain.

I felt an arm slide across my waist. Gyda grasped my hand, fingers closing around mine. *"Now,"* she shouted, and then pulled me to the tower, right through the middle window, both of our bodies curving like willows, as graceful as two sleek cats.

We landed softly on the floor. A cloud of dust billowed into the air, particles dancing in the moonlight.

The others soon followed, shadows pouring through windows, feet making trails through thick dust.

I blinked the grit from my eyes.

The room was cavernous and filthy.

Owls hooted overhead, perched on black rafters about two dozen feet above. I saw piles of once-bright feathers, a mass of black candle stubs, and three black cauldrons, gray with dust.

A large tapestry depicting a single dead tree hung from the far wall—it was unraveling in the middle and brown with age.

There were wooden cages, all sizes, and a black stone hearth. A sunken bed stood against the far wall, covered in dirt and leaves. Glass vials lay scattered across the shelves and the floor, some whole, some broken into shards.

I saw books, dozens of them, piles on the floor, stacks leaning against the bed, heaps jumbled together near the cauldrons.

Lionel appeared at my side. She reached over her shoulder, searching for her bow, but she'd left it on the ground far below. She frowned, then looked up at the owls above us. "I have a bad feeling about this place, sister."

Madoc hit his head on a black cage that hung from the rafters and swore. "I agree, Quick. This tower throbs with dark magic. It feels almost . . . almost as if it has a heartbeat."

"Aye," Ink said. "I can feel it . . . *pulsing*."

Gyda kicked a glass vial to the side, and its oily contents splashed against the wall, leaving a red stain. She leaned in toward me, mouth near my ear. "I can hear that Jade Fell witch on the wind. Can you?"

I listened . . .

"*Yes*," I said.

The wind began to move in great gusts through the windows, in and out, in and out—

"The tower is *breathing*," Lionel shouted, a deep voice cutting through the roar.

"Do you hear it?" Gyda yelled. "Do you hear the whisper behind the wind?"

"*Yes*," I screamed.

The wind began to hiss like a cat, spitting out ancient words that I didn't understand, words that shook my heart and wove my veins into cobwebs . . .

I turned, my heels in the air, my toes scraping through dust. Sven du Lac stood, head bowed, dark hair covering her face. She clutched a large leatherbound book in her wiry arms, embracing it as I'd embraced the swelling moon.

"*The Jade Fell witch knows we're here*," she said.

The wind swept through the tower, a giant gust that swirled the feathers, the cobwebs, the dust, the glass shards, into a churning funnel of filth . . .

It spun five feet . . . ten feet . . . twelve feet high in the center of the room—

The funnel began to take the shape of a woman.

"*Careful*," Sven shouted. "*Stand back.*"

The dust-witch began to scream, a howling, screeching wind that stretched her dust-mouth wide, that made her dust-cheekbones go sharp, that made her dust-hair stand on end.

The six of us moved backward, pressing our bodies against the far tower wall—

The witch howled and raged, her dust-hands clenched into fists, shoulders back, chin thrust forward—

My skin started burning, ripping . . .

Thin lines of blood opened across my arms as I watched, three, five, ten—

I clamped my hands over my ears. Streaks of blood opened across the tender skin of my chest. I turned to Ink and saw blood dripping from her forehead and the ends of her fingers. I turned to Madoc and saw blood pouring out of his nose, down his face . . .

"*Run!*" Gyda shouted. "Jump out the windows *now*."

We jumped.

We threw ourselves out into the night and slithered down the stars.

SIXTEEN

❋

We awoke at the foot of the tower, our heads throbbing, our skin crusted with dried blood.

It was a misty dawn, eerie, an orange sun in a filmy blue sky, white fog rising off the trees.

"Witchy weather," Sven said, eyes upward, wiry arms wrapped around her thick book.

We rose and stretched and groaned. Flying on Sly Barbaric Mushrooms all night didn't lead to a pleasant morning.

Teel and Galath stood at the edge of the trees, toasting slices of bread over the fire. They greeted us with raised eyebrows, him tall and lean, her thin and petite, both of them staring at the book Sven carried.

"That tower witch get the better of you?" Galath ran his thumb across a cut on Sven's chin.

Sven grinned. "I found *Skinn Lykill*. It was worth a few cuts from some old witch-ghost."

Teel handed Sven a slice of bread with melted cheese. "It was a risk. Are you sure she is fully contained within that tower?"

Lionel glanced at the Glee Starr girl. "If I know anything about magic, and I do, I'd say her ghost is held there by her own spell, one she wove when still alive. We are safe."

A Quick named Amma jumped down from one of the trees. She was plump and strong, with beautiful eyes. She faced Sven, raised a finger to her throat, and made a slicing motion. "Someone should have boiled that Jade Fell witch down to the bone."

Gyda made the Elsh sign of truth. "And crushed her bones into dust, as the Sea Witches did with the Cut-Queen. It's the only way. Otherwise, they can leave a trace . . . a ghost, a memory, a scent."

Ink described our night to the other Quicks as we ate breakfast. I found myself caught up in her story, even though I had actually been there and seen it all myself. Ink folded words into stories so seamlessly it felt like a spell—the trademark of any true storyteller.

Afterward, we gathered around Sven as she set *Skinn Lykill* on the stump of a tree. She undid the gold clasp and lifted the heavy front cover.

The Quick stared at the first page for a moment, then let out a small sigh. "As I expected, it's written in Old Vorse."

Ink nodded. "You will have to get a Scholar to translate it for you . . . which will be tricky, as most are itinerant— they roam from library to library in search of esoteric knowledge."

Sven met the storyteller's gaze. "I know of a Scholar who roams this forest every summer, though she will take some time to find."

"Gretel." Teel thoughtfully traced her blue tattoo with her fingertips. "She's an odd one."

"She knows every language, alive or dead," Lionel added.

A pretty Quick with short brown hair and sad brown eyes stepped forward. "It's said she searches this forest for the lost library of a legendary tree wizard. The library moves with the wind and shifts with the sun, so it's nearly impossible to find."

Sven smiled. "I've heard that story as well, Pip. And I believe it."

"We see Gretel a few times each year." Galath glanced at Ink. "She has long white hair and long white limbs, and she rides a giant white reindeer. She often watches us from a distance as we hunt—she'll approach if invited, but otherwise keeps her distance."

Sven tilted her head and narrowed her eyes. "Gretel will want to know about the other books in that tower."

"But you have to find her first," Gyda said.

I reached out and ran my fingers down a page of the book, over strange texts and stranger illustrations. "It appears you now have a quest to find a Scholar, Sven du Lac. Gyda has a quest to find a sword. Madoc has a quest for vengeance, and I have a quest to find my sister."

The Quick leader looked at me. "It is good to have quests, Torvi. It is Vorse."

"Stefan used to say that the Butcher Bards are roamers and artists who seek out danger and share a desire for adventure." Ink rested her hand on the hilt of her knife and gazed up at the sky. "He used to say that each of us is a hero in search of a quest. He was right, of course. And here I am, the only one without a crusade."

A slow smile spread across the storyteller's face. She reached into her pack and pulled out a small book, bound in black leather. "I also took something from the Jade Fell witch. *Ash and Grim*. It is a book so rare it is considered half myth. And it is written in Old Elsh, so I can read it." She paused. "I pledge here and now to learn its forgotten stories and share them with the world. This will be my quest."

It took us several days to cut across the Brocee Leon Forest toward Lake Le Fay.

We moved leisurely, taking our time, setting up camp early, drinking *Vite* and eating stew, talking, boasting, singing the old songs.

We could all die by that lake, fighting the wolves. It was on our minds even as we feasted and laughed by the fire. Gyda was the only one among us who was safe. She'd dreamed of her death and knew it didn't end at the hands of a wild-eyed priest.

If one believed in dreams, that is.

The Quicks were right to enjoy the journey, and I couldn't hold it against them. Even when we stopped to have a languid meal by a forest stream . . . or when we wasted an afternoon climbing a grove of hop trees to fill our packs with the sweet black fruit . . . or when Sven called a halt so she could watch a pretty deer eat tree moss in a shaft of sunlight.

In fact, the only time I saw the Quicks live up to their name was when they were on the hunt. We ran out of meat on the second day, and the Quicks, bows in hand, took off after a pack of wood elk. I ran with them for as long as I could, but I was soon outpaced. All their former idleness disappeared when they chased their prey, replaced by intense focus and silent action. They cut across the forest floor like hawks cut through the sky, wings in, feathers sleek as silk.

The Quicks took down two of the elk, and I was glad to have missed the slaughter—I never did like killing animals. We spent the rest of the evening smoking the tender meat, and I was twitching with impatience by nightfall.

For the first few days of our travels, I fought the urge to bolt, to simply run, dagger in fist, until Morgunn was in my arms and my Butcher blade was buried hilt-deep in Uther's neck. I was getting closer to my sister, and I could taste it. I could feel it in my skin, in my bones, in my heartbeat.

But I needed the Red Sparrows. It was why we'd done it all, sacrificed Stefan to the Drakes, entered the Brocee Leon Forest, drugged ourselves on Sly Barbaric Mushrooms to conquer a tower and find a book.

If she's survived this long, she'll last another few days.

I remembered how Morgunn's voice grew breathy and sweet when she drank *Vite*. I remembered how her eyes would dance when she was about to cause mischief. I remembered all the little things about my sister as the miles wore on.

Ink read to us from *Ash and Grim* at night as we ate. She began with "Three Songs for a Drowning," which was about the love between an Arctic Syren and an Iber sailor, and the bargain they made with a wizard that ended in trickery, seduction, sacrifice, and poison.

It stirred me to the core to hear a story that was so rare. *How many years have passed since a Vorselander last heard this tale?*

"What else have you learned from the book?" I asked Ink when she'd finished the first story.

Ink gave me a sly smile. "I have learned many things. New stories, mostly, which are priceless in themselves, but it seems that this collection of tales is also a puzzle, where every story builds on the one before it, adding clues, revealing secrets . . . until, by the final tale, an observant reader will be able to uncover a key that opens a doorway to another world."

I raised my eyebrows. "Little wonder the book is so rare,

then. If all the previous readers walked into other realms, taking the book with them . . ."

Sven pursed her lips and blew out a puff of smoke from Madoc's pipe. "There is a legend among the Quicks about an archaic book that opens a pathway to an Elver jarldom on the other side of Hel."

Gyda nodded. "The druids have this legend as well. The realm is called Heartbreak, and it is said to be a mysterious, beautiful, and dangerous place. The humans who visit rarely return, and if they do, they are . . . different. Odd. Some reek of secrets, and some stink of magic, and all smell of oakmoss, peeled birch bark, rotting leaves, and freshly dug soil."

Madoc rubbed his chin and looked thoughtful. "Finding this Elver jarldom would be a noble quest. Ink could write tales of our adventures there, and I could craft songs, and we could spread them across Vorseland when we returned."

Gyda shook her head and then patted Madoc on the arm. "One quest at a time, Bard. One quest at a time."

Our last night in the Brocee Leon Forest was a pensive one.

Even the hope of seeing Morgunn again couldn't snap me out of a deep melancholy. I watched the seven Red Sparrows after our supper, marveling at their relaxed postures and easygoing conversations on the eve of battle.

Have I made the right choice?

If one of them died on the banks of Lake Le Fay, it would be my doing. Mine and Madoc's.

Viggo would have said that slaying Uther and her wolves was the right thing to do, a triumph of good over evil, and this was worth any risk. He would have said it was heroic. He would have said it was Vorse.

The morning of the final day broke clear and bright. We'd reached the edge of the forest, and the trees had thinned. I could see the sky again, and I felt a surge of hope, a burst of faith in the gods.

"Sometimes all it takes is a bit of sunshine and a balmy breeze to shake off the gloom," Gyda said as we walked side by side, her arm brushing against mine.

"Stop reading my thoughts, druid."

"We've chosen our path, and it is a virtuous one. The only thing left for us to do is follow it to the end."

"Truth," I replied, and then heard Ink and Madoc echo it behind us.

"Truth."

"Truth."

We stood on the bank of Lake Le Fay, a line of Quicks and Bards, our boots in soft sand. We watched the night breeze ripple across the lake's placid surface, bringing us the scent of clean, cold water.

We heard the wolves before we saw their fires. They howled at the moon, long, endless wails that soared across the lake and hit our ears like a slap across the face.

It made my blood go as crisp and cold as snow.

"The wind is in our favor," Sven said, voice low, "but Uther will sense our coming all the same. I've no doubt she has the nose and instincts of the damn wolf she thinks she is."

I met Sven's gaze. "So we attack tonight. While they sleep."

Sven nodded. "When the howling stops and the fires die."

We crouched in the long grass, waiting.

"Remember what you learned," Ink whispered to Gyda and me. "Remember the Amber Dance. Just breathe."

"The steps will flow through you," Madoc said. "Don't get in their way."

"Don't think too much, don't feel too much," Ink added. "Don't think of your sister, Torvi. Don't think of Melient, Gyda. Don't feel wrath or vengeance. Be the fox hunting the rabbit. Be breath and blood and hunger and heartbeat, and nothing more."

Gyda reached out and gripped my forearm in the dark.

"You can smell a wolf-priest," Sven whispered. "They rub

ash into their skin like the Long Death followers—they feel it brings them closer to their god. So use your nose if it's too dark to see their glossy yew berry eyes. They reek of fire."

I remembered the young wolf-priest who had come to our Hall, how she'd smelled of dirty skin and meat and ash.

Could I kill such a creature?

My mother would not have believed me capable of it. She would have said I was too much like my father, too softhearted, too un-Vorse.

She had insisted that I help Viggo slaughter sheep the previous autumn, though I felt ill each time my blade sliced through their woolly necks. Killing wolves should be easier, since I liked the sweet, harmless sheep and hadn't wanted them to die.

"There might be other captives besides Torvi's sister," Sven continued. "Be careful, Sparrows. Use your knives for close fighting. Make no mistakes." She paused. "Spare one or two— I want them questioned. I would know more about these wolf-priests and what plans they have for Vorseland."

"What about their magic?" Teel asked. "Shouldn't we fear this?"

"Yes," Gyda said. "But they need their poison to cast spells. Without it, they are left with the same weapons as any wolf— their teeth and claws. The yew berry holds them back as much as it gives them power. They move slower on the drug and are easily distracted."

Moments passed.

Slowly.

Slowly.

It was long after midnight when the howling stopped and the fires across the lake grew dim.

Sven rose to her feet, bow in hand. "Now," she said. "*Now.*"

We ran.

We followed the small Quick as she circled the lake, hugging the shore, silent feet kicking up soft sand.

Something scratched at the corners of my mind as I raced toward the camp, something the Drakes had said . . . what was it? *Hel.*

I emptied my thoughts. I became nothing but breath, blood, hunger, heartbeat . . .

Sven slowed as we reached the outskirts. We halted beside her and stood, *savalikk*, peering ahead into the shadows.

I counted two dozen tents, sturdy swaths of waxed, tightly woven wool pulled taut over wooden frames. I counted a dozen firepits scattered along the shore, scarlet embers glowing against the dark night.

I remembered what Gyda had said that first night she'd come to our Hall: *The yew berry poison makes them love the smell of fire and the sound of screams.*

We saw no guards. The wolves didn't need guards. They had Uther.

I heard a twig snap underfoot, then another—

Madoc bolted to the left, dagger in hand.

He returned a few moments later, his tunic splattered with blood. He and Sven exchanged glances, and then he nodded and wiped his blade on a patch of grass at his feet.

So there had been a guard after all.

We waited several long moments as Madoc scouted the area. He returned, shaking his head. Sven raised an arm, then drew it out in a wide arc. She grabbed an arrow from her quiver and clenched it in her fist.

Scatter.

Kill them all.

Ink was at my side as we darted through the camp. The rest would choose their own paths. Mine was now tied to the story-teller's.

We headed toward the last tent at the far end, nearest to the lake. It was similar to the rest, though the walls were decorated with strings of wolf teeth and a dozen or so wolf tails.

I slipped through the flap and crept forward in the dark, knife ready.

Fortune favors brave women.

I would kill these wolves. I would not flinch when the time came.

I waited for my eyes to adjust to the light—a small brazier was in the corner, casting long shadows across a pile of furs and sheepskins. I moved toward the heap, Ink behind me.

I crouched low, reached into the mass of pelts, and grabbed a chunk of stinking, ratty locks in my fist.

I pulled the wolf up by her hair, put my Butcher Bard blade to her throat . . . and hesitated.

"*Kill her, Torvi,*" Ink whispered. "*Now, before she screams——*"

I looked down into the wolf's face. I wanted her to see me before she died.

Short nose . . . violet eyes . . . dark, curly hair . . .

Morgunn.

SEVENTEEN

❋

I opened my fist and dropped my blade.

Morgunn threw off the furs and rose to her feet. Her small body was covered in streaks of soot and ash.

"*Torvi*. Why are you here? Why did you come?"

"I'm here to rescue you," I whispered. "Why else? The Butcher Bards saw the red cloth I tied to the tree, and they found me the night you were taken. This is Ink—" I nodded at the storyteller. "There is a band of Quicks outside, killing wolves. I have so much to tell you, Morgunn. Are you well? Have they hurt you?"

My sister regarded me coolly and said nothing. She looked *rangy*, her curly hair a mess of snarls. She looked hungry, raw, carnivorous. Uther had been starving her, as she'd starved her other wolves.

I put two fingers to my heart and said a quick prayer to Stray that Sven had found the wolf leader and cut out her heart.

Morgunn lifted a reedy arm and drew a cross over her chest with her thumb—the Elsh sign of warning. "You coming here . . .

It means your death," she said. "I would have let you go on liv-ing in Viggo's hut, Torvi. You should have stayed. I thought you would stay."

She was high on yew berry poison. I could see it in her eyes. The pupils were large and glossy black.

I finally understood. Morgunn hadn't wanted me to come. She wanted to stay here with the wolves.

I heard shouts outside, but whether they were the howls of dying wolf girls or the howls of dying Quicks, I could not say. The screams sounded far away. Far, far away.

I felt Ink stiffen beside me. I turned around—

Uther.

She rose from the furs like a giant, like Logafell from the sto-ries and the songs. Six feet tall, taller even, and built like an ox.

She was beautiful. Strong jaw, wide-set eyes, copper-colored hair to her waist, thick and tangled, muscles gleaming in the firelight.

Her gaze flickered from me to Ink. "Who are these girls, Morgunn?" Her voice was deep, as deep as Madoc's. "Why haven't you killed them?"

Morgunn stared at me and didn't answer. Uther stretched, arms above her head, and then slowly yawned.

The wolf-priest who had come to our Hall all those months ago had been skittish, like a wild animal, but Uther was calm, almost languid.

I'd come across it before, this lazy fearlessness. I'd seen it in the old woman churning butter, and in the cool gaze of the Drakes, and, occasionally, in the eyes of Sven du Lac.

"I suppose that noise is the sound of your little friends out there in the night, trying to slay my wolves." Uther spoke our Vorse tongue with ease, the soft Fremish accent faint and controlled. She was no dense, boorish beast, despite her size.

I realized then how truly dangerous this wolf leader was.

Out of the corner of my eye, I saw Ink raise her arm—

Her Butcher Bard blade slid into the right side of the wolf's neck. Uther blinked, stepped forward, and hit Ink across the jaw. The storyteller fell to her knees, then toppled over onto her side.

"*Ink.*" I dropped to the ground, put my palm to the storyteller's cheek, and then felt her wrist for a heartbeat. Yes, it was there, slow but strong.

"Stop it, Uther. There's no need." Morgunn gestured toward me. "Torvi is my sister. She came here with a band of Quicks to try to rescue me."

"Your sister? Ah. Then she must drink." Uther reached up, yanked the blade from her neck, wiped it across her dirty tunic, and tossed it onto Ink's body.

The blood began to flow down her chest. She grabbed a scrap of linen from the corner and wrapped the cloth around her neck. It quickly turned red.

I heard more shouts from outside, screams and howls roaring into the night.

"Is that the sound of dying Quicks? Or is it the sound of my dying wolves?" Uther shrugged. "Everyone sounds the same when they die . . . and it makes little difference in the end. I can always get more pups. This country of yours is full of them. Every village from here to Frem has a litter or two."

Morgunn had fetched a vial from a fur-lined pack near the bed, and she held it out to me now, its oily orange hue shimmering ominously in the firelight.

"You're the only family I have left, Morgunn. But I will not drink that poison."

Uther smacked me across the face. My lip began to bleed, small, fat droplets down my chin.

My sister held the vial out to me again. "Prove you love me, Torvi. Drink."

"No."

Uther hit me again. My nose poured blood, a silky, warm flow down my face, down my neck.

I took the vial. I pulled the cork, and the smell of ripe fruit filled my nose . . .

Fruit and cold winter storms.

My mind flashed again to that night in the Hall, the starved young wolf-priest with the bulging blue eyes, the smell of dirty skin and ash.

Perhaps all these wolves had once been girls like my sister, taken from their homes and fed poison until they lost themselves to it.

The yew berry juice tasted of apples and snow. I threw the empty vial into the corner of the tent and wiped my mouth with the back of my hand. It came back covered in blood.

"Yew berry juice is better than mead. It's better than *Vite*." Morgunn's voice had a soft, melting quality now, a quality I'd heard in the Long Death fanatics at the Night Wild, when they were speaking of their goddess, Klaw. "Uther showed me how the nectar of yew berries feeds the same longing as mead but also opens my mind and lets me *see*. I no longer feel fear or sorrow, Torvi. I do not think of our mother, buried in the earth, or of our father, off at sea. I do not think of Aslaug, turned to ash. I am at peace. I feel only my love for the goddess Skroll, and my joy in the flames."

"The redhead must drink as well." Uther nudged Ink with her bare foot, and the storyteller stirred. "Get up, girl."

Ink sat up slowly, shaking her head. She grasped her Butcher Bard blade and returned it to the sheath around her neck.

Morgunn held out another of the orange vials. Ink stood. She looked at me, and I nodded. She took the poison and downed it in one swallow.

I heard screams again, out in the night.

The yew berry juice began to work its way into my skin, my blood, my bones. I started to flush from it, cheeks hot, chest red.

It felt like a gulp of *Vite*, burn, burn, burn. No wonder Morgunn took to it.

Ink leaned against me, clutching her head. We stood side by side as the poison bled into our minds.

Morgunn began to whistle, long and low.

I blinked, blinked again . . .

The shadows began to dance. Furry black creatures scuttled across the floor of the tent. I watched them as they watched me, open black mouths spitting harsh black sounds.

"*Back*," I whispered, "*get back, beasts.*"

They moved in closer . . . closer . . . until they were rubbing up against my ankles like a pack of purring cats. Their shadow-fur was as slick and glossy as Morgunn's yew berry eyes.

"Ink," I said, "do you see them? Do you feel them?"

"Yes. Don't be afraid, Torvi. They aren't real."

I wiped another stream of blood from my face, glanced at my sister—

And jerked backward. I could see into her, *through* her, right through her skin, through her ribs, right into her glowing red heart, pulsating in her chest, dazzling as fire, golden as the sun—

Her heart was screaming, howling out its hunger for fame, for power, for glory—

I slammed my hands over my ears to block out the sound. "You want to pull the sword," I yelled. "That's what this is all about. You want to find Esca's sword."

Morgunn ran to me then, straight into my arms as I'd yearned for her to do earlier. "*Yes*," she said. "You finally understand. I'm the one—I'm the Vorselander who will pull Esca's blade. It is meant for me, no other. I knew this from the moment Gyda told us of the druid legend." She squeezed me tighter in her arms.

"I'm the one who will win the jarldom, Torvi. That's what this was all for . . . Father leaving, Mother's death, the wolves capturing me and burning our Hall. I'm going to win a jarl's throne, like a hero from the sagas."

"Oh, Morgunn," I whispered. I pressed my face into her tangled, stinking hair. "You can do that with Gyda and me. We can take you there. You don't need these damn wolves to get a jarldom."

My sister's arms dropped from my waist. "Gyda will never let me pull the sword. She wants it for herself. Besides, she doesn't know the path—she was trying to get it out of these wolf-priests. That's how she got captured. But Uther understands that the sword is mine . . . that Esca's jarldom is mine."

"I won't let you stay here, Morgunn." I pressed my palms to my eyes, trying to clear the yew berry haze. When I opened them again, I could still see Morgunn's heart beating in her chest. I looked down. The shadow-beasts had curled up at my feet.

"I won't leave you behind," I repeated. "I've risked people's lives to rescue you, Morgunn. I lost a friend to the Drakes. I won't let you stay here with these wolves, drinking poison and burning villages. You aren't in your right mind—you don't know what you're doing. I'd rather kill you myself than leave you to these vile creatures."

Uther stepped between us. "Enough talk. Wolf her, Morgunn, sister or no."

Morgunn stared at me, glossy eyes fixed on mine. "I can see inside you, just as you can see me, Torvi. I can see how much you want Esca's sword for yourself. It's shining all around you. I can *smell* your need for it—you smell like greed and victory."

"That's not true, Morgunn. I don't care about the sword—I never have . . ."

It was so hard to think . . . My mind felt as if it were wading through water . . .

"I knew you'd try to stop me, Torvi. I knew you wanted the sword for yourself. Uther warned me. Mother always said that I would be the one who would do great things, that I was true Vorse, not you. Why would you try to take this from me?"

"No, Morgunn. I don't—"

My sister tilted her face to the sky and began to howl.

I felt Ink's fingers sink into my arm. "*Oh, Hel.* It's a tooth-and-claw spell, Torvi. Run. *Run!*"

Too late.

The howls slid into my ears, sharp and oily, like knives into skin. I felt a splash of blood drip down my earlobes, down my neck—

Ink and I fell to our knees, twitching, writhing. The pain, *Hel,* the pain . . .

"It's a wolf spell," Ink spat between clenched teeth. "All you can do is endure until it runs its course—"

I howled like a wolf. I gnashed my teeth like a dog. We

foamed at the mouth and crawled on all fours and rolled and shook and wept.

Days passed. Weeks. Seasons. Years. I died and was resurrected, like the Cut-Queen, like a witch.

When the spell finally subsided, Ink and I were on the ground, curled into each other, gripping each other skin to skin, bone to bone, limbs entangled, a mess of blood and dirt and tears.

We couldn't speak or move. We simply shivered together, eyes closed, basking in the sudden stillness, in the absence of burning, searing agony.

The blistering pain in my ears subsided. I could still hear battle noises outside, screams, howls, Quicks shouting to one another, running feet.

I could hear the soft voices of Uther and Morgunn.

"Escape into the Brocee Leon. Head to the Skal Mountains and take up with Sinthe and her pack of wolves. Follow their trail—you know the way."

"No. I won't leave you, Uther."

"You will. If you stay here on your own, those Quicks outside will get you. Sven du Lac is the leader of this pack. I can smell her—we've crossed paths before. My wolves were doomed from the moment Sven set foot on the shores of this lake. I'll have to start over . . . new villages, new girls."

"Then let's run north together. I'll help you recruit wolves on the way."

"No. I have something I need to do first, a tribute that must be paid to Skroll at the Tree of Sorrow." Uther paused, listening. "It is growing quiet out there. Time to go, Morgunn."

I heard the soft rustle as the tent flap shifted, then closed again.

I opened my eyes. Uther stepped over Ink and then lifted me in her arms, easily, as if I weighed no more than a spell carried on the wind.

She strode out of the tent, into the night, and I didn't fight her. I had no strength left after the poison, after the wolf magic, after Morgunn's betrayal. I was as hollow as a hollow-eyed North-Fairy from the sagas. I was as limp and heedless as a sleeping child.

THE STONE TREE

EIGHTEEN

--- ✳ ---

Uther hanged me from the thickest branch of the Tree of Sorrow. The leader of the wolves placed me at its base, almost gently. I curled into a ball and moaned in pain. Remnants of Morgunn's wolf spell still rippled through me—my blood stung, my breath burned.

Uther pulled a small torch from her pack, lit it, and angled it into a crook of the tree so that it could cast its light across the clearing. I flinched and tilted my head to the side.

I was in a ravine, rocky sides opening up to the night sky. I could smell running water—a stream was nearby, though it was too dark to see it.

Uther unwound the long, thin leather belt that encircled her waist in tight loops. She tied one end into a noose and slung it over a limb.

The tree was a tall, dead oak, twisted and gnarled and bone-white.

The wolf leader knelt on the ground near me and tied my hands behind my back with a leather rope—though it mattered little, since I couldn't move my arms. My body was cold, stiff, dead.

Uther began to pray to Skroll, her deep voice rumbling through the narrow canyon, words of worship and sacrifice, some in Vorse, most in Fremish.

I had faced my death on my family steading when the snow sickness blew in on a spring blizzard. I'd faced my death with Madoc on the night we camped next to the Salvation monks.

I was afraid of pain, but not of death itself. I'd conquered this by the rowan trees, when I'd dug two graves and screamed out all my sorrow and fear.

Would Viggo be waiting for me in Holhalla, even though I hadn't burned his body so that his soul could rise up to the gods?

He would. I was certain he would.

I thought of Viggo. Only Viggo.

Uther grasped my hair in her fist and pushed my head through the leather noose until the strap sat snug under my chin. She gave a slight grunt and then yanked the other end of the leather belt. The tree limb groaned.

I was lifted off the ground by my neck.

Up . . . up . . . all the way, until my feet began to swing.

I'll see you soon, shepherd.

———————

I was not yet dead.

Of this, I was certain.

I hurt too much to be dead.

I hung, limp, floating in and out of consciousness, waiting to suffocate, waiting to die.

I was nothing. I was a leaf on the breeze. I was a half witch caught in midair. I was a dead girl on the wind.

My body twitched in the predawn, my bootheels knocking together, my Butcher blade tapping against my chest.

The wolf leader had given me back my knife after she'd tied my hands.

I heard screeching and forced my swollen eyelids open. White death-jays were beginning to circle above my head, yellow-tipped wings, black beaks. They playfully darted in and out of the oak's branches, looking forward to their coming meal.

Let the Bards find my body, I prayed. *Let them find me, Stray, and burn me so that my soul can float up to Holhalla. Don't let me swing from this tree until these death-birds eat away my flesh, until I'm nothing but a tangle of dull black hair and leathery ligament and sun-whitened bones, a somber sacrifice to a Fremish god.*

The warriors in sagas often thought of their loved ones as they lay dying—this theme echoed through many of Aslaug's fireside stories. I closed my eyes and let my mind drift.

I remembered holding Morgunn as an infant in my arms. She was a beautiful child, black curls and plump cheeks.

I remembered my father, his violet eyes, his soft beard, the way his voice changed when he spoke of the sea.

I remembered my mother, her strength, her courage, how safe I felt when she was near.

I remembered Aslaug, the way she looked when she sat beside the fire, her heart full of stories.

I remembered Viggo, the soft skin of his stomach, the warmth of his chest when I pressed into him, the curly hair on his forearms, the way his lips slid gently against mine, the purr in his voice when I lay close to him . . .

I thought of Stefan and the marvelous Night Wild. I thought of Gyda, bare skull in the rain. I thought of Ink, red curls, shy smile.

I thought of Madoc, of his beautiful voice lifted in song, of his body next to mine at night, of his scent, of his silky brown hair, of the long night we spent waiting for the Salvation monks to cut our throats and take our bones.

The wind jerked my body, and I wept with pain. The Vorse did not cry. But I was half Elsh, and the tears ran.

I heard footsteps splashing through shallow water, somewhere in the dark.

Uther had returned to make certain I was dead.

I opened my eyes . . .

The woman running toward me was too small to be the giant wolf leader. Her graceful frame was silhouetted in the pink, slanting light of the setting sun . . .

It was Stray.

She was coming to take me to Holhalla to be with my mother and Aslaug and Viggo.

She was so beautiful, so very beautiful in the early-dawn light, bright eyes under short blond hair . . .

I was ready to die. I was ready for the pain to end.

Come to me, Stray . . .

NINETEEN

❦

I *dreamed.*

Blood dreams, death dreams, a ring of fire around my neck . . . It *burned*, oh, Stray, how it burned . . .

I dreamed I was in a cave, flames casting shadows on rock walls, my body pressed against wooden casks.

I screamed that I was dying. I screamed that my flesh was ash and that I was nothing but bones. I screamed that Fetch, the faceless Elsh god of death, was rubbing his numbing oil into my skin, preparing me for the grave.

I screamed for someone to give me a drink of mead so that I could enter Holhalla with the taste of ale on my tongue.

I dreamed of Gyda, chanting, sweat dripping off her brow, tossing things into the fire, dancing around the flames . . .

I dreamed of Madoc, holding me, crying softly, whispering in my ear. I dreamed of Sven du Lac and the Red Sparrows, drinking mead and singing songs of the Rover King. I dreamed of Ink, grasping my hand and telling me the story of a girl named Torvi who fought a wolf-queen and rose from the dead.

I felt sunlight, warm silk on my eyelids.

I yawned and stretched into the balmy light.

I was alive.

I opened my eyes. I lay under a pile of furs in a small, grassy clearing surrounded by pine trees, beneath a wide blue sky. Birds chirped above. People talked and laughed in the distance.

I spread my arms. My fingertips touched a warm body— someone was sleeping next to me under the furs.

Madoc.

I smiled. I sat up and tugged the hides back from his face—

It was not my sensitive Butcher Bard. It was Uther.

The wolf-priest was sleeping, eyes closed, lips parted slightly.

Am I still death-dreaming?

I reached out and touched her. I ran my hand over her tangled hair. I traced her nose with the end of my thumb. She slept on.

"Torvi."

I flinched and looked up. Madoc stood, palm to his heart, tears in his eyes. "You're awake. You're alive."

I rose, and the Bard took me in his arms. "Your neck is bruised almost black," he said.

I held him against my shoulder and stroked his hair. "I dreamed I wore a chain of fire," I whispered. The words came slowly, painfully, like soft skin dragged over sharp teeth.

"You nearly died, Torvi."

I nodded, my chin rubbing against his chest.

"Madoc?"

"Mmm?"

"Why the Hel is Uther sleeping next to me?"

"Don't worry. She's bound at the wrists and ankles." He released me, leaned over, and lifted the hides. The shafts of two arrows protruded from a seeping wound in Uther's torso. "She's dying, Torvi. We can't pull the arrows, or she will die even faster. Sven and Gyda hope to get some information from her before her soul is taken by Skroll."

"How did you capture her?"

"The Red Sparrows tracked her for twenty miles across the Brocee Leon. Those Quicks have the instincts of feral cats. Uther is more vulnerable when not surrounded by her pack of dogs." He paused. "We killed every one of those beasts on the banks of Lake Le Fay. She's the last."

I took a breath and let it out slowly. "Did you find Morgunn's trail? I'm sure Ink told you she was headed north to the Skals to join another pack of wolves."

"She did tell us," Madoc replied, "and we searched but found nothing. Your sister disappeared into the Brocee Leon without a trace, Torvi. I'm sorry."

I nodded. "I expected as much. She's lost to me now. I doubt I will ever see her again." I paused. "In some ways, it would have been better if she'd died during the snow sickness. If I'd buried her with our mother by the rowan trees."

"You don't mean that, Torvi. You're simply grieving."

I nodded. "Perhaps. Though right now I believe it would soothe my heart to have her safely tucked into the ground at our own steading rather than wandering Vorseland as a flame-hungry wolf. I've grown used to grief. This . . . this is something new. I'm afraid of my own younger sister, Madoc. Of what she will do." I reached up and put my palm to his cheek. "Will you breathe easier now that your revenge is complete?"

"Perhaps. I wish Stefan were here."

"As do I." I scanned the little clearing and watched as butterflies danced over green grass and a trio of yellow flush-birds sang on a low branch of a sapling blood tree. I reached my arms toward the small patch of blue sky and stretched again. My body felt . . . *strong*.

"How long have I been out, Madoc?"

"Four days."

"I'm starving."

Madoc smiled. "That's a good sign. How's your throat?"

"It hurts."

I looked down at the sleeping form of Uther. I felt no anger for her taking my sister and turning her into a poison-drinking wolf. For hanging me from a tree as a sacrifice to her god.

"Why put her next to me, Madoc? Was there no other place to leave this Fremish monster in an Endless Forest?"

"Gyda ordered that you be taken to this clearing—she wanted you to get some fresh air and sunshine. She thought it would help you wake from your death-sleep, and it did." Madoc paused. "Sven suggested we put Uther next to you in case she dream-slipped and shared a reverie with you of your sister, of where she was headed."

"Dream-slip?"

"The Fremish are dream sharers. They share their dreams with anyone who lies near them."

"She shared nothing with me. I dreamed only of pain . . . and of Gyda, you, and Ink . . . and a cave filled with mead."

"We carried you to a nearby Butcher Bard cave—we needed to take you somewhere after Gyda cut you down from the oak. You were near death, Torvi. I think . . . I think you did die for a little while."

I met his gaze.

Madoc blinked, and tears ran down his cheeks. "Gyda saved you. She brought you back from the dead. I don't know what those druid spells cost her—she is resting inside the cave. She still tires easily. Sven said she paid a high price for that sorcery, one the gods will collect someday. Gyda is a true friend, Torvi. No one could have done more."

"Take me to her," I said.

Madoc fetched a nearby Quick to guard Uther, and the two of us walked the half mile to the cave through the cool, dark

Brocee Leon. I wove between trees, soft green moss grazing my skin, soft black earth melting under my bare feet.

I'd believed I was on my way to Holhalla, and to Viggo . . . to now find myself still in Vorseland, in an Endless Forest, still alive thanks to a druid with a heart of gold . . .

It stirred me somewhere deep and raw. I was changing, my heart, my blood, my bones. A part of me was being forged, like steel placed in fire.

Viggo had once said there was steel in my veins.

The entrance to the Bards' cave was cleverly hidden behind a large spider tree. Hundreds of its white spindly branches wove an intricate pattern of rings that entirely obscured the opening. Madoc and I slipped behind the web and into the cave.

A large fire burned in the center, and the cavern was bright and very warm. I began to sweat almost immediately. I threw off my cloak and looked around. Casks of mead were stacked in neat piles, just as they had been in my death-dreams. Several had been emptied and tossed aside. Water trickled down from somewhere far above. The ceiling was so high it faded into darkness.

The walls of the cave were streaked with ripples of milky-green stone—this was a Jade Cave, then. They were common in the Skal Mountains and were famous hiding places of the Jade Fells— they had, in fact, given the Mountain Witches their name.

"Ink and the other Quicks are off hunting." Madoc nodded to a figure huddled next to the fire. "There she is, resting."

Gyda lay with her cheek on her arm, her short blond hair

sweetly tousled. I knelt beside her. "I hear that you saved my life, Pig Witch."

She opened her eyes. "I'm no Pig Witch."

I reached out a hand, and she grasped it. I pulled the druid to her feet and clasped her in my arms.

Gyda looked at Madoc. "Is the wolf leader still alive?"

He nodded. "And will be for a while yet. I know you have questions for her. There will be time."

The three of us walked to a deep stream that ran near the cave, silvery water twisting over stones between a grove of thin white willows. We dropped our clothes on the mossy bank and jumped in naked, too dirty and hot to care who saw what.

The cold water washed away the smell of fire, of wolves, of death. It made my blood sing and my heart hum.

We began to lazily tread water, our toes sliding over slick river stones, our lips spreading into smiles whenever our bare limbs brushed underwater.

I noticed Gyda had several delicate cuts under her skin, as if she had been sliced open from the inside.

"Did you get wounded during the wolf attack?" I asked. "Is this from a wolf spell?"

The druid shook her head. "This came with the magic I used to heal you. It will pass."

I put a wet palm to her cheek. "Thank you," I whispered. "Thank you, druid."

"Are those tears in your eyes, Torvi?"

"No."

"You're getting as softhearted as this here pipe-smoking Elsh Bard."

I laughed.

"Gyda killed three of the wolf-priests during the battle," Madoc said. "She did well."

"And Madoc took down ten, not counting the scout he killed before we attacked."

"And all I did was get myself hanged," I said with a frown. "You both proved better Butcher Bards than me."

"No, Torvi," Madoc replied gently. "You are part of our family now. Our success is your success. We are one."

I felt a sudden wave of fellowship wash over me at this, toward my two companions, toward Ink, toward Sven and all the Quicks.

Is there anything better in life than having brave, true friends?

Some time later we lay on the riverbank, staring up at the cloudless sky.

Madoc pulled his pipe from one pocket and a flask of moon-gold cider from the other. "Which would you like?" he asked the druid with a smile.

"Both. I did save a dead girl, after all."

Ink took me in her arms when she returned from the hunt and held me for a long while. She muttered soft things into my temple—quotes from the sagas about friendship and heroes brought back from death.

Teel, the young Glee Starr Quick, found us all sitting beside the stream as twilight crawled in, smoking pipes and drinking mead and talking softly of irreverent, pleasant things. "The dying wolf is calling for the druid," she said, eyes on Gyda. "You had better come."

We followed the Quick, weaving through the trees in the gathering dark. I heard a Great Owl hoot above me and took it as a good sign.

Uther lay where I had left her, on the furs in the small, grassy clearing. She was surrounded by Quicks. Sven held a torch, and the orange light shone down on the brawny wolf.

She looked smaller than when I'd first seen her, tall and muscled, in the tent with my sister. Her beautiful face was pinched with pain, and blood oozed from her wound each time she took a breath.

The Quicks had cut her bonds, though two of the archers stood with bows raised as a precaution.

Uther gestured with two fingers for Gyda to draw near.

"*You're the one who wants to find the path to Esca's jarldom.*" Her voice rumbled in her broad chest, deep but weak. I had to strain to catch each word. "*I saw your ache for Esca's sword—I saw it glowing within you the first time we met.*"

Gyda rubbed her skull with her palm and then dropped to her knees beside the wolf-priest. "Yes. I am the one searching for Esca's forgotten lands."

"*I tried to burn you and a Quick some weeks ago. You escaped and took the archer with you.*"

"Yes, wolf. His name is Melient. He has returned to his Quick companions and freely roams this forest, no thanks to you and your wolves."

"*My wolves are all dead.*" Uther slowly lifted her hand and rested it on Gyda's head, like an Elshland monk offering a blessing. "*I did not tell Morgunn how to find the key to Avalon. She begged me, yet I did not tell her. Without it, she will never find the sword . . . I didn't want her to find it. She has too much chaos in her blood. She is a wolf, not a jarl.*"

Gyda kept her head bowed, *savalikk*, and let the Fremish priest rake dirty fingers through her short hair.

"*There is a tunnel through the Skal Mountains. It was built by Fremish stonecutters in the age of the sagas and leads to Esca's jarldom in the Green Wild Forest—it is the only path that still lies open to his forgotten lands. You must go straight north from here. Follow the Mort Darthur River until you reach the base of Imp's Ear Peak. There you will find a Fremish wizard in a small hut beside a sky-blue troll-stone. The wizard will be young, beautiful, and mischievous.*"

Uther's voice faded. She put a hand to one of the arrow shafts in her side, took a breath, and pulled. The arrow slid out, followed by a splash of crimson. "*I want to die. Skroll is coming for me. I can hear her footsteps echoing through the trees . . .*"

Gyda pressed her hand to Uther's wound, and blood seeped between her fingers. "Tell me how to find the door, wolf. You will tell me this before you die."

Uther sighed deeply, and her giant frame rattled, rib cage shaking. She put her hand to the leather pouch at her waist, opened it, and pulled out a small statue. The figurine was part woman, part owl, with large, staring eyes, and two hornlike tufts of hair. "*Here, druid. Skroll has ordered me to give this to you— she has changed her mind and now approves of this quest to find Esca's sword. Show this trinket to the wizard and then make the trade. He will know what it means.*"

Gyda took the statue and clutched it to her heart. "Thank you, wolf."

Uther took another deep breath and yanked the remaining arrow from her torso. She dug her dripping red fingers into the dirt beneath her and opened her mouth wide.

"*Skroll,*" she shouted. "*Skroll.*"

The queen of the wolves died in blood, screaming for her god.

It was a good death.

I had hoped to interrogate Uther about Morgunn and the wolf-priest leader Sinthe, but she died too soon.

Perhaps it was for the best.

My sister had run off to drown herself in yew berry juice and rampage the Skal Mountains with another pack of wolves.

I'd failed her.

I would not run after Morgunn again and risk my friends' lives trying to rescue her.

I would help Gyda obtain Esca's sword. I would keep this oath. My companions had helped me find my sister once, and I would not ask them to do it again.

———————

Madoc taught the basic steps of the Amber Dance to the Quicks that night.

"We are archers at heart," Sven said, "but we carry knives and need to know how to use them."

"I thought you only taught the Amber Dance to other Bards." I glanced at Madoc and put my hand on the hilt of my blade. "You were very clear about this in the shepherd's hut, after Uther burned my home."

Madoc shifted into the first stance and smiled at me over his shoulder. "I've changed, Torvi."

The Quicks had lost a companion on the banks of Lake Le Fay—Pip, with the brown hair and sad brown eyes. They had burned his body and completed their dawn-to-dusk mourning. The archers were now back to their boisterous, cheerful ways—they would weave Pip's name into their songs and into their stories. He was not truly dead.

The graceful archers picked up the Amber Dance as easily as breathing, and we all flowed through the steps together, four

Butcher Bards and six Quicks, moving through the forest shadows. Afterward, we feasted on forest deer and yellow butter mushrooms. Gyda and I ate like half-starved Aradia Witches, fresh from a monthlong journey through the Spice Desert on a black-and-white dune ship.

TWENTY

--- ❈ ---

The blood trees soared above us, blocking out the summer sky. Sunlight streamed down in thin, ethereal strands, like the silvery-blond hair of Midnight in the *Sea and Ash Saga*. We'd stopped at a crossroads in the Brocee Leon Forest. One stone arm of the signpost pointed to Tintagle, and one arm pointed north, to Imp's Ear Peak—the highest point of the Skal Mountains.

Ink, Gyda, Madoc, and Sven du Lac leaned against two thick tree trunks, smoking their pipes. The Quick leader carried *Skinn Lykill* in her pack, nestled against her hip—she never let the book out of her sight.

The Mort Darthur River flowed behind them—it was nearly eight feet wide, with a swift current of melted snow from the tips of the Skals. The water had a violet sheen to it, created from mineral deposits it picked up during its course down the mountains. Mists of purple-hued droplets hung in the humid forest air and settled on our skin.

"It's the color of your eyes in moonlight, Torvi." Ink nodded toward the river.

"Sea Witch eyes," Lionel added. The tall Quick knelt down on the bank and slipped her fingers into the water. She caught a fish in one hand, threw it onto the bank, and then brought up ten more.

We roasted the fish on thin sticks over a small fire. It was our last meal with the archers before we turned north to find the Fremish wizard and the tunnel to Esca's jarldom. Sven du Lac and the Red Sparrows would return to Tintagle and seek word of the Scholar Gretel.

I embraced each of the Quicks in farewell. Teel was bruised and battered from the wolf battle—she put a hand to her sore ribs each time she laughed, but it didn't stop her all the same. She chuckled softly into my neck when she said good-bye.

Galath had taken a knife to the shoulder during the attack. I kissed each of his cheeks instead of clasping him in my arms, in the way of the Fremish.

I held Lionel longer than the rest, Sea Witch sister that she was. She'd emerged unscathed from the battle, which came as no surprise. Only Uther could have posed any real challenge to her in close combat—the Quick was built like a god.

Sven du Lac was last. She gripped my forearm, her small fingers wrapping tightly around my skin. "I promise to come to your aid if you ever have need of me." She turned to Gyda, Ink, and Madoc. "Same goes for you, druid, and you two Butcher Bards. Send word. I'll be there."

Madoc placed his hands on Sven's shoulders and touched his forehead to hers—an Elsh gesture of gratitude and honor.

"I owe you, Quick. I obtained the vengeance I've craved since Uther murdered my Butcher Bard family."

They stayed like this for some moments before Sven gently pulled away. She looked up at Madoc, her eyes bright and mischievous. "We rescued a book from a tower, massacred a pack of meddlesome wolf-priests, and drank copious amounts of mead in a Butcher Bard cave. What more could we want from an adventure?"

I laughed. "Good luck finding your Scholar, Quick."

Sven put a fist to her heart. "Good luck finding your sword, Bards."

"*Heltar*," Gyda and I whispered in unison.

Gyda, Ink, Madoc, and I watched the Quicks stride off down the Tintagle path, the air ringing with their cheerful voices. We stared after them until they disappeared, bodies swallowed by trees and shadows.

The world felt smaller suddenly. Less vivid.

I hoped I would see them all again. Soon.

Who knew?

Gyda leaned against the stone sign and sighed. She had dark circles under her eyes, and I could see the thin crimson streaks from the druid magic under her skin, radiating up her neck.

"I can sense your heavy hearts, companions," she said, voice low. "I will finish this quest alone. Follow those merry Quicks back to the tree town. I will find you when I have the sword."

"Never." I slid my arm around Gyda's waist and pulled her to my side. "You save my life, druid, and you expect me to abandon you at the first fork in the road? I'd rather drink poison and follow the wolf-priests straight to Hel."

Madoc nodded. "We will return to Tintagle when your quest is complete, Gyda, and not before then. I got my revenge, and Torvi found her sister. It's your turn."

"Truth," Ink added. "We go nowhere alone, and everywhere together."

Gyda grinned, and then she tilted her head back and laughed. "Fair enough, Bards. We travel the Imp's Ear path and hunt up this Fremish wizard."

We followed the Mort Darthur River for five days.

On the second day, we passed through a tree town named Glaston. It was smaller than Tintagle but just as bright and lively. It had a large inn called the Straight and Narrow, run by a band of seven sweet, handsome brothers.

We made a bit of coin singing and telling stories among the treetops, as we had in Tintagle. It was time for me to start earning my keep, so I told one of Aslaug's favorite tales, about four young Fremish thieves who stole a formula from a Scent Witch for a perfume called Gentle Air, which turned all who wore it into cunning, imaginative liars.

Madoc sang the comic song "The Fevered Mother," about a woman who feeds her loud, greedy children a poisoned soup, only to watch them return as ghosts and be more troublesome in death than they had ever been in life. The audience joined in on each refrain:

> *"Have a bite, child, have another, eat it all, eat it up, eat it up, eat it up."*

We all took long drinks of ale after each chorus, and soon the entire inn was sloshed and joyous.

"Are all tree town taverns run by packs of beautiful siblings?" I asked one of the brothers when he brought my fourth mug of mead.

He smiled at me shyly. "You have visited Tintagle. Yes, we've heard about those sisters. We plan to close the Straight and Narrow for a fortnight this fall and travel to this other tree town to meet these Pinket Trills."

"You will like them," I said. "Very much, I should think."

On the fifth day, the trees began to thin. The sun broke through and streamed down in thick yellow rays. I smiled as it warmed my skin.

We reached the end of the forest path around high noon. I

stepped out of the dark woods and into a mile-long stretch of verdant plain. The fresh air was a relief after the dankness of the forest, and I breathed in deeply.

I shielded my eyes. The rolling green landscape spilled out before me, ending abruptly in a line of majestic blue-gray mountains cutting into the blue sky.

I'd seen a depiction of the Skal Mountains on a tapestry in Tather Hall, and I had imagined them many times since . . . But nothing could compare with actually standing facing white-capped crags. It was like kneeling before the gods.

Ink pointed. "The Imp's Ear. It's the tallest and the most oddly shaped."

The Skals' highest peak did look like a pointed ear, and the snow pooling at its tip only made the similarity all the more striking.

"There are rumors that the Jade Fells dance with alpine beasts in its snow-filled curves," Ink said. "On warm summer nights, they build a giant bonfire, tear off their clothes, and frolic naked among the wolves and bears and mountain goats, howling and casting spells."

"I very much doubt this is true," Gyda replied, "but I'd like to witness it all the same."

I laughed. "As would I."

I turned, scanning the green plain, and spotted a single black apple tree in the center of the meadow, its branches heavy with dark, aromatic fruit. "Maybe we should pick an apple and see if a wizard appears. Black apples are common in Elsh fairy tales, are they not? They summon witches and bring on storms."

Madoc smiled. "It's worth a try."

The four of us sat in the shade of the fruit tree, enjoying the bittersweet taste of the black apple peel mingling with the crisp honey flavor of the white flesh underneath.

We picked several and savored them slowly as we crossed the wide plain.

From the edge of the Brocee Leon, the Skal ridge appeared to be a few miles away, no more . . . But it took us three days to reach the foot of the mountains, covering fifteen to twenty miles a day. We passed soft cobalt lakes and endless green meadows, saw countless herds of elk grazing and a white arctic bear eating berries with her cubs.

A small forest lay at the base of Imp's Ear, not nearly as large as an Endless Forest, but pretty all the same—blue fir trees and red-tipped wick trees cradled the foot of the mountains like a crimson-indigo quilt.

"The hut will be here, in this woodland," Gyda said. "I can feel it."

The druid was right. I was munching on my last black apple when I saw it.

The wizard's cottage lay between two lush wick trees, their large, fat, curving roots hugging its frame like a mother cradling an infant. It was thatched in the Fremish style, black reeds over a black door, yellow-painted stone walls.

It was decrepit, half ruined. I counted several large holes in the roof, and the whole building seemed to slant to one side, as if it were about to crumble into dust.

Madoc turned and pointed. "And there's the blue troll-stone, just as Uther said."

The troll-stone rose about fifteen feet into the air in front of the hut. I could just make out its features as we drew closer— eyes, long pointed nose, chin, hunched shoulders—though wind, rain, and time had worn away most of the details.

"It must be one of the few left from the sagas," Ink said. "When the trolls came down from the Far North to fight in the first Witch War, they died by the hundreds. They fought hero- ically until the sun rose and turned their flesh to charcoal-blue stone. Dozens used to dot fields across Vorseland, but most have been eroded to unrecognizable lumps."

I ran my palm across the giant knees of the troll as I passed. The cold stone had once been flesh and blood, and I still could sense it, the heartbeat that had once flickered inside.

I wondered if Esca's tree would feel this way, like an animal caught in a stone cage.

The worn wooden sign on the door of the hut read: PUZZLES SOLVED AND QUESTIONS ANSWERED. In smaller letters under- neath were the words KEYS, DOORS, POTIONS, PERFUMES, AND RESINS.

I glanced at my three companions and then knocked.

Despite what Uther had said, I still expected an older man or woman to come shuffling to the door, milky eyes, red-tipped nose, clawlike hands. When the heroes in the sagas went searching for oracles, or prophets, or sorcerers, the mystics they found were generally elderly and wise, with cunning eyes and a grim smile.

No one answered my knock, though I tried three more times. I turned and walked through the wick trees to the back of the hut. There I found a small, grassy area and an abundant, well-tended garden.

A young man was hanging linens on a rope strung between two blue fir trees. He saw me but made no move to come closer. He simply smiled and smoothed the edges of an undyed linen sheet with his palms.

He was very beautiful, with a willowy frame, wide eyes, straight, refined features, and thick, short brown hair that curled at his temples and the back of his neck. He wore a long, loose tunic made of fine wool. It was dyed a deep, rare shade often referred to as Fremish blue. The tunic had billowing sleeves and pockets of all shapes and sizes—the classic sorcerer's robe.

I called out to my companions, and they joined me in the garden. The wizard finished with the laundry, then crossed his arms and scrutinized us. "And what do you all want, I wonder? Spells? Keys? Answers? I provide all these things."

His words dripped with the silky Fremish accent—it was an

inflection I'd always found lovely. Even Uther's voice had been alluring, in its way.

Gyda pulled the half-owl, half-human figurine from her pocket and tossed it toward the magician. He caught it in one hand.

We drew closer as he gazed at the statue, which sat open on his palm. He looked up and met Gyda's gaze. There was a mischievous glint in his clear brown eyes, and it made me rather like him.

"You were sent here to ask me about a key," he said softly. "Come inside. We need to talk terms."

"Vorse words sound better when spoken through Fremish lips," Gyda whispered as we followed the wizard through a back door into his hut.

"Truth," I replied.

The cottage was far bigger than it appeared on the outside, with high ceilings and sturdy wooden beams. There were three wide, airy rooms, all of which had only three solid walls, the fourth left open to face a central seating area and a square stone hearth.

"Hearth magic," Ink said with a smile.

One of the rooms held the typical potions and vials and cauldrons of every magician. Half-melted candles littered a stained workbench; drying herbs of all colors and kinds hung from every corner and every wooden beam.

The second room contained the wizard's heavy black-oak bed frame, upon which lay several charcoal-colored blankets, doubtlessly woven from the wool of the feisty black mountain goats that roamed the Skals.

The third room was a simple kitchen with a stone-pile fireplace for cooking, a table, and several shelves containing various vegetables, fruits, and dried beans.

"I am Talon," the wizard said, turning to me. He did not hold out his hand in greeting but merely fixed his eyes on mine.

I put my hand to my heart. "Torvi."

Talon greeted Ink, Madoc, and Gyda in the same way, dark eyes on theirs. Ink was shy as usual and hid behind the hood of her cloak, keeping her face in shadow.

The wizard motioned for us to sit by the hearth fire. His wide-sleeved tunic made a gentle rustling sound when he moved, and I found it strangely calming.

I sat down on a bench made soft with furs and sheepskins, and Madoc sat beside me. The fire was nothing but red embers—it was too warm for flames. Talon had left the back door of the hut open to let in the summer breeze, and it was scented with garden herbs, the sweetly resinous wick trees, ripening fruit, and . . . mountain.

The Skal Mountains smelled of iron and stone and strength. They smelled of the sagas. They smelled of the gods.

"You are correct," Talon said, his gaze on the storyteller. "This hut is under a spell. What you see in here is real, everything else an illusion. I do not want passersby to believe I live in this kind of luxury—it helps keep away thieves.

Though they would be fools to steal from me. A few have tried and failed."

Talon glanced toward the potion room, a shrewd look in his eyes. I recalled a passing reference Ink once made when discussing Fremish magic—she said many of the complex and potent spells called for extracts that were distilled using something called *skull-drip*.

I scanned the line of vials and flasks and shivered.

Talon moved to the kitchen and poured us each a mug of a drink he referred to as sun tonic. It was a pale green liquid that smelled of grass and tasted of tart summer berries.

"It's made from things I grow in my garden," Talon said as he handed me a cup. "Herbs and fruits. Nothing more."

"Nothing more . . . such as essence of thief or oil of brigand?"

Talon laughed. It was a surprisingly sweet sound, youthful, almost innocent. "I don't believe that would taste very pleasant, do you?"

Gyda chuckled as she took her cup from him. "I prefer my tonics to taste refreshing, not villainous." The druid sipped deeply, keeping her gaze on the Fremish wizard. "Aren't you going to ask us what kind of key we need?"

He shrugged.

"We need to know how to find the tunnel, the one that leads to Esca's forgotten lands," I said. "We believe that there is a secret door and that you know how to open it."

"We killed a wolf-priest to get this information," Madoc added. "A bishop."

Talon drank his mug of green elixir in one swallow and then nodded slowly. "I am the fifteenth wizard to live and work from this hut at the foot of Imp's Ear Peak, and no one has asked about the Avalon tunnel in all this time. Why now?"

Gyda put her hand to the Butcher blade at her sternum. "The time has come for a Vorselander to pull Esca's sword."

"And are you the person who will pluck this blade from the stone tree?"

"Perhaps."

"What is your price?" I asked. "We have some coin, though not much."

Madoc rose and faced the wizard. "We are Butcher Bards. We can trade in art. We trade in stories and in song."

Talon's eyes sparkled with the mischief I'd noticed earlier. "I have the only key to the Avalon tunnel, and therefore I can ask any price I wish. Gold has its uses, especially in the summer when the Night Wilds are in full force." He paused. "Opening the path to the forgotten lands . . . This is a spiritual endeavor, a sacred journey, and I can't take coin for such a thing. I'll need something a great deal more valuable."

"That sounds ominous." Gyda gave the wizard a wary look and then turned to us. "You do not need to pay his price. I can do this alone."

"You risked your life for me at Lake Le Fay," I said. "Let me do this for you, Gyda."

"I wouldn't dream of letting you go on this adventure without me," Madoc added.

Ink reached out and rested her hand on Gyda's arm. "We want to help you. Let us."

Gyda laughed and tossed back the rest of her tonic. "Fair enough."

Talon went to her and made a gesture with one long-fingered hand. I didn't recognize the movement—it was Fremish, curved, quick, mysterious.

"From the druid, I will take the scar from the top of her left hip, though the memory of how she received it is dear to her."

He turned to Ink and made the same odd Fremish gesture. "From the storyteller, I will take the memory of a tale whispered to her by her first lover, at dawn, on board a ship crossing the Quell Sea."

Madoc took a step backward when the wizard approached him. Talon merely raised one eyebrow, paused for a moment, and then moved closer. "From the singer, I will take the only memory he has of his true mother, the one who left him at a Night Wild. It is a memory of scent, of iris and cedar, of clean skin, fine wool, and long, myrrh-scented hair."

Talon shifted, and his tunic rustled softly against his willowy frame. My turn. "From the hanged girl, I will take the memory of her sister, of their childhood together, of all the sweet moments up until the fire."

Talon returned to the kitchen and refilled our cups with tonic. "You may refuse these requests," he said as he handed them to us again. "But know that I will respond with a demand for something of even greater value. So proceed with caution."

I shook my head. "I will not make this trade. Morgunn may be a poison-drinking wolf-priest, but she is the only family I have left. Choose something else, wizard."

He stared at me for a long moment and then made another gesture with his hand, a quick flick of his wrist near my stomach and a waving motion over my head.

"I will take your firstborn child, to raise as my own in the Fremish faith, in the way of the wizards."

Ink flinched. Gyda and Madoc swore.

I raised my hands, palms out, and shook my head. "I will never have children. That path is closed to me now—it ended the day I buried a Vorse shepherd by a grove of rowan trees."

Talon simply nodded. "The price is the same regardless."

"Then I consent."

"Do you all agree to this price?" He looked at us slowly, giving everyone time to answer.

"Yes," said Madoc.

"Yes, wizard," said Gyda.

"Yes, Talon," said Ink.

"It is done." Talon turned with a soft swoosh of his Fremish tunic. He went to the room with the black-oak bed and moved it to the side with a hard shove. He knelt down and lifted a white wool rug, revealing a black iron ring.

The wizard grasped the ring and opened the trapdoor. We gathered around him and looked down. I saw a flight of stone steps descending into shadows.

"The tunnel exits into a cave that lies within the Green Wild Forest, in Esca's forgotten lands. His jarldom is protected from the outside world, as described in the *Moon Serpent Saga*, and it will remain so until the sword is pulled and the magic released."

"So this is why you live here in this hut," I said. "You guard the path to Avalon."

Talon bowed his head in assent. "Me and all my brothers and sisters before me."

Ink straightened and glanced at Talon. "Why haven't any ambitious Fremish folk tried to win the jarldom for themselves? If Uther knew why you were here, so do others."

"Only someone of Vorse blood can pull the sword," Gyda replied. "Besides, the wolf-priests don't concern themselves with legends and jarldoms. They care for little but poison and flames."

"The druid is correct," Talon said with a nod.

I stared down the stone steps and then turned to the wizard. "And how did Fremish wizards come to guard a Fremish tunnel in the north of Vorseland?"

He met my gaze, the mischievous glint back in his eyes. "That is a long, dark story, best told on a long, dark night."

We lingered in Talon's hut for the rest of the day, finally falling asleep in our cloaks before the fire. Though the cottage was of Fremish build, with strong wooden timbers and a thatched roof instead of sod, it reminded me of Viggo's hut in the hills. Enough that I dreamed of the shepherd and woke at midnight, my heart aching and my eyes damp.

I pressed my palms to my wet cheeks and frowned. My Elsh blood was coming through, encouraged no doubt by Madoc. I slid out from under the Bard's arm. I rose, stretched, and crossed the room to the back door of the hut.

The wizard's garden smelled of Frem—lavender, thyme, rosemary. I breathed in deeply. I smelled freshly turned earth and mountains . . .

And pipe smoke.

"Torvi."

I turned. Talon sat on a fat root of the wick tree, one knee tucked into his elbow, a long-stemmed Fremish pipe in his hand.

"You can't sleep," he said.

I shook my head.

"And you want to ask me something."

"Yes." I seated myself on the tree root, close enough that the ends of Talon's billowy tunic tickled my fingers when the wind blew.

"You want to ask me if I can change my appearance to look like a certain shepherd from your past. The answer is yes, I can."

"Then do it," I said.

A cloud floated in front of the moon, and everything dimmed. I blinked, and the moonlight returned.

Viggo.

Broad shoulders, wide forehead, gray eyes, pink scars.

It was him, from the shape of his elbows to his plump earlobes to his lower lip that was ever so slightly fuller than his upper.

I reached out and ran my hand down his chest, throat to torso. I pressed my face into his neck, pressed my wet eyes into his skin. "*Viggo*," I whispered, and then again, "*Viggo*."

I felt hands on my shoulders, gently moving me away.

"Don't," I said, my eyes still closed. "Don't push me away."

"Is this really what you want, Torvi?"

I paused. "No. No, it's not."

"Good."

I opened my eyes. The wizard had returned.

Talon sat holding his pipe cupped in his palm, his eyes calm, brown curls damp with dew. "I used your memories of the shepherd to take on his appearance," he said softly. "You would be going to bed with a Fremish sorcerer and your own recollections, nothing more."

I tilted my head and glanced up at the snow-capped peaks above me. "I want something real, Talon, not an illusion."

He nodded. "May I suggest an alternative?"

He stood and walked to the garden. I followed. He reached

forward, unclasped my cloak, and then spread it on a patch of grass near a row of lemon-scented thyme.

"What about the Bard?" he asked as I drew near. "Something is growing between you."

"Yes, and it is stronger than one night spent with a Fremish wizard."

Talon arched an eyebrow at this but did not seem insulted. I began to loosen the leather belt that held his flowing tunic tight to his waist. "I am not yet ready for what is to come between Madoc and myself. My heart is still healing. Yet . . . yet I still ache for closeness."

Talon pulled the bright blue Fremish tunic over his head, tossed it onto the ground, and then glanced away, almost shyly.

He was beautiful. Sleek and slender and delicate. I moved forward, and he backed away.

"You have to be with me, Torvi, and not him."

"That is fair."

I moved forward again and slid into his arms.

When the sagas told of wizard love, they used words of earth and sky, words of fresh soil and resinous tree sap, of milky stars and citrus lightning and honey-scented rain.

When the songs told of wizard love, they used words of witchcraft, of melting beeswax candles, of whispered midnight chants and ink-stained skin, of ripe fruits bubbling in black cauldrons, of supple flesh that smelled of moonbeams and shadows.

It was all these things and more.

Afterward, I lay curled into him, both of us naked under the dark sky, the night breeze stroking our skin.

"How will you use my companions' memories?" I asked him softly, my fingers spreading across the warm skin of his torso. "It seemed a cruel price."

He turned his head and gazed at me warmly. "Some people come to me who are heart-hurt, who cling to dark, sad memories that eat away at them like a disease. I will use your friends' cherished recollections to replace these people's bitter memories with something joyful, something healing. This will allow them to recover."

I thought about this for a few moments. "I approve."

He laughed softly and pressed his palms into my lower back. "Once upon a time, a young wizard traveled north with a band of Fremish stonecutters." Talon's voice was soft, his lips near my temple, his skin dissolving into mine.

"Are you going to tell me a story?" I asked.

"We wizards always follow lovemaking with a story. It is our custom."

I dug my fingers into his hair and kissed him. "Please continue, then."

"The stonecutters had been hired by a jarl to cut a path for trade through the Skal Mountains, connecting the Green Wild Forest with the Brocee Leon. The wizard, a woman named Sov, was to brew tricky and dangerous fissure potions that could slice through rock and stone—"

Talon told me the story of the Avalon tunnel as I held him close, the air filled with the scent of Fremish herbs, my body satiated, my heart content.

———————————

We dressed sometime in the night, shivering in the predawn chill, and were sleeping fully clothed on the grass when Gyda found us at sunrise.

"Well, Torvi," she said softly. "You have been a farmer, a traveler, a hanged girl, and now you are a lover of wizards. Who will you be next?"

I laughed and gently untangled myself from Talon. "Is Madoc upset?"

The druid shook her head. "He understands."

"That Bard is truly exceptional, I think."

"Yes. Just like his Butcher Bard brother." Pain flashed in Gyda's eyes at the thought of Stefan. I took her in my arms and kissed her on the temple.

"He will return to us, Gyda."

"Will he?"

"The hanged girl is right, druid. Stefan will return to Vorseland. I read it in the stars." Talon smiled, and the druid eyed him warily. He rose to his feet and then wandered off through his garden, leaning over occasionally to touch leaves and caress half-ripe fruits.

"Come, Torvi," Gyda said. "I'm eager to get into this tunnel."

Talon prepared us a delicious breakfast of fresh greens with flaxseed oil and soft-boiled, lilac-colored eggs collected from wild forest hens. He sprinkled flakes of Fremish salt over the food, and it added a floral taste, subtle and savory.

While we ate and sipped a few more rounds of sun tonic, Talon made each of us a torch from oiled linen wrapped around sturdy wick tree branches. I enjoyed watching his long fingers deftly craft the lights—he moved with the skill and grace of someone long used to mixing intricate potions.

"These are spell-lit—they will last six days, perhaps seven." Talon handed me a torch and then one each to Gyda, Ink, and Madoc. "Move quickly. Do not linger in the tunnel. It . . . wears on people who aren't used to moving underground and living in endless dark."

I nodded. "We will."

Madoc put his hand on his knife. "Yes. We will be careful, wizard."

Talon paused for a moment, eyes on Gyda. He opened his mouth and closed it again. I had the feeling he was about to per-suade us not to go. But in the end, he merely narrowed his eyes and shrugged. "You may hear noises, but do not follow them. Do not veer off the main tunnel."

Gyda chuckled. "This sounds like something from the sagas—a wise mystic warns the brave heroes not to turn off the path through the enchanted forest, and they agree, most sin-cerely . . . only to find themselves doing just that when they spot a group of beautiful Winter Elvers dancing under thick moonlight, their voices raised in song."

Ink and I smiled, but Talon and Madoc looked grim.

The wizard went to the trapdoor. He lifted the iron ring and opened it. "The stone tree grows within Esca's ruined Great Hall, but where the Hall lies in relation to the tunnel's exit, the cave, I do not know. Good luck, Bards."

My companions lit their torches with one of Ink's fire staves and began to descend the stairs. Talon touched my arm, and I held back.

"Be careful, Torvi." His Fremish accent was soft and silky, as it had been the night before. My cheeks grew warm.

"I will, Talon."

His fingers touched the back of my neck, and he kissed me, his lips moving softly, gently, against mine. "Thank you," he said.

"Will we ever meet again?"

"Yes, I believe we will."

"You're a sorcerer. Don't you know everything?"

He laughed his sweet, innocent laugh. "No, not everything. Less than some, more than most."

He kissed my cheek and then my neck and then a spot behind my left ear. With a rustle of his tunic, he turned and disappeared outside, into his garden.

I lit my torch and stepped down into the tunnel to Avalon.

❧

TWENTY-ONE

*D*o you hear something?" *Madoc was a few steps ahead of me, his* shadow stretching long through the torch-lit dark. He stopped walking and tilted his head.

I lowered my torch and listened. "I hear our footsteps echoing off these tunnel walls, nothing more."

"I swear I just heard laughter, Torvi."

We didn't know how long we'd been wandering the Fremish tunnel—with no sun or sky, it was hard to mark the passing of time. Ink thought we'd been inside for four days, but perhaps as many as six. The days blurred together. Gloom and murk. Cold, stale air. Eerie echoes. White whisper bats swooped above us, their wings tickling the tips of our ears.

The tunnel was narrow, five feet wide and twelve feet tall, and after a few days without sunshine or the sight of the sky above, we were tense and miserable.

Madoc had passed the time by asking Gyda to use her druid magic to conjure up a false sun or a fleet of cave horses to carry us swiftly to the tunnel's exit and then accused her of being lazy when she said that wasn't possible. Their good-natured bickering kept us entertained and helped us bear the gloom.

Gyda came to a stop beside Madoc, one hand holding her torch, one hand on her knife. "The only entrance is through the wizard's hut. No one else is in this cave, Bard. You must be hearing things."

Madoc lifted his light and stared down the length of the dark tunnel. "A section could have caved in. Or perhaps someone found the exit in the Green Wild Forest."

Ink halted and tilted her head to the left, as Madoc had done. "I hear it, too. Laughter, high and resonant."

"Yes," Madoc replied. "Children's laughter."

I peered forward into the shadows. "Do you see something up ahead? An orange light? It's no bigger than a star, but it's there."

We walked forward toward the faint glow and soon came to a section of the tunnel that had been closed off by a rockslide. The light filtered in through a gap in the rocks.

The laughter was clear now, soft, young voices on the other side of the fallen stones. I began to move the rocks away, and the rest joined me, all of us grunting and sweating with the strain.

"We'll need to be careful," Madoc said. "A band of Jade Fells could be on the other side of these stones."

Gyda grinned at him over her shoulder. "Afraid, Bard?"

Madoc frowned. "Of the Fell witches? Yes."

"It could be a grimalkin." Ink grunted as she set down a small boulder. "Their howling sounds like children's laughter, but if you get too close, they will leap onto your chest and rip out your throat."

"Grimalkin . . . you mean a cave cat?" Gyda laughed. "That's just a fairy tale, told to children to keep them from exploring caves."

Ink shook her head. "The grimalkins are real. I once read an account in an old Elsh book of beasts about a woman who was traveling through the Skal caves searching for cavern sage, when—"

"*Who approaches?*" The voice rang out as clear as a bell from the other side of the rocks.

"Four Butcher Bards on a quest," I called out. "And who are you?"

I heard more laughter and excited mutterings. "We've decided we like Butcher Bards," the voice said, "though we've never met any. You are free to enter."

I lifted away the last stone, and it left a hole big enough to crawl through. "I'll go first," I said. I took my knife in one hand, slipped into the gap, and landed feetfirst in the middle of a cluster of cone-shaped cave stags, rising up from the floor like small white towers.

Gyda, Ink, and Madoc followed.

The cavern was as lush as a jarl's Great Hall. Fires roared in several braziers, giving the enormous room an amber hue. The walls were marbled with streaks of jade stone, and rich tapestries hung from every corner, depicting scenes of trolls, trees, wolves, feasts, battle.

I counted a dozen beds scattered about, all piled high with thick sheepskins. I saw a long wooden table, well made—it held golden plates and cups fit for any luxury-loving jarl, each of them shining sun yellow in the firelight.

I smelled incense, fruity with a hint of herbal earthiness, and noticed a plume of white smoke rising from a thurible that hung in the corner.

Ten children watched us, none older than twelve, each with long hair coiled into tight braids.

A girl with bright red hair stood in the center of the group. She had a grave, melancholy air about her and bright, intelligent eyes.

"Did we just enter a fairy tale?" I asked.

Gyda laughed, and the girl joined her—she had a charming, infectious giggle that contrasted with her stoic demeanor.

"I'm Pellinore," she said. "You've wandered into our home."

I noticed she had three small pale green dots tattooed at each of her temples. I scanned the other children and saw the same.

"You are Jade Fells," Ink said. "You are Mountain Witches. You sleep during the day and prowl the night like wolves. You drink blood and eat the hearts of your dead."

The girl put her fist to her heart. "No. We are rogue Jade

Fells. We have forsaken our people, and we make our own way. We roam the caves under the Skal Mountains, searching for ancient, forgotten treasure."

I held out my hand. "I'm Torvi. This is Madoc, Ink, and Gyda. We are trying to free a sword."

Pellinore invited us to share their meal—fire-roasted cave mushrooms and a simple wild-garlic broth. We dined on golden plates and drank mountain ale from golden cups, like gods.

My three companions and I smiled our way through the supper—we were all feeling merry and lighthearted, having left a dark tunnel and entered a dazzling, magical cavern.

The rogue Jade Fells did not ask us questions as we ate, instead laughing and joking among themselves in the selfish, sweet way of children everywhere. They were drinking too much mead, but I wasn't about to tell them so.

As the leader, Pellinore kept her attention on us and only partially listened to the others.

"Do the Jade Fells truly eat the hearts of their dead?" Gyda asked after Pellinore poured her another mug of mead. "What does human flesh taste like?"

I kicked the druid under the table, but she merely winked at me.

Pellinore gazed at Gyda, eyes bold and unashamed. "Yes,

they do, but it is ceremonial. It is not vulgar and violent, and it's not why we left our band of Fells."

"Why did you all leave?" Ink sat next to Pellinore. The two of them looked like sisters, same red hair, same bony frame. I noted with interest that Ink was less shy than usual.

The children seemed to like Ink's question, and their answers were swift and varied.

"We left because the Fells are murderers."

"We left because it was dull."

"We left because we wanted to find treasure."

"We left because we wanted to find adventure."

"We left because a Fell prophet told Pellinore we would rule a jarldom one day."

I exchanged a look with Ink. Her eyes were dancing. She liked children, as did I. I missed the Arrows suddenly, though I'd known them for only a brief time. I wondered if they'd run off again to fight wolves or if their father was keeping them in line.

"Vorselanders wanting to rule a jarldom . . . I'm hearing a lot of that lately." Madoc gave Gyda a wry look.

The druid grinned, and the children went back to their food and drink. They began to discuss their next cave exploration in high, excited voices. Many of them quoted the lyrics of an Old Vorse song called "Mountain Hoard," which had several lines about a golden girl who sat on a golden throne in a cave under the Skals.

Madoc took a sip of his broth, eyes on Pellinore. "How do you find food, living down here?"

Pellinore gestured to a corner of the cave. "That tapestry with all the warriors feasting at a long table—it conceals a passage that leads to a hidden alpine meadow. We get what we need from there, and from the caves themselves. Does the mead taste familiar, Butcher Bards? It's your own, left in one of the caves on the southern side of the mountains."

Madoc and Ink laughed.

"Yes," Madoc said. "I knew it was moongold cider, though it's aged past the fiery stage and mellowed a bit. It must be twenty or thirty years old."

"Older, even," Ink added. "It's been in that cave since our grandmothers were young, I think."

"How long have you all been living here?" I asked. I was still enthralled by the splendor of the cavern, the gold, the ornately carved beds, the wooden chest of silver trinkets that I'd just noticed sitting near a tapestry depicting two sleeping trolls.

"We've lived here since last autumn."

"And you found all these riches in that time?"

Pellinore smiled from ear to ear and lifted her chin proudly. "We are small and can wriggle into places where no adult can go. Trolls used to wander these caves in the time of the sagas. They kept many treasure hoards. Hundreds died on the battlefield during the first Witch War, and their gold was never found. Until now."

The blond girl sitting next to me pounded her fist on the table to get my attention. "You should know that we don't just want this treasure because we are greedy and gold-hungry, like other Jade Fells. We have a quest."

Gyda chuckled at this, and I gave her a warning look. These children took themselves very seriously. "What is your quest?" I asked.

A boy across the table turned to me. He had floppy dark hair and thick eyebrows. I'd marked him as the quietest of the children. He wore a haunted expression despite his youth, and in his dark eyes, I saw a glimpse of the world these children had come from.

"The life of the Fells is one of violence and grim ritual," he said. He crossed his arm over his thin chest and touched his fist to his shoulder. "All of us in this cave have chosen to live another way, one that doesn't make our hearts ache and fill our nights with dark dreams. We will not go back."

He paused and let his gaze linger on mine. "There is a jarldom on the outskirts of the Myrk Forest. We are going to buy it."

I raised my eyebrows.

"Men are greedy," he added. "With this amount of gold, we could probably purchase half a dozen jarldoms in Vorseland. We could have gone after Esca's jarldom as well, but we want the Myrk Forest throne. It's farther south, with a milder winter, and the Myrk Forest tree towns are known to be some of the prettiest, wealthiest, and liveliest in Vorseland."

"The last Myrk jarl died without an heir," Pellinore added. "We've heard that his remaining relatives are weak, sniveling creatures who crave gold more than power. In a few months, we should have enough to pay their price."

"Will they sell a jarldom to children?" Ink rubbed her chin and looked thoughtful. "I know many stories of children inheriting jarldoms, but never of one being sold to a child."

Pellinore touched her fist to her shoulder, as the quiet boy had done. "They will sell to us. We will make them. And all ten of us will rule as equals. We will hire advisors and mystics, and we will succeed. As Olivar said, none of us here will go back to the life of the Fells. We'd rather die."

I let the redheaded leader pour me another mug of mead and considered telling her about our own quest. I glanced at Gyda, and she nodded.

"We also seek to gain a jarldom," I said. "By pulling Esca's sword from the stone tree. We made a bargain with a Fremish wizard, and he showed us the entrance to the tunnel—it will take us to Esca's forgotten lands. This is what we were traveling through when we heard the sound of laughter and followed the sound here to all of you."

Pellinore lowered her clever green eyes for a moment and then raised them to meet mine. "There is a young prophet among the Fells, a boy named Resin. He had a vision of two young female jarls sitting on two bloodred thrones. I am one of those jarls. Are you the other?"

"I am not. It is Gyda here who will inherit the jarldom."

Gyda shook her head. "I'm not concerned with who pulls the sword, as long as it is a woman."

I watched Pellinore's expression slowly shift from gravity to mirth. She giggled, and the sound was filled with such innocent joy that I couldn't help laughing as well.

"We are all characters straight from the sagas," Pellinore said. "Listen to us . . . wizards and tunnels and treasure and swords and prophecies and lost jarldoms."

"It's true. This is the life." Olivar began to laugh as well, and it was sweet and low and hinted at the deep voice that would come as he aged.

Pellinore knelt on the bench and began to pound her fist on the table until the golden cups shook with it. *"We are living the life of heroes."* Her voice rang out through the cave, bouncing off the walls, soaring up to the shadowed ceiling high above.

The other children joined her, small fists pounding on strong wood.

"Heltar," I cried out.

"Heltar," echoed Ink and Gyda and Madoc.

"Heltar," the children shouted.

When everyone had drunk too much mead, especially the children, a rogue Jade Fell boy by the name of Safir began to sing one of the Frey songs, a sad, sweeping melody about the Boneless Mercies' fight with the giant in a Skal Mountain cave.

We sat *savalikk* as Safir moved from verse to verse. Even the youngest of the children, a girl of five with wispy blond hair and a feisty look in her eyes, was silent and still.

When Safir finished, I told the story of Olli from the *Blood Frost Saga*, of how she journeyed on her own to the Skal Mountains to find her sister, Eela, and recover the magical sword Eela had stolen from an Elsh hedge-fighter.

Afterward, the yawning children began to wander off to their comfortable beds. The flames died, leaving bright red embers. I and my three companions, half drunk on moongold cider, fell onto a pile of furs near the largest of the braziers and nestled into the fire's amber glow as if it were a soft golden quilt.

I slept deeply.

"Torvi."

I opened my eyes slowly, trying to shake off my dreams.

Pellinore's hand was on my shoulder, the ends of her red braids touching my cheek. She held a torch in her fist.

"Torvi, come. I've already woken the druid. Someone has asked to see the both of you."

I wriggled out from Madoc's arms. Gyda gave me her hand and pulled me to my feet.

We followed the girl across the cavern, weaving around the beds of sleeping children. Pellinore stopped at a tapestry in the far corner, the one that depicted a group of men and women hunting a boar through a sunlit forest.

We slipped behind the hanging. Pellinore led us down a narrow passage, down and down, past milky-white cave stags, past a small rust-red pool, crimson droplets cascading from above.

We stopped in front of a small alcove, glowing with the light of two braziers in the corner. A girl sat cross-legged inside on a comfortable bed of sheepskins, her pale eyes watching us. She wore a plain brown robe. Her head was shaved to the skull, and her skin was dusted with bright pink powder.

Gyda silently pulled her knife and then shifted into the first stance of the Amber Dance. "*Pig Witch*," she whispered.

"*Druid*," the girl replied.

Pellinore stepped between them and held out her bony arms. "Peace, mystics." She glanced at Gyda. "This is Elm. We found her wandering the caves a few weeks ago. A band of Jade Fells summoned her people to them to perform a pig ritual. When they didn't like the prophecy, they slaughtered all but Elm, leaving her to die alone in the caves."

Gyda lowered her dagger. "I'm sorry for your loss, Strega."

The Pig Witch nodded. She rose to her feet and went to the

druid. They were of a similar height, though the witch was much younger. "Pellinore has asked me to read for you. She believes your quest is important. Are you willing?"

I knew how much Gyda hated the Stregas, and I knew how much she wanted Esca's sword. I could guess her answer.

"Yes, I'm willing."

Elm touched the side of her nose with one finger and then smiled. "You can return to your hatred of us Pig Witches tomorrow. Tonight, I give you a vision. Wait here."

Elm disappeared for a few moments and returned with a white whisper bat, held gently between her two small hands. She murmured a stream of words into its ear, and it went limp in her grasp.

"Your knife, druid."

Gyda handed her Butcher blade to the witch. Elm took it and dropped to her knees. She sliced the poor bat open from wing to wing.

The druid turned away, as did I. We had seen many beasts killed on the road, for food, for survival, but we loathed using animals like this, for prophecy.

Yet this girl was trying to help us. I straightened and made myself watch.

Elm slid her fingers into the slit in the bat's belly, and blood ran down her wrist. The Pig Witch began to shake, the trembling jolting her slender spine. The whites of her eyes turned a faint milky red.

Aslaug had told me of the Strega prophecies, of glistening pig guts and steaming entrails.

There were songs about the Pig Witches and their dark readings, ones that the Bards liked to sing on snowy, shadowed winter evenings. There had been a Bard in Tather Hall during our last visit, a stocky young man with a broad back and a broad smile and a voice like sunshine warming cold skin. He sang a song about the Stregas, one of treachery and prophecy, one of hairless skulls and wide eyes and blood-drenched skin, one of the love between a Pig Witch and a jarl and the war it started.

Elm went still, *savalikk*. She closed her eyes. "*Tree of bone*," she whispered, "*tree of ssstone, the tree-crone sssits the throne. Toss the dice, mortal sssacrifice. Eye for eye, tooth for tooth, bone for bone. A purehearted sssspell-speaker must kneel. Ssspill her blood, sssoul for sssword.*"

The Pig Witch sat back on her heels. She wiped her bloodied hands on her tunic and then rubbed her eyes. "The tree requires a flesh offering," she said, "or it won't give up the blade. The offering must be of a magical person—a wizard or a witch, one who is noble, who is brave, who is Vorse."

The druid glanced away for a moment, expression grim, then held out a hand to Elm. "Thank you."

The Pig Witch rose to her feet and gripped Gyda's forearm. "You owe me nothing, druid. There is a tale among the Stregas that speaks of an ancient sword and a heroic female jarl who will become a legend. I believe in myths, and I believe in quests, and I want yours to succeed."

We said farewell to the rogue Jade Fells the next morning, after a loud, merry breakfast of hard-boiled eggs from white alpine grouse and golden goblets filled with summer cloudberries.

"We will meet again." I grasped Pellinore's bony hand in mine and shook it.

She nodded, bright eyes, solemn expression. "Yes, I sense this, too."

"I hope you get your jarldom." I put two fingers to my heart. "I will say a prayer to Stray, the Elsh god of luck."

Pellinore tilted her sharp chin down and crossed her arm over her chest, fist to shoulder. "I hope you get yours as well. I will say a prayer to Feral."

Feral was the god of rogues and mischievous children. Pellinore had chosen well.

All the rogue Jade Fells wanted to shake our hands before we left. Ten children and four adults—it took a while. We were all laughing by the end.

"This is the north end of the mountains," Pellinore said. "You are near the exit." She reached up and embraced me.

"We will meet again in a Great Hall," I said. "We will feast and trade boasts and get stumbling drunk, and they will write songs about us."

Pellinore grinned. "Farewell, Bards. Think of us rogue Jade Fells at night when you sit beside the fire."

"We will. I swear it." I climbed through the hole and slipped back into the dark.

TWENTY-TWO

❋

We traveled the Avalon tunnel for two more long, gloomy days.

When I finally stepped out of the tunnel and into a large blue rook cave, I laughed with relief.

The cave was filled with hundreds of the cobalt-colored birds, roosting in a space the size of my Hall back home, before it burned. Blue rooks were known for being brave and loud—their screeching was deafening, rising above our howls of happiness.

Madoc raised his torch toward the entrance, and a dozen rooks squawked and began to circle above our heads. "The cave opening is covered by Snow Plum vines," he shouted, nodding to the plants.

"Careful." I strained to hear Ink's low voice over the birds. "Don't burst one of the fruits. The juice will burn your skin."

We slipped through the tangle of plants slowly, inch by inch. I could smell the ripe sweetness of their poisonous liquid mingling with the crisp, clean scent of fresh air.

I slid my leg through the last tangle of vines, my foot carefully gliding past three shiny black plums.

I was free.

I looked up and saw the sky for the first time in days. I stretched out my arms and howled like a wolf.

Ink, Gyda, and Madoc joined me. Hel, it was good to get out of that tunnel.

"I could never live like the Jade Fells," I said. "The lack of sunlight and fresh air, the thought of an entire mountain pressing down from above. It's unnatural."

"Agreed," Gyda replied. "I need to feel the wind on my skin. I need to see the day passing, the light changing, the sun moving across the sky."

Madoc waved a hand across the landscape in front of us. "Red pines. My favorite tree in Vorseland. If you press your nose into the cracks of their bark, you can smell butter and honey, like the sweet butter drinks served at the Night Wild."

"The Green Wild Forest doesn't have the soaring blood trees of the eerie, magical Brocee Leon." Ink's face was tilted upward toward the sun. "It gets too cold here. But this is still the largest of the Endless Forests. It reaches all the way to the Wild Ice Plains and the Faroe Glaciers, where the giants used to roam."

We set up camp in a clearing next to a small lake and ate supper as the sun sank behind the trees—hard sausage from Madoc's pack, fried with a handful of waxy red forest potatoes that Ink found growing in among the roots of a red pine sapling.

The northern nights were cool even in summer. My

companions smoked their pipes after we ate, and the night drifted by slowly, crawling toward midnight.

I shared Madoc's snug wool tent. I'd grown used to sleeping next to him. My dreams were softer and less melancholy when he dreamed beside me.

A thunderstorm came in the night, crackling lightning, roaring thunder, cutting rain.

"I love night storms," Madoc whispered in my ear as he pulled me closer. The oiled wool of the tent kept out the rain, and his arms around me kept out the cold.

We woke the next morning to a damp ground and balmy weather under a cloudy sky.

Madoc prepared a simple breakfast, which we ate standing up, enveloped by summer breezes and deep, fresh forest scents. I refilled our leather flasks from the spring-fed lake—the water was cold and clear and tasted of snow and stone.

"Are there any old legends of Esca's Great Hall?" I asked as I handed out the flasks. "One that speaks of a landmark, a hill or river? It would be useful to have a direction before striking out, or we could be stuck wandering this forest for months."

Madoc leaned against a red pine, arms crossed. "Wandering this forest for months . . . the thought is not entirely unpleasant. It's a very peaceful place, this Green Wild wood."

Gyda took a sip from her flask and then pushed back the hood of her cloak. She put a palm to her heart and began to whistle.

The notes were beautiful, lonely, and haunting. I'd never

known music to summon a scent, but Gyda's whistle evoked all the smells of the Night Wild, of trance sage wafting past warm skin on a cool night, of wood smoke, exotic fruit, bubbling cauldrons, spiced mead, thyme-scented linens, night roses.

Ink was the first to spot the bird. It circled above us, three loops, four, and then it slowly descended, resting on a lower limb of a nearby red pine.

The yellow-horned owl was one of the largest birds in Vorseland, three feet from yellow ears to yellow claws. They were rare, preferring the deep woods to civilization. I'd seen a horned owl only twice in the Ranger Hills, both at sunset in autumn.

The owl watched us from its branch, unblinking, unmoving. Gyda touched two fingers to her forehead and then her lips. "Show us the path to Esca's Great Hall," she called out. "Show us the path to the stone tree with the sword."

The owl tilted its head, shook its blond feathers, and spread its blond wings. It rose back into the air. It began to dip and soar between the trees, its feathers stroking the sky.

We followed Gyda's Whistler owl for days. We circled frigid lakes, climbed hills, crossed babbling brooks, and tramped through grassy meadows covered in wildflowers. We saw no one.

The owl perched on a branch above our tents at night, hooting softly whenever Gyda stirred in her sleep.

Finally, as the evening sun began to sink on the fifth night, we came upon a large, flat hill. It was blanketed with bright north-poppies, their blue-and-crimson petals gleaming in the dappled sunlight.

It stood on the crest, untouched by time, like something from a fairy tale.

Esca's Great Hall was enormous, built in the old style, the roof resembling the wooden boards of an upturned longboat. Unlike modern Great Halls, where the wood was left bare, Esca's Hall had been whitewashed with chalk from Elshland, and it shone bright and clean in the evening sun. Colorful round shields lined the walls, a hundred or more, each as vivid as the day they were painted.

Gyda fell to her knees in the poppies. "*Heltar*," she shouted. "*Heltar.*"

It's no easy thing to meet your dreams head-on. We stood by, silently letting the druid come to terms with the final leg of her quest, not speaking, not rushing her forward.

While Gyda knelt at the base of the hill, the yellow-horned owl circled the sky, finally coming to land on the white roof of the Hall, where it regarded us coolly. Gyda rose to her feet and raised her hand to the bird. It watched her for a moment, head tilted to the side, and then disappeared back into the sky.

We began to climb the hill, our boots slicing through poppies. We passed several outbuildings and empty pens—I imagined there had once been dozens of shacks and huts leading up the hill—but the spell had not protected them, and they had fallen in time and dissolved into dust.

"The air smells different here than in the forest," I said softly. "It smells of . . . magic."

I was the first to reach the main steps, but I held back so that Gyda could lead. She touched the two doors gently, as if stroking a lover, then she put her shoulder to the heavy wood and pushed.

"We are the first people to enter Esca's Hall since the sagas," I said softly as my bootheels hit the floor behind the druid.

Gyda turned and took me in her arms. "*Heltar*," she whispered in my ear.

The main room was cavernous. I saw a high table, still covered with a linen cloth and set with hammered metal dinnerware, as if the Hall had been emptied only moments earlier. Several other tables stretched the length of the room, each lined with fur-covered benches. There was a grand central stone hearth with several hanging cauldrons—it was big enough to heat the room and prepare food for an army.

A crimson throne sat on a small platform at the far end of the Hall, behind the high table. It was carved from a blood tree, and the wood was so highly polished that the red hue seemed to shimmer in the slanting sunlight that beamed down from the opening in the roof.

"Esca's red throne," Ink whispered with a nod.

There was a tale in the *Moon Serpent Saga* about Esca's red throne, about how he quarreled with a witch in the Brocee Leon Forest after she'd stolen his Iber horse and sacrificed it to her god. Esca forced the witch to fell one of the blood trees, carve a throne from it with her bare hands, and then carry it, strapped to her back, all the way to the Green Wild wood.

We approached the stone tree last. It rose up from the center of the Hall, thick, gnarled, and misshapen, with bulbous growths on the side of its twisting trunk, like one of the sinister tree gods from Ink's *Ash and Grim*. Its thick branches had been woven closely into the wooden ceiling, as if stitched together by one of the Seam Weavers from the east, and its large, curving roots surged out of the Hall floor like the twisting tentacles of a giant sea creature.

I put my hand to the trunk. The stone did not feel dead and cold—there was life inside, a very faint pulse tapping against my palm. I shivered and then climbed up onto one of the roots and gazed on Esca's legendary sword.

The blade was simple. No jeweled hilt, no golden shaft, just pure steel wrapped with a leather strap to give it a grip. The final two feet of the sword were embedded in the thick trunk. I touched the edge with my thumb, and droplets of blood bubbled up from my skin—it had not dulled in all the years since it had been cast into the tree.

My blood went hot, my skin flushing. Staring a myth in the face . . . It takes courage.

"Wrath," Gyda said, climbing up beside me. "The sword is named Wrath."

Several letters in Old Vorse had been carved into the stone

290

beneath the sword. I traced them with my fingertip. "Can you read them, Ink?"

She shook her head. "Like Sven's book, only a Scholar would understand them."

"We know what the words say." Gyda touched the hilt of the sword with her hand and then grasped it in her fist. "The *Moon Serpent Saga* tells of it. Obin carved the words after casting the blade . . . *Whoever pulls this sword will inherit this jarldom.*"

I met the druid's gaze and nodded. "Do it, Gyda."

She wrapped both hands around the hilt, pressed one foot against the trunk for leverage, and pulled.

Nothing.

She tried again. Then again.

I tried. Then Ink. Nothing.

Nothing.

Nothing.

Gyda sat down on one of the tree's thick stone roots, wrapped her arms around her knees, and sighed. She didn't swear or howl in frustration. She simply sat without speaking for a long, long time, and we let her be.

Day passed into night. We gathered wood from the forest and started a roaring fire in the central hearth. We wandered down hallways, opened doors that had been closed for centuries. The air smelled of dust and stone and ancient wood.

Madoc snared a snow hare, and we had rabbit stew with wild

onions and salty, savory pine moss. Gyda found an ancient bottle of *Vite* in one of the Hall's many cellars, and we drank our fill.

After our supper, I sat against one of the carved wooden pillars, knees up, belly full. I glanced around the grand room, at the high ceiling, at the paneled walls carved with scenes of Esca's adventures, at the ancient ash tree, at the sword protruding from its stone trunk.

"We've entered a legend," I said quietly. "We are walking through a myth."

Madoc looked at me fondly. "Life is strange, Torvi."

"Indeed," Gyda added. "Strange and sad and marvelous."

We tried to pull the sword for three days. We fortified ourselves on *Vite* and strong forest food. We strained and sweated and swore.

Gyda woke me on the third night, gently shaking my shoulder until I opened my eyes. I slipped from Madoc's arms and followed her to the thick stone roots of the tree.

"Do you remember what the Drake told us, Torvi?"

I nodded. I did remember. *Esca's sword will not be wielded by a Boar Island wizard.*

"Do you remember what the Pig Witch said?"

"That we will need to sacrifice a spell-speaker, one with a

pure heart. I've thought of this a thousand times since we left the tunnel."

Gyda took me in her arms. Her hands gripped my waist, and my fingers clutched her shaggy blond hair.

"Do you love me, Torvi?"

"Yes."

"Then you must sacrifice me to the tree to free the sword."

"Never."

She sighed and let me go. We walked to the main doors and slipped outside. I sat down in the field of north-poppies, facing a large wooden barn, and Gyda sat next to me, cool night air, big night sky.

"It's so quiet," she said. "A mead Hall should be raucous, even at night—warriors snoring, dogs barking at cats, cats hissing at dogs, people making love in dark corners, chickens squawking on the roof, logs crackling, owls hooting from the rafters."

I looked over my shoulder at the Hall. "It will be that way again, Gyda. Once we figure out how to pull that sword, we can start filling this place with all those things."

She slid her arm around me, her fingers resting on my hip bone. "We know how to get the sword, Torvi. The Pig Witch saw it in her vision."

I didn't answer.

"Remember back in Viggo's hut in the hills, the first night we met the Butcher Bards? I told you that I dreamed of my death."

"Yes."

"The druids will often try to bring on dreams during the full moon. When I was fourteen years old, I made a strong brew of valerian root and lemon balm and drank it during an autumnal moon. I dreamed of a woman with dark, curly hair and violet-colored eyes. I dreamed she slit my throat at the foot of a tree made from stone." She paused. "I will not allow us to simply turn around and retreat. You must do this, Torvi."

"Never."

"It is right that a woman takes this long-forgotten jarldom and makes it her own. You know it is right. I can see it in your eyes, even as you tell me no." Gyda put her palm to my heart. "I can feel it in the pulse of your blood and the shifting of your bones."

"I will never sacrifice you, Gyda. Let's leave the sword for someone else. Let's return to wandering, to being simple Butcher Bards."

The druid eyed me calmly. "You are meant for greater things, Torvi."

"I am not."

Gyda clenched her hand and put it to her heart. "You are. We druids aren't known for palm reading, but we do practice the art on occasion, and I've seen your life line. Your path is long, with many twists and turns."

I opened my hand and stared at my palm for a few moments

and then reached forward and took Gyda's wrist. "And your own life line?"

She opened her fist. "Short."

I dropped her hand. "I won't do it, Gyda. I won't run my Butcher blade across your throat and spill your blood onto the ground just to inherit a sword and a Great Hall."

"Even if it's my greatest wish in all the world?"

I began to weep then, like Madoc, like the half Elsh I was.

Gyda and I did not return to our beds. We drank centuries-old *Vite*, we smoked pipes, we talked about big things and small things and everything in between.

Gyda sang a druid song about the earth and the sky, and how they made love, and the sky gave birth to twins, the sun and the moon. I told her every joke I could remember, from silly, simple childhood puns to the lazy, thoughtful shepherd jokes that Viggo would share with me when we were out in the hills with the sheep. She told me of her childhood, of the odd, quiet lives of the druids, of their ancient rituals, of how she was conceived during an Ostara festival when her mother danced around the hilltop bonfire with all the other youths on the island and afterward lay with a masked young man on a fur-covered mound of snow.

I taught her to braid my hair. She shared with me the vilest of druid swear words. I told her about the first night I spent in Viggo's arms.

We danced the Old Vorse dances across a field of

north-poppies. We laughed and sang and sat in silence, gazing up at the stars.

We lived an entire life in that one night.

We fell asleep in each other's arms.

Morgunn found us at dawn.

TWENTY-THREE

---❦---

I woke to *Morgunn's touch, her fingertips fluttering on my cheek like* butterfly wings.

We said nothing for a few long moments, just looked at each other.

Beside me, Gyda shifted in her sleep and then opened her eyes. She swore and grabbed her knife.

The druid hadn't seen my sister since that last night in Viggo's hut. She was much changed. Morgunn had always been robust and round-cheeked, with dewy skin and dimpled arms. Now she looked hollow. Starved. Her hair hung in thick knots, tangled with bits of feathers, sticks, fur, and leaves. Her skin was dull and streaked with dirt. She wore a foul-smelling wolf cloak, and she had lost her boots—her bare feet were black with filth, the nails torn and bloody.

"How did you find us?" I whispered.

Morgunn sat back on her heels. "Uther dream-slipped."

Gyda swore again.

Morgunn snapped her teeth like a dog at the druid before

turning back to me. "It's why I begged to be Uther's sleeping companion. She slipped me images nearly every night, images like Imp's Ear Peak and the wizard."

I moved into a sitting position. "So you found Talon, and he let you use the tunnel."

"I found the wizard two days after you did. At first, he refused to bargain with me, but in the end, he made the trade. He had a deck of Elsh Fortune Cards, and he consulted with them several times. I'm sure they told him what I've known all along—that I was meant to pull Esca's sword." Morgunn nodded over her shoulder. "I assume you used druid magic to find the Hall?"

Gyda narrowed her eyes and kept her hand on her blade. "No, I bought a Whistler spell at a Night Wild."

"I had to rely on wolf magic. I found this place by scent. It took some time." Morgunn turned back to me. "I've barely touched the yew berry juice since I left the wizard's hut. I wanted to be clearheaded when we met again. I didn't want to kill you on sight."

I looked up at the brightening morning sky and then scanned the Green Wild Forest, stretching out on all sides as far as the eye could see. The air smelled of wet earth and pine, and a cool breeze wafted up from the dark, shaded woods. I wondered how far we were from the coast and the Far North. I'd heard that the lands past the Skal Mountains were far less populated than the southern part of Vorseland. I stood up and stretched. "You need to eat, Morgunn."

"I drink moonlight," she whispered, pulling her shaggy cloak tighter around her shoulders. "I eat the stars."

Gyda laughed, and it was harsh and raw. "That's wolf talk. You're half starved, Morgunn. Come."

We went back inside the Hall and woke Ink and Madoc from where they slept beside the central stone hearth. They opened their eyes, stretched . . . and then swore when they spotted the wolf-priest lurking behind me. They seized their Butcher blades and jumped to their feet.

I held up my hands. "Madoc, this is my younger sister, Morgunn."

Madoc lowered his knife but said nothing.

Ink kept her blade raised, and shifted into the first position of the Amber Dance. "Yes. I remember her."

Morgunn bared her teeth at my companions, then shoved past them and walked to the base of the stone tree.

"Go ahead," I said. "Pull it."

She grasped the blade with both hands. She pushed her dirty, bare feet against a stone root and pulled until she was cursing, until her skin ran with sweat that smelled of yew berry poison, until she was growling like a dog.

For all that Morgunn said she lived on stars and moonlight, she ate like a wolf. She consumed half a dozen eggs and a large wedge of cheese.

My three companions stared at my sister warily, hands hovering near their blades.

I grew melancholy as I watched Morgunn eat. My younger sister was emaciated, addicted to a Fremish poison, and covered in filth.

I had failed her.

She finished her food and began to eye the half-eaten cheese on my plate.

I handed her the food. "What trade did you make with Talon to gain access to the Avalon tunnel?"

Morgunn flashed me a defiant look. "I traded the memory of our mother. I remember nothing of her now except a hazy image of a tall woman. She's dead anyway, what does it matter?" She paused. "I still have all my memories of you, Torvi. He did not take those."

I sighed. "You were too young to remember Father after he left, and now you've bargained away our mother. I'm all you have left, Morgunn."

She shrugged and gestured to the stone tree. "Do you know how to release the sword?"

"Yes."

"So why haven't you done it?"

I didn't answer.

"Are you afraid? You always were a bit of a coward. Tell me, and I'll do it for you."

"No."

She bared her teeth again. Next to me, Ink and Madoc flinched. My sister was half beast. It was unnerving to watch her shift from girl to wolf.

"I will use my tooth-and-claw spells, Torvi." Morgunn's voice was raw, guttural, with none of the soft tones I remembered. "You will tell me anything to stop the pain."

"I have my own magician. Gyda's magic is more powerful than a few wolf tricks you learned on the road." I didn't know if that was true, but I said it with conviction. "She can slit your throat with one dark, bloody thought," I lied. "I've seen her do it."

"It's true," Ink said.

"It's true," Madoc echoed.

Gyda's eyes met mine, and then she nodded slowly. "And I don't need poison to wield my magic, unlike some."

Morgunn grabbed a hard-boiled egg from Gyda's plate. She popped it into her mouth, chewed, and swallowed. "You won't kill me, Gyda. It's against your druid religion."

"I will if you attack Torvi."

"Eventually you will run out of the yew berry juice, Morgunn," I said. "Yes, I heard the vials clanking inside your tunic pockets. It won't last forever, and when it runs out, so does your magic. It will take you days to fetch more. Weeks."

Morgunn shoved back the bench and jumped onto the table, crouching in front of me. She clenched the front of my tunic in her grimy fingers and pulled my face close to hers.

"So we are at a standstill, sister."

"Yes."

She made a soft growling noise in the back of her throat. "*Holmgang.*"

I broke free of her grasp and slammed my hands on the table. "You want to skin-fight me for the right to pull Esca's sword?"

Skin-fights were Vorse duels, fought naked or nearly so, with no weapons. Some were to the death, but most were fought until one of the participants begged for mercy.

A Holmgang was a skin-fight that followed the rules set down in the *Blood Frost Saga*. It was rarely invoked. The loser endured a brutal punishment.

"Yesss," Morgunn hissed. "We will duel in the way of the sagas. The loser will forfeit her sword hand. The winner will inherit the jarldom." She paused. "You are bigger than me, but you're no warrior, as I am. It's a fair fight."

I felt my three companions watching me as I considered this. Holmgangs were considered antiquated and brutal . . . but they were still a respected form of combat. Esca himself would have approved.

I thought about the other paths that lay open to me. We could attack Morgunn and imprison her in one of the locked storage rooms under the Hall. Try to drain the poison from her body, drag her back to Talon, and beg him to help turn my sister back into a girl again.

But if cornered, Morgunn would use her wolf magic. The only reason she hadn't done it yet was that she was sure of winning.

My sister had always been unsentimental and confident. Our mother had seen these qualities as heroic. As Vorse. But even Uther had detected the chaos in her blood. Morgunn wasn't meant to rule a jarldom, and I would have to prove it to her.

I put my fist to my heart and bowed my head.

"As you wish. We will skin-fight at nightfall."

We spent the rest of the day praying and sleeping, as was the custom for a Holmgang. I prayed to Stray, and Morgunn prayed to Skroll.

Afterward, I thought she would seek a shadowed corner to rest before our fight, but she crawled under my furs near the central hearth fire and curled up against me like in the old days, the stone tree towering behind us.

I wanted to curse and shove her away.

I wanted to pull her closer and wrap her in my arms.

Gyda and Madoc disappeared down the west hallway, off to pray to their gods. Ink stayed nearby, keeping a close eye on the wolf. All three were troubled that I'd agreed to the Holmgang, but they understood why I'd done it. It was either this or we fought a battle of Bard and druid and wolf in this lonely Great Hall. I couldn't let it come to that.

Morgunn stank of unwashed skin and sickly sweet yew

berry, of wilderness and violence, of ash and fire. She was bony, smelly, and dirty . . . and yet familiar. Achingly familiar.

I'd missed my sister, her short, tiny frame and her small nose and her soft, lyrical voice. I'd missed the way she sighed with pleasure when eating her favorite food or drinking *Vite*. I'd missed the way she talked in her sleep and sang to herself when she thought no one could hear her.

She was all I had left from my old life.

"You really remember nothing of Mother?" I whispered after we'd both awoken from our nap.

She rubbed her eyes and shook her head and looked like the sister I remembered. "I remember Aslaug and the servants and our Hall. But nothing of her."

"Well, our mother used to tell me that I was good for nothing but marrying," I said. "You were the one she thought was true Vorse. She used to say I'd been born first so that I could watch over you and help you achieve glory."

Morgunn's gaze met mine. "So why aren't you?"

"Because she was wrong, Morgunn. No one is born to merely help another person on her path to greatness. We are all equal in the eyes of the gods, each of us capable of bravery, honor, compassion, and triumph. That is what it means to be Vorse."

Morgunn made no reply, and we were both quiet for a while.

"Our father is the son of a Sea Witch," I whispered a little later.

Morgunn raised her eyebrows. "He is?"

"A Drake told me at the Night Wild—it's why we smell of Fremish salt, and why our eyes look violet in moonlight."

She smiled, and suddenly her starved face was full of life, full of mischief. "We are half witches? Truly?"

"Yes. We can go to the Merrows and claim blood ties. And we can find Father—all the sailors visit the Sea Witches eventually. Come with me."

"I will. Just tell me how to pull the sword first."

I sighed. "Morgunn?"

"Yes?"

"Take a bath. You stink."

She bared her teeth at me and no longer looked like my sister. "No. I smell like what I am. I smell like a wolf."

She pushed back the furs and rose to her feet.

I stood and removed my Butcher blade. Morgunn unclasped her wolf cloak and let it drop to the ground.

Gyda and Madoc returned as we began to strip to our thin linen underclothes. The Bards embraced me and whispered prayers in my ear. Gyda held me longer.

"You were meant to pull this sword," she said softly. "I've known it from the first moment I saw you." She touched her forehead to my own and then released me.

We moved one of the feast tables to the side to clear a large open space. Gyda had found a drum in one of the bedchambers, an ancient style made from cedar and deer hide. She began to beat a rhythm on it—it was the custom for a Holmgang to be fought to the sound of drums.

The Bards stepped back, and I turned to face my sister.

Morgunn and I began to circle each other.

She looked even younger without her cloak and tunic, even more gaunt.

She attacked headfirst, butted me in the stomach, and then shoved me across the room and into a carved wooden pillar.

I spun out of the way as she came at me again, this time slamming her fist into my lower torso. My head snapped forward, and I bit my tongue. I gasped and spat out blood.

Morgunn was smaller than me, but she'd gone feral since leaving home. She wouldn't hold back out of sentiment or love.

I dropped into a crouch and punched my sister in the back of her right knee. She crumpled to the floor.

Morgunn went still. I leaned over her, and she jerked to the side and kicked me in the face. My nose poured blood.

We bled, we bruised, we sweated, we swore.

Skin-fights were often joyous things, held in brightly lit Halls, fought between pent-up warriors who'd grown bored during a long, dull winter. People took sides, shouted insults and encouragement, passed *Vite*, and roared with laughter. I'd seen three in my life, all at the Tathers' steading.

This fight was not joyous.

We grimly kicked, shoved, and flung each other across Esca's Hall, until my limbs shook, until my lungs burned. My nose was swollen, my face crusted with blood. I had a black eye, and so did Morgunn. I coughed and spat more blood onto the floor. Morgunn wiped her bleeding bottom lip with the back of her hand.

It went on and on.

We circled the open hearth, both of us limp from exhaustion. The drumbeats echoed through the Hall, keeping time with my heartbeat until I could no longer tell them apart.

Morgunn dropped to all fours and began to move like a dog, eyes narrowed, barking, howling, sidling through the shadows like a wolf on the prowl.

I heard Gyda yell my name, and I glanced to the side.

"End it, Torvi," the druid cried. "*End it.*"

I gave one last, lung-sizzling shout. I jumped through the fire and slammed my body into my sister. I pressed my knee into her back. I dug my fingers into her filthy, tangled hair and pushed her face toward the flames.

"Mercy," she whispered. "Mercy."

"I won't do it," I said. "I won't." I stared at Morgunn, at her tiny right hand. "I couldn't even kill the chickens on the steading."

Morgunn cursed. She raised her arm and punched me in the sternum. "There is honor among dogs," she said as I gasped for breath. "You will do this, Torvi. You will do this or Skroll will spit upon me and take my magic."

"Do it, Torvi," Gyda said. "You know you must."

Ink and Madoc said nothing. They did not understand the Holmgang and what it meant to us Vorse. They looked troubled and anxious, but I couldn't comfort them.

I crossed the room and took a one-handed, single-blade battle-ax from where it hung on the wall near a tapestry depicting two wolves howling at the moon.

Morgunn retrieved her clothes and began to dress. I noticed that she wore the same tunic that she'd had on the night she disappeared, though it was so dirty and torn I hadn't recognized it at first.

Madoc handed me a flask of *Vite*, and I drank deeply. I gave it to Morgunn, and she guzzled it like water.

My sister clasped her wolf cloak around her neck. She took a great, shuddering breath and placed her hand on the end of the nearest table.

She closed her glossy yew berry eyes.

I filled my lungs with air and then let it out slowly through pursed lips. I put two fingers to my heart and said a prayer to Stray.

I lifted the ax . . .

And brought it down hard.

My sister's small hand fell to the floor with a soft thud.

Blood spurted across my face, my neck, my arms, my tunic, the table.

I began to weep.

My sister clutched her bleeding stump to her chest and did not cry. Her tunic filled with blood. She fumbled in her pocket with her left hand and drew out a vial. She drank it down, and then another, and another, while her arm bled and bled.

I bound her wound with a piece of linen, but it's all she would let me do for her. "Let me go, Torvi," she said as I wrapped the cloth tight around her wrist, her blood dripping down onto my feet. "Just let me go."

"Stay," I said. "Please."

She shook her head and moved toward the front doors of the Hall. I followed her outside. I stood next to her under the stars and smelled sweat and blood and trees.

"Don't go, Morgunn."

She changed before my eyes, the poison settling into her bones. I blinked, and she was a stranger to me suddenly, a wounded wolf-priest, nothing more.

Morgunn tilted her face up to the sky and howled, once, twice. She turned and loped off into the night, her right wrist still clutched to her chest, her shaggy wolf cloak flowing behind her.

Ink and Madoc drew near and wrapped me in their arms.

Gyda stood nearby, hand on knife, staring out into the dark. "Morgunn's story has not yet ended," she said. "You will meet her again someday, Torvi. Mark my words."

———————

"This is a spell," Gyda said as we all gathered around the tree. "And every spell can be broken. If this one can be undone, if I can be resurrected like a witch, then I know you will be the person to do it."

I gripped Gyda's tunic in my fists and pulled her to me. "I

will free you from the tree. I will never stop looking for a way to break this curse."

I held her for a long time. I was shaking, but she was calm.

Madoc opened the Hall's main doors to let in the morning air, to let in the first light of dawn. The druid knelt at the base of the tree, close to one of its large stone roots. She grinned at me and then let out a small laugh, as if this were nothing, as if we were simply sitting by the fire in Viggo's hut, telling stories.

"Just do it, Torvi."

She was very brave.

As brave as my sister.

Braver.

I screamed, chest out, arms out, eyes shut, heart splitting in two.

"Just do it, Torvi."

I put my hand to the back of Gyda's neck and ran my fingers through her short hair. "I love you," I said.

I pulled my Butcher Bard blade and held it in my quivering hand. I screamed. I screamed until my voice filled the Hall, until the building brimmed with my howls, until I stopped shaking, until I went still, *savalikk*.

I took a deep breath and moved into the fifth stance of the Amber Dance. *"I'll see you soon, Gyda."*

I slit my friend's throat, just as the Butcher Bards had taught me.

I howled when the knife went through her skin. I howled

when her blood splashed over the stone roots. I howled when she slumped over onto the floor.

I dropped my Butcher blade and kicked it into the corner. I would never use it again.

I fell to my knees and held the druid in my arms. I clutched her to me as her skin paled, as the light went out of her eyes.

The ancient ash began to shed its stone shell, chunks falling away and landing on the wooden floor with a crash like bones breaking, like thunder cracking across the sky.

The tree shook itself, brown limbs shifting, green leaves unfurling.

A black hollow appeared in its side, stretching vertically, as if the trunk were being slit with a knife.

Gyda blinked, and I flinched. She wasn't yet dead. She put one hand to her neck, then broke free of my embrace. She rose to her feet and stumbled toward the hollow.

The druid stepped inside and bowed her head. The bark closed over her skin.

She was gone.

I put my palm to the trunk and wept.

I was Torvi of the Ranger Hills. I was drenched in tears and drenched in a druid's blood.

"*Heltar*," I cried out.

"*Heltar*," echoed Madoc and Ink.

The three of us stood shoulder to shoulder in Esca's Hall, staring at the tree that held my friend.

"There's no going back," Ink said softly. "You pull that sword and you will set yourself on a path that can't be altered."

Madoc took my hand and held it to his heart. "Be sure this is what you want, Torvi."

I stroked his temple with my thumb. "I will take this blade for Gyda and for Vorseland."

I reached up, wrapped both of my bloodied hands around the hilt of Esca's famous sword, and pulled.

TWENTY-FOUR

❧

I sat on Esca's red throne, and I ruled over an empty stretch of the Green Wild Forest.

My companions and I tracked down three bands of Quicks just outside Esca's borders. The intrepid archers, always up for an adventure, spread word of my tale to every tree town and Night Wild in northern Vorseland. They hired every band of Butcher Bards who crossed their path and sent them to my Hall.

The Elsh storytellers crafted tales, and the Elsh singers crafted songs. Word began to spread.

Pulling Esca's sword had released the spell that kept his land hidden from the world. The old paths and roads were opened, and my jarldom now sat in the center of several trade routes that led to the Far North, to Finnmark, to Blue Vee, and to the thriving port of Ector on the Vorseland coast.

People began to drift in by the dozens, from southern Vorseland, from Elshland, from Frem, from Finnmark. Like the Butcher Bards, I denied no one who was courageous and honorable.

Madoc found gold in Esca's small treasure room behind the throne. The lock had crumbled into brown flakes, but the coins shone as if freshly minted.

I hired Mason monks to start building four tree towns, one in each corner of my hundred-square-mile jarldom.

I offered a large reward to any Orate Healer or hedge witch who could find a cure for the snow sickness.

I feasted with a troupe of half-starved Finnish Relic Hunters, and they agreed to clear the old roads through my woods in exchange for their right to eat what they caught and claim any ancient trinket or coin they might find in the forest while doing their work. It was a common-enough bargain, and I made it willingly.

The dozens turned into hundreds.

I gave the newcomers land, and they supplied my Hall with dairy and meat and metalwork.

I welcomed all magicians, wizards, and witches. I sat them at Esca's high table and gave them food and mead. Afterward, I watched these sorcerers cast spells on the tree. Dozens. Hundreds. I watched mystics cast spells of breaking, spells of rebirth, spells of renewal and restoration, spells of finding, spells of reverse concealment, spells of woodcutting. A Fremish wizard even tried an ancient spell that claimed to "frighten trees into submission."

Some of the spells took days to perform while some took only moments. Some used long, tongue-twisting words while some were enacted using only the sorcerer's breath or a twitch of her eyebrow. Six of the spells called for a vial of children's tears, three required a splash of my blood, two used the crushed bones of criminals hanged from ash trees, and one used the pick-led eyeball of a rare woolly mammal from the Wild Ice Plains.

Eight of the spells called for an animal sacrifice, which Gyda would have hated. I let the mystics try the spells anyway. The druid could scold me later, when I'd freed her from the tree.

Spells upon spells, and yet the druid remained lost to me.

Nine months passed, and I gave birth to Talon's daughter. I named her Lash. She was a happy baby, plump cheeks and dark curls, with violet Sea Witch eyes. She smiled at everyone and everything.

Talon came for his daughter when she was just shy of her first name day. He'd known he would father a child with me when he asked for my firstborn in payment.

Wizards. They are a mischievous, tricky band of mystics.

I thought I might fall to my knees when he arrived and beg him to release me from a promise made so thoughtlessly all those months ago in his hut.

I thought I might weep in the way of the Elsh.

But I did none of these things. I embraced Talon and offered him food and drink. We spent the night talking beside the fire, and he told me many things, things from his past and things from his future.

He laughed with joy when he held his daughter in his arms.

I asked Talon to try his Fremish sorcery on the ash tree, though I'd paid dozens of Fremish wizards to do the same. He spent an entire night at its side, casting spells. When he came to me at dawn, he was pale with exhaustion, and his knees and hands were shaking. He'd done all he could. Tricky and mischievous, yes, but he was also virtuous.

I let the Fremish wizard take Lash away with him to the country of his birth, though it broke my heart. I was a Vorseland jarl, and I would keep my promises, to wizards and to everyone.

Before he left, Talon went down to one knee and swore he would bring my daughter to visit me often, even if I was traveling and far from home. He would find me and let me see my daughter at least once a year.

I believed him.

When my grief was still fresh, I traveled south with Ink and Madoc to the Brocee Leon. We found Sven du Lac and the Red Sparrows in Tintagle. After a night of rejoicing in the Wayward Sisters Tavern, after mead drinking and story and song, I persuaded the Quick to leave her forest and join me in Avalon.

I now had an army, though a small one. Sven du Lac began recruiting among the Green Wild Quicks the day she arrived in the Great Hall, and the Red Sparrows grew in number, week by week. I referred to them as my *Riddari*, the Old Vorse word for an army of soldiers, warriors, and knights.

We all feasted together in the evenings on deer from my forest, on mushrooms and wild herbs drizzled with honey from the fat, cheerful north-bees that built their hives in the hollows of the red pines. We gulped mead that Madoc brewed in the cellar—my Hall needed a brewer, and he'd proved skilled at mixing potions, having learned the basics at the side of his foster mother, an herb witch.

Madoc sang most nights, and Ink told stories, many from the book she'd taken from the black tower. We drank and played Jacobs beside the roaring hearth fire. The Quicks slept outside in the trees on all but the coldest nights—they needed to feel the sky above them.

My Riddari headed south to hunt the Fremish wolf-priests whenever they crossed into the Vorseland Borders. In the beginning, I ordered a few of the wolves to be captured alive and brought back to my Hall, to see if they could be made to see reason once the toxic juice had left their bodies. But they were all too far gone, addicted to the yew berry with little thought of anything else. Each of them quickly wasted away for want of their poison.

Sven du Lac still searched for a Scholar to translate the book she'd found in the black tower, for Gretel had disappeared from the Endless Forests. There were rumors that she'd led a battle in Elshland during the recent Tome War. A library was uncovered in the ruined Elsh city of Pomplea, and the Scholars, the Elshland Clerics, and the spell-scripture Vicars all claimed the library as their own and went to war to prove their right to its books.

Sven and Ink believed that Gretel had perished on the battle-field, along with many other Scholars.

I found Esca's hidden library by chance while exploring a narrow passage that led from Madoc's mead cellar to the dairy barn. Even jarls have to clean their own Halls on occasion, and Madoc and I were sweeping the tunnel of cobwebs and mice droppings when I leaned against a panel of the wooden wall, and it opened.

I discovered stacks of archaic volumes inside, similar to the ones in the Brocee Leon tower, except these hadn't been ex-posed to wind and air and birds, and sat instead on neat shelves.

The books were written in Old Vorse, and so I, too, was now eager to find a Scholar. One of them might be a grimoire, and if so, it might contain a spell to break the curse that kept Gyda in the tree.

A band of Butcher Bards had been sleeping next to the main hearth fire since the past Mabon. They were friends of Madoc and Ink and had been livening up my Hall with their art for weeks, dancing, singing, telling stories, weaving tapestries for the walls, painting the wooden pillars with scenes from their lives.

Two of the Elsh artists were sisters with clever expressions and dark, curly hair like my own. I offered Sonja and Helvi a sack of coins and told them to roam the earth and return when they had found me a Scholar. They took the coins and were off.

I spent many of my days meeting with other Vorse jarls to

discuss boundaries and alliances. They often wished me to marry their sons or their brothers or themselves. I refused them all.

When the jarls finally realized they couldn't claim Esca's lands through marriage, they would try to get them another way. There would be war. There was always war. The sagas had taught me this.

I hired a passing band of Woodwork nuns to build Avalon's first Ovie. My jarldom would have a school for training girls and women in the art of the Seventh Degree.

I slowed the trade of boneware by the Salvation monks. Anyone caught selling boneware in my jarldom was publicly beheaded, and I sent out bands of my Riddari to capture any of the monks who moved through the Green Wild Forest.

Pellinore and the rogue Jade Fell children acquired their Myrk Forest jarldom, though I had to stand on the tribunal and argue at length for their right to do so. They had a round table built for their Great Hall, and all sat as equals. They hired an army of Ovie-trained women.

Whenever I couldn't sleep, I went to the stone tree and sat at its base. I leaned my head against the trunk and thought of Gyda and Viggo and my daughter, Lash. I let bittersweet memories drift through my mind and stir my heart.

Madoc shared my bed. He was a tender, experienced lover, and we suited each other well. I slept deeply when my naked skin was pressed into his.

And if I sometimes still dreamed of the green Ranger Hills, of sheep and sky, of a dark-haired sister and a gray-eyed shepherd, if I sometimes still dreamed of a simpler life, of seasons passing peacefully by . . . then I was no different from all else who longed for their lost childhood of easy summer days and snug winter nights.

And if I sometimes still dreamed of returning to the road, of traveling to Elshland and Frem and Finnmark, of visiting ancient cities and hopping a ship to unknown ports, of going on another quest, however dangerous, however likely to fail . . . then I was no different from the Quicks on their endless hunts through the Endless Forests. I was no different from the Relic Hunters, chasing their bits of antiquity. Or the Vorse jarls, chasing power. Or the wolf-priests, chasing flames. Or the itinerant Scholars, chasing knowledge.

I was no different from all who walked the earth, searching for something larger than themselves.

EPILOGUE

---　❖　---

D o you hear that, Torvi?"

"The knocking?"

"Yes."

"No, I don't hear it."

Madoc laughed.

We lay sleeping under a pile of furs and sheepskins, drowsily listening to the birds sing their sunrise songs outside the window.

"You can come in, whoever you are," I called out, "as long as you bring food."

Ink entered, followed by two curly, redheaded toddlers. They were twins, born three years ago on a cold winter's solstice. Their father was Melient, the Quick who had escaped Uther all those years ago with Gyda's help. He was an honest, kind man. Ink had chosen well.

"I do not have your breakfast," Ink said, laughing, "but I do have these two troublesome girls. Will they do?"

Tiv and Link climbed on top of my bed, giggling, red curls bouncing.

"And how are you today, my wee little warriors?" Madoc asked.

Link grinned and flexed her tiny arm. "Strong. Stronger than yesterday."

"That is good," I said, smiling. "That is Vorse."

Tiv crawled into my arms and began to play with the ends of my long, dark hair. I looked at her mother and thought of the first time I'd seen Ink, hood drawn, in Viggo's hut. We'd been through much together, and I loved her deeply.

"There is a glint in your eye," I said to the storyteller, "and I know you wouldn't wake me this early without just cause. What has happened?"

"Someone is here. Someone you will wish to see." Ink glanced at Madoc. "Both of you. He is waiting in the main hall."

———————————

I didn't recognize him at first. The forked scarlet beard hid his easygoing smile, the red cloak hid his frame.

But Madoc knew him instantly. He gave a shout of joy and grabbed the Butcher Bard in his arms, tears running down his cheeks.

"Such a soft heart," Stefan said with a laugh. "It's one of the things I missed most about you, Madoc."

"You found us again," I said. My eyes were damp, but I was grinning.

Stefan released Madoc and embraced me. "Tales of Torvi of the Sword have even reached us mysterious Drakes on our mysterious island."

I held the Bard tightly. He smelled faintly of moongold cider and Elsh brickle-leaf and something else, something exotic— hot air blowing across white sand, foreign spices on northern skin, foreign words on an Elsh tongue.

"I want to hear everything," I told him. "Everything you've done, everywhere you've been, everything that's happened to you."

Stefan laughed again. "That story will take a while."

Ink joined us, the twins at her heels. The girls ran off to play with the pack of sweet deerhounds lazing about near the main hearth, and the four of us retreated to a quiet corner at the far end of my Hall, away from the travelers who still lay sleeping near the fire.

We talked all day and late into the night. Stefan regaled us with his adventures, and we shared our own. He told us what he could of his life with the Drakes. He had sworn to keep their secrets and was not a man to break his word.

I told him of the books in Esca's library and how Gretel the Scholar had taught me to read Old Vorse. Yes, the Scholar still lived, and I'd found her. She'd arrived three years ago on her white reindeer, the two Butcher Bard sisters behind her.

"Gretel was wounded in the Tome War," I said, "and she carries the scars across her arms, hands, and cheeks. But otherwise, she is as hale as ever, despite her age. She stayed with me in the Great Hall for two years and is one of my dearest friends."

"And where is she now? I'd like to meet her." Stefan stroked his newly clean chin. He had shaved his scarlet beard earlier in the day and exchanged his red Drake cloak for a simple Vorse one, woven from the wool of the agile black sheep that roamed the Skal Mountains to the south. He looked ten years younger. He looked like himself again.

"She has returned to roaming the Endless Forests. I like to think of her wandering through the sea of trees, on her grand, gentle-eyed white beast. She is a creature of wisdom and goodness, and our world is better for it."

"Speaking of a better world, you have done well here, Torvi." Stefan had allowed his hair to grow long, and it fell over his shoulders in soft waves. "I spent a night in a tree town tavern called the Crone and Spider on my way here. A lively place in a growing village. The people seemed content. I also passed by a thriving Ovie, filled with eager students."

I nodded. "The Woodwork nuns built it in the new Stave style—they like to train the girls on the slanting roofs, to improve their balance."

"And I watched an army of Quicks practicing archery in an open field as I climbed the path to this Hall."

"Yes. I believe they'd rather be roaming the woods, but they chose to stay and keep my borders safe from wolf-priests and other threats. I pay them well, and as my Riddari, they know they are free to go whenever they please, to follow quests, to seek adventures, to right wrongs, to wander."

"I recognized three of the archers," Stefan said with a smile.

I chuckled. "Yes, the Arrows. They found their way here two summers ago. They are still troublemakers, through and through—if one of them starts some mischief, the other two are sure to join in. Things are never peaceful with them around. But they are three of the best archers I have. They led the crusade to clear this forest of thieves last winter, and each year they drive hundreds of wolf-priests back to Frem. The Bards already sing of them and their adventures." I paused. "They still speak fondly of you . . . and of Gyda."

Stefan put his hand on mine. "This is what she would have wanted," he said, reading my thoughts.

I paused for a moment and then turned to the tree that rose up in the middle of the Hall. As the years passed, it had begun to change subtly, until a figure began to emerge from the trunk, one that resembled the druid—short hair, strong chin, muscled frame, kind eyes.

"I read all the books in Esca's library, searching for the spell to break Gyda from the tree. I tried simple spells and complicated spells. I tried spells that used sweet-smelling herbs and spells that used fermented, foul-smelling animal blood. I tried them all."

Stefan's eyes met mine. "Then we need to find you more books."

Ink laughed. "That's what I keep telling her."

"The Scholars did not win the Elshland Tome War," I said. "The books are in the hands of the Clerics."

"There are other books of magic, and ones nearer to hand," Ink replied. "Like the ones still in the Fisher Ives tower."

"Yes," I said. "I need to visit the tower again."

Ink knew why I held off returning to the Brocee Leon. The Fisher Ives tower was my last hope to save Gyda. If it failed . . .

The four of us sat quietly for a while, and it was an easy and comfortable silence, as if no time had passed since that first night we'd all shared a fire on the road.

"So," Madoc said. "Shall we smoke, like old times?"

The Bards lit their pipes, and the scent of brickle-leaf filled the air. I watched the smoke lazily float to the ceiling, to the ash tree's limbs that stretched across the length of the Hall. Ink's twins lay sleeping at her feet under the table, next to two deerhounds. Melient sat nearby, sharing a cup of mead with the storyteller.

"Will you stay here, Stefan?" I asked softly. "Or will you return to the Drakes?"

He met my gaze, eyes dancing. "I have good news, but it is woven into bad news. Are you ready to hear it?"

I put my hand to my chest, reaching for the hilt of my Butcher blade, though I'd stopped wearing it years ago, on the day I used it to slit Gyda's throat. "Yes," I said. "Tell me."

"On my journey here, I heard tell of a young, dark-haired witch who lives in the black tower in the Brocee Leon—the same tower you just mentioned, Ink. This witch has started casting dark, evil spells, and they are rippling through the forest, blighting trees, causing sickness. Many have tried to stop her, and few have lived." He paused. "They say she is missing her right hand."

I put my palm to my chest again and didn't speak for several long moments.

"That is the bad news," I said finally. "What is the good news?"

"I plan to travel to the Brocee Leon Forest and stop your sister, Torvi. Will you join me?"

———————————

It was said of me that I ruled my jarldom with a troubled heart. Perhaps it was true. The songs told of my journey from a shepherd's hut in the Ranger Hills to Esca's lost jarldom, ending with me seated on his throne, his sword across my knees and my gaze on the horizon, dreaming of the open road.

They called me Torvi of the Sword.

Madoc was half wild with joy at the prospect of leaving. He'd stayed in Avalon to help me build my jarldom, and I loved him for it, but he was a roamer to the blood, to the bone. And he longed to see his home again—he had not been back to Elshland in five long years.

We would first visit the Sea Witches in the Merrows and meet my father's family. I would stay with them until they'd taught me about the magic that courses through my Sea Witch blood. And when I'd mastered what I could, I would set out to stop my sister from casting spells in a black forest tower.

Ink finally solved the riddle of *Ash and Grim* and uncovered directions to a ruined tree town in the Myrk Forest that contained a magical door, one that supposedly led to an Elver realm on the other side of Hel. Perhaps we would find this door and visit this other world. The thought stirred my questing heart.

I often thought of the time Viggo said I needed a quest, all those years ago, in the small loft of his shepherd hut. He'd known me well.

Ink would not travel with us. She would stay with her daughters and Melient, and she was content with this, for now. She and Sven du Lac would sit on the throne in my place.

"You will not let the northern jarls take this land or this Hall," I said.

"No, we will not," they both replied.

I took each in a tight embrace. "I will be gone for a year, perhaps more. I won't return until I've found a spell that will break Gyda's curse . . . and until I've dealt with Morgunn, once and for all. I'll save her if I can."

Sven nodded. "You have many quests before you. Which is fitting and right for the woman who pulled Esca's blade."

Ink put her fist to her heart, then reached out and gripped

my forearm, in the way of warriors, in the way of heroes. "You are a living saga, Torvi of the Sword."

I laughed softly and then kissed her on both cheeks. "Not yet, storyteller. Not yet."

Stefan, Madoc, and I set out on the road to the Skal Mountains, three of the original five, together again. It was a brisk spring morning, the sky stark blue, the sun bright yellow.

I carried Esca's freshly oiled blade strapped securely to my back. I had studied the weapon at Avalon's Ovie, with students from all over Vorseland, and I'd mastered the Seventh Degree. I would keep up my training on the road—Stefan had learned swordplay, among other things, during his time with the Drakes, and we could spar together.

I didn't glance back at the Great Hall as I walked away, just as I had avoided one last look at Viggo's hut all those years ago. It felt unlucky.

I paused. I heard a trio of midnight crows cawing from a tree limb somewhere high above, though it was long past their hour of song. "Something tells me this first quest to stop my sister in the black tower will lead to another quest, and then another," I said softly. "An endless series of crusades that will have us crisscrossing Vorseland and Frem and Iber and Elshland."

Stefan laughed, head tilted back, long hair glossy in the sunlight. "What more could we want from life?"

I remembered Aslaug suddenly, and how she used to sit beside the fire and whisper to me that great stories began with a journey and a quest.

What more could we want from life, indeed.

The sea took my father and the snow took my mother. The Fremish priests took my sister and turned her into a wolf. Uther sacrificed me on the Tree of Sorrow. Gyda the druid saved me. I loved a dead shepherd named Viggo and will carry him in my heart always. I pulled Esca's sword from the stone tree, broke a myth, and inherited a jarldom. I am Torvi, and this is not the end of my story.

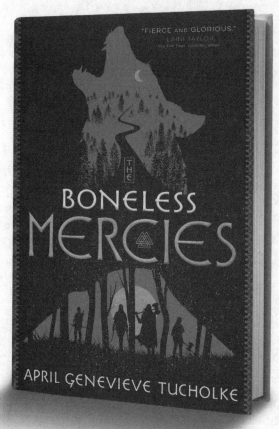

Turn the page to start reading Torvi's favorite saga about
Frey, the Mercy who fought the giant Logafell,
in *The Boneless Mercies*.

ONE

⚛

They say *dying makes you thirsty, so we always gave our marks* one last drink.

I reached for the flask of black currant *Vite* I carried in my pocket and put it to her mouth. "Here," I said. "Drink this, lamb."

She took a long sip. I pulled the flask away and wiped a drop from her lips. They felt plump and warm under my fingers, like a red plum in August just picked from the tree. I called all our marks *lamb.* Even the big ones with thick beards and hands the size of boulders. Even the mean ones with cold, shriveled hearts and dried blood under their fingernails. This *lamb* was neither.

She was covered in black silk, head to toe. The silk clung to her curves and moved lightly through the air as if woven from soft summer breezes. I wanted to touch it. I wanted to wear it. Our thick Vorse wool and furs and leather kept us warm, but they were utilitarian and plain next to her delicate dress.

"You're from Iber." Runa stared at the woman's clothing as well.

The woman nodded. "I grew up with soft white sand instead of snow. The sun shone bright and brazen, and women had fire in their blood."

She'd hired us herself. She wanted to die. Her husband, children—all dead from sickness. How she ended up in a dark, sod-roofed house on the other side of the Black Spruce Forest, I didn't know.

The woman in silk was tall, taller than me, taller even than Runa. She had deep brown eyes and pointed ears like the Elvers in Vorse fairy tales. She took another sip of *Vite* when I offered it, and then slipped a gold coin into my hand.

"What's your name?" she asked.

"Frey," I said. I didn't ask hers in return.

She sighed and leaned against me, her soft arm against my hard shoulder. I pulled her black hair away from her cheek, gently, gently, my knuckles across her skin. Her hair felt heavy on my palm, and it bore scents of the south. Myrrh and frankincense.

"We will do it quick, lamb," I said. "As promised." She looked up at me. Her smile was swift and kind and sad.

I motioned to Ovie in the shadows near the cold hearth, and she came forward, taut but quiet, like a snow cat on the hunt. Juniper, our Sea Witch, began to pray in the corner by a pile of hides and an old loom. Trigve stood by my side, and Runa simply watched us from the doorway.

Ovie handed me her knife—it was better made, sharper than mine. I took it and slit the woman's neck. A flash of sharp silver, and it was done. The woman kept her eyes on mine until the end, never looking at the knife. I caught her as she fell to the floor.

Juniper finished her prayers and came over to us. She put her hand on the mark's chest, and her curls fell over the dying woman's cheeks. Juniper's hair was blond, with a faint shimmer of pale, pearly sea green, the same as all the witches of the Merrows.

We waited for the mark's breath to slow. Slow, slow, and stop forever.

"I bet she was fierce when she was young." I closed each of her eyelids with a gentle push of my thumb. "Fierce as the Iber sun. I wonder if she was banished here, to the frigid north, for some fierce, heroic deed . . ."

Runa looked at me, sharp.

She said it was dangerous, this way I had of thinking about our marks after they died, imagining how they had lived, dreaming how their lives had played out, the twists and turns they had taken. She said all that dreaming was either going to get me into trouble or turn me soft.

Runa wasn't soft—she would have made a good Mercy leader. She could have gone off and started her own Mercy pack. Though when I admitted this once to Juniper, she'd just shrugged and said leadership took imagination as well as strength.

Runa stood then and began to explore the cold, empty house. I knew she was looking for food and clothing and weapons. I caught her halfway down a shadowed hallway leading to more dark rooms, old bearskins hanging in the doorways.

"Leave it, Runa. The job is done. Let's get out of here."

She'd glared at me, mouth tight above her pointed chin. "There might be something hidden—treasures from the south, desert jewels we could sell for enough gold to book passage aboard a ship . . ."

"*No.*" Ovie's deep voice echoed down the corridor. "We will not steal. Leave her things alone, Runa."

Trigve and Juniper stood silent behind Ovie, though Juniper fidgeted, at war with herself. Her thieving urge was strong. Siggy had told us time and time again that the gods were watching and that they would punish a Mercy who took anything other than coin from a mark.

And yet . . .

I cut a lock of the Iber woman's hair before we left. I slipped Ovie's dagger under her head, metal scraping the cold stone floor, and sliced.

Runa had taken things in the past from our marks: simple, useful things. She kept a strong coil of hemp rope in her pack and all other sorts of stolen odds and ends: strips of leather and metal hooks and pieces of old wool and vials of potions and tonics. Runa usually did as she pleased, and I admired her for it.

Afterward, we waded into a nearby stream to wash the blood from our hands. We tried not to get blood on our clothing. Whenever we met people on the road, their eyes flashed to our black cloaks . . . and then to the old red stains on our plain wool tunics. It reminded them that one day their blood might be staining our clothing as well. People didn't like to think about this.

The woman in silk hadn't wanted us to burn her. She'd asked us to leave her there in the forest, with the worn front doors of her home left wide open. The wolves would come and take care of everything after nightfall.

"That's how they do it in Iber," Trigve said. "I've read of it."

Walking away and leaving the woman's body to be torn apart by beasts in the night took all my discipline, all my steel. I ached to set her body on fire and let her soul drift up to Holhalla while her flesh turned to ash. Or even to put her safe in the earth, six feet deep, as the Elsh did with their dead.

How someone preferred to die said a lot about how they'd lived. The woman in black silk had wanted to die bloody.

And if she'd wanted a wild death, who was I to take it from her?

They called us the Mercies, or sometimes the Boneless Mercies. They said we were shadows, ghosts, and if you touched our skin, we dissolved into smoke.

We made people uneasy, for we were women with weapons. And yet the Mercies were needed. Men would not do our sad, dark work.

I'd asked my mentor, Siggy, about our kind one solstice night, when the light lingered long in the sky. I asked when the death trade had begun, and why. She said she didn't know. The bards didn't sing of it, and the sagas didn't tell of it, and so the genesis of the Mercies was lost to time.

"Jarls rise and jarls fall," she whispered, her dark eyes on the last orange streaks of light flickering across the horizon. "The Boneless Mercies remain. We have roamed Vorseland since the age of the *Witch War Chronicles*. Perhaps longer. We are ignored and forgotten . . . until we are needed. It has always been this way." She paused. "It is not a grand profession, but it is a noble one."

I didn't answer, but she read my thoughts.

"This isn't a bad life, Frey. Some have it much worse. Only fools want to be great. Only fools seek glory."